What is a Paddywack?

And Other Important Questions

Other Books by Paul Lubaczewski:

I Never Eat…Cheesesteak

A New Life

Cult of the Gator God

Also from Dreaming Big:

A Spoonful of Sugar

End of the Sojourn

What is a Paddywack?

And Other Important Questions

By

Paul Lubaczewski

What is a Paddywack?
Copyright © 2021 by Paul Lubaczewski

Content Editor: Katie Schmeisser
Copy Editor: Morgan Mitchell
Editor-in-Chief: Kristi King-Morgan
Formatting: Amanda Clarke
Cover Artist: Paul Lubaczewski
Assistant Editor: Maddy Drake

Printed in the United States of America

ISBN-978-1-947381-45-2

www.dreamingbigpublications.com

Contents

As a rule, I tend to leave my early childhood alone when I'm writing. Five or six was an idyllic time when I had no idea how the world really is. That was going to change soon enough. This was written with a time of my life in mind when I was ten or elven and we were about to be forced to move, but in many, many ways this is all about the little stream I loved as a boy.

What is a Paddywack?

Dad had left. He had even taken a suitcase this time. This wasn't Mom and Dad's normal fight at all. As he watched his father throw the suitcase into the back of the car, tears started running down Alex's face. He couldn't do anything now to stop Dad, so Alex just left the house. Just left, he couldn't really bear to watch it anymore. He didn't want to have his mother come to him and tell him, "He'll get over it," again. He just wanted to be alone with his pain.

Alex stumbled out the basement door of the rancher, having a hard time seeing because of the stinging tears that blinded him. The door opened up to a patio area where the side of the hill that the house sat on had been left gouged out in construction to give it easy access to the basement. There was a destination in mind, this was not just some random heartbroken meandering. Past the back yard was a haven, a place he could hide where none of this could touch him. The creek. It was just a little splash across trickle of a thing. It never got more than a few feet deep, never over your head. But it was nice, quiet, and above all, a peaceful place to go and hide for a while when the world got to be too much.

Soon Alex was through the fence in the backyard, clicking it shut without any thought, an automatic action drilled into his head by many reprisals for failing to close it. As he walked to the woods, the long uncut grass of the back half of the property whipped at his knees and bent in the light breeze. He walked like a somnambulist the whole way, occasionally tripping on an unseen clod of dirt, but moving steadily in one direction, sanctuary.

He didn't even notice as he started to work through the fence-line trees and into the woods proper, all of his movements were now operating on auto-pilot. His brain finally started to re-engage when he heard the burbling of the little creek. This was his happy place. A place where nobody came. Neither of his parents would trouble themselves to walk this far to look for him. This was safety and solitude. Alex wanted that more than anything right now.

In a little while, he made his way to the creek itself. It had a little trail that ran along both banks, so it could be crossed and re-crossed anywhere really. There were plenty of rocks sticking out of it. It really was just a trickle except in the most extreme rainstorm, but he'd only ever seen it jump its banks once in his young life. It ran flat and mostly straight in its little valley, just two gentle slopes slowly going down until they reached here. A place of gentle burbling water and absolute isolation; well, unless he brought Sean down here with him. That was rare though. Sean may be his best friend, but sometimes a guy just needs his own territory.

Alex never went far anyway, so maybe it was just exciting for him to be alone. Today he didn't want to stop walking. Alex may have been an only child lacking the socialization of a sibling, but he knew his emotions well enough to know if he stopped walking, he'd start thinking about everything and he had already cried enough today. Since Alex knew what was downstream (it mainly ran behind people's houses until it hit the lake that it emptied into), he thought today was as good a day as any to find out what miracles upstream had to offer.

Soon there were bright spots where the trees weren't so thick, replaced by large-leafed plants growing near the banks of the creek. This was as new as the direction he'd chosen. Alex reached a spot where a bridge crossed the creek and even at his short height, he had to stoop a bit to get under the darkened area beneath it. Here his feet got a bit wet. There weren't enough stones to navigate here and stay out of the stream, but he didn't want to go over the road. He didn't want to lose the sense of privacy he felt in the woods.

On the other side of the bridge, the woods quickly got deeper and stiller. The trees went farther and higher than near his house, and there wasn't the underbrush that there was in his wood. Alex began to wonder where he was. Was he getting close to the highway now? He thought he must be, he'd been walking an awfully long time now.

The banks were getting higher as well. Walking down by the creek seemed even more isolated than before in the shadows. The trees themselves with their canopy so much higher than he was used to made everything begin to get dark and foreboding to him. But Alex still walked on. Walking was the really important part of this.

The reality was, Alex was walking on legs that were running out of energy. Finally, tired and directionless in his mind, he flopped down on the bank to rest himself. What he had been afraid would happen if he stopped began almost immediately. Alex found himself staring at his reflection in the still water by the side of the creek, he could see the sadness in his face. Eventually, his reflection was broken by expanding concentric circles where his teardrops fell. After seeing that, it was like a dam had broken inside of him. In an instant, he was bawling away with all the force that a tired nine-year-old could bring to bear on a situation. His eyes screwed up tight, his shoulders hunched over tight, mucus dripped from his nose. Alex didn't care at all, no one could see him, and nobody cared, least of all his parents.

"BOY! BOY!" bellowed a voice from around the bend in the stream, breaking into his train of self-pity.

Alex broke off crying. It took a second and there were still a few quaking sobs as he tried to wind down. Eventually, he was able to sob out between deep, shuddering breaths of air, "Who...who's there?"

"Come closer, boy, come 'round the bend so we can talk a bit better," the voice said.

Alex got up. He tried to creep closer to get around the bend to see who awaited him there. He tried to creep, but he kept slipping into the creek, so the splashing quite ruined the effect for him. He was stunned though to see when he arrived, there was no person awaiting him. There was just a bend in the river, and a hollowed-out area going under the bank, a dark hole surrounded by rocks and mud.

"I still don't see you!" Alex said in a plaintive voice.

"Oh, I don't think you want to be seein' the Man of the Woods, my boy. But you may want to talk to him," the voice now came seemingly from the hole in the bank, where it appeared to echo around inside.

"Do I?" asked Alex, perplexed at the thought of talking to a disembodied voice in the hole.

"Well, a body who's cryin' like you wuz just now," the voice cackled, sounding both high pitched and old at the same time, "well, a body like that might want to talk about what be so terrible to him."

"I dunno," Alex said skeptically. "It's not like you'd be able to fix it. You're stuck in a hole!"

"Oh, you might be surprised about that one, my boy. But regardless, sometimes, sometimes it just helps to tell someone what be ailin' you," the voice soothed and purred.

"My dad LEFT! And he's NEVER coming HOME!" Alex suddenly blurted.

He hadn't believed he had wanted to talk, so he was surprised at how much he shared. Alex found he wanted to say it, to get it out of him, so he could look at it. So he could analyze it in some way and examine it more closely. But once it was out of him, the weight of it came crashing down on him, and he flumped down on the bank like a puppet who had had his strings cut.

"I tol' you, you couldn't do nuthin'," Alex sobbed.

"Well," the voice mused, "I wouldn't be too sure of myself on that part. Would it be my understandin' you'd be wanting your Mum and your Da back together again?"

"Of course, I do!" Alex sobbed.

"More than anything at all?" the voice purred.

"Yeah!"

"Well, then maybe we could have what they call an arrangement. I get lonely, my boy. Do you have any friends or other boys you know?"

"Yeah, a few," Alex sniffled, his curiosity overcoming his sadness for a minute.

"Are any a bit slow of wit? I feel myself quite overwhelmed talking to a bright boy like you. Maybe someone duller to join you that speaks down to my own level?" the voice asked.

"Well, Timmy lives pretty close to here, not many people like him though. He talks slow and he doesn't always put his words together right. But I don't mind him," Alex said.

"If you could bring this Timmy to visit me, boy, I think maybe I could arrange your Mum and your Da to have themselves a making up and kissing," the voice said happily now.

"You really think so?"

"You just bring this, uhh...Timmy to me, and I'll take care of the rest, I promise!"

With that, there was a feeling he couldn't explain, but it felt like the encounter was over. Alex got up and started trudging for home. He began to suspect he was already in trouble for scaring his mother. If he thought about the idea of coming back with Timmy at all, it went like this, *Well, Timmy never gets to go out and do anything cool, nobody likes hanging out with him, and his parents are poor. If it will get Mom and Dad back together, just to get Timmy to take a walk in the woods, how great would that be?*

Alex was right about Mom being mad. She hugged him and cried at him for a while when he got home. But, for whatever reason, she also seemed so happy he was alright that she forgot to ground him, which was a bit of a surprise.

Timmy lived in a trailer with his parents on the top of the hill that eventually led down to Alex's street and finally ended at the creek. Getting him to come along was easy enough. A few days later when he was sure his mom wasn't mad at him anymore, Alex called up there and just asked if he wanted to hang out by the creek. Most of the kids in the neighborhood knew how protective Alex was of his time at the creek, so Timmy was absolutely enthusiastic.

Around noon, he met Timmy near where the bridge crossed the creek.

"Why aren't we just going behind your house?" Timmy asked as they scrambled down the bank by the side of the bridge that led to the creek itself.

"It's neater here," Alex explained. "The trees are bigger and older down there."

"If you say so," said Timmy, dubiously climbing down to the water with him.

Timmy's concern vanished as they began to splash along in the creek. In theory, they were trying to stay dry and stay on the rocks, but in practice, little boys somehow manage to "slip" early and often. The other thing that makes boys get muddy when approached with a small body of water is all the things that live in it like minnows and crayfish and turtles. These need to be chased so both boys can look at them in more detail. It doesn't count if you see the crayfish, but the other boy doesn't.

It didn't take long at all for Alex to forget why they had even come down here. They weren't talking much, except to point things out to one another. That was the power of this little haven in Alex's heart. He was actually enjoying Timmy's company, which is something he rarely really did. Nobody really did, but your parents would get mad at you if you said so, and who wanted a clip by the ear and hearing, "Well, he can't help how he is, what's your excuse?"

The real reason they were back here came rearing up when they rounded the corner in the stream and there it was, drawing the eye, all black and foreboding. There was the hole that had spoken to him before. The only sound now was the burble of the water, but Alex still felt his skin go cold just looking at it.

What should he do now? Should he say something? Had he just imagined it before?

His quandary ended when Timmy piped up, "Hey! I wonder where that hole goes?"

"I don't know, I never looked. Maybe you should go find out?"

Alex couldn't believe it might be this easy!

"You think I won't? You think I'm scared?" Timmy replied defensively.

"Nope, but you said you wanted to look, and there's only room for one of us," Alex replied as calmly and reasonably as he could manage.

Carefully and obviously scared, but convinced his tough guy points were on the line, Timmy splashed across the creek. Alex remained on the bank, watching him with bated breath. He wasn't even sure anything would happen at all, and if so, what would? The man of the woods had said he just wanted to talk, hadn't he?

"Boy," said Timmy, bending his head to peer in, "this goes back for a bit. I'm gonna poke my head in."

Alex could no longer see Timmy's head at all now as the boy peered into the darkness. Suddenly, Timmy's arms stiffened out at his sides, flying straight out. Alex could hear a muffled cry of fright come from him as if a hand was over his mouth. Then in almost an instant, his body just vanished completely inside, as if something had just sucked it in like something out of a cartoon!

Horrible cracking noises came from the hole now, along with the voice he'd talked to before. Whoever the speaker was, it was now saying gleefully, "Snick! Snack! Your ribs to crack! Let's see all your bones!" This was soon followed by a noise that, if you pressed Alex for what it sounded like, he probably would have said it sounded like what happened when the Cookie Monster finally got his cookie at the end of the skit.

Alex had fallen back and was scrambling madly to get back up the bank, and as far away from the darkness as possible. His feet skidded and slipped, as did his hands as he tried to get away to high ground for the comfort it might provide. His eyes were locked on the void under the bank and while he watched, a bright red trickle started coming out, where it joined the creek in a little colorful swirl in the current.

The noises inside the little cavern stopped now for a second.

"BOY!" the voice cackled out. "Thank you for yer gift to me! A lovely gift it is! I'm bettin' now that if ye get yourself home, things will be different now! A thing for a thing! We had a bargain. I'll keep my end, never you fear! But before ye go, if there's someone else the world would be a better land without, see if you can't think of yourself another wish! I'll be here a-waiting for ye!"

There was a short burst of evil-sounding, cracked laughter from the hole and then the horrid eating resumed. That was all Alex could take. He got back to his feet and ran. He stumbled a few times and fell once, but he was a determined little boy. In no time at all, bloody and scratched, covered in burrs, he reached the bridge.

He felt he could stop now. Alex ducked under the bridge and found a rock he could sit on, dangling his feet into the water. He just stared at the water trickling by him in the dim light that reached down here. At first, he couldn't think of anything at all, his mind was just numb from what had happened. Soon, that changed to the recurring thought, *Oh my god, I am in SO MUCH trouble!* This continued for quite a while as if it was on a loop, which caused him to start sobbing quietly.

But even that energy ran down. In a gasping, heaving of his shoulders, he tried to stop hyperventilating and start breathing normally again. Alex started washing his arms and legs off in the water so he wouldn't be such a mess when he got home so Mom wouldn't yell at him. After that, he began pulling the burrs and stickers off his clothes one by one, letting them drop into the water, watching them carefully as they floated away.

Now that he was calmer, he began to think, Maybe I won't get in trouble? I mean, I didn't do anything! I was trying to be nice to Timmy! Nobody else does! Maybe I shouldn't even mention I was with Timmy? I mean, why would I hang out with Timmy? Nobody likes that kid! Maybe nobody will even ask?

Finally, with this train of thought firmly in place, Alex started the long trudge back home. He was absolutely exhausted by the time he made it to his backyard again. But it had changed, it had become his backyard with his dad in it! All thought of what had happened vanished now, he ran the rest of the way and flung himself into his dad's waiting arms.

"You're a fag, Alexis!"

There followed a thump on his shoulder as he got off the bus, which caused him to stumble. Alex didn't even look, he knew it was Logan. It was always Logan. He didn't know why that guy was like this at school. Back home, they sometimes played together, but on the bus and at school, Logan was nothing but abuse and names.

Alex was getting so sick of it. If it wasn't for how Logan got in school, he'd almost enjoy being there. His parents wondered and worried over why his grades had gone down in a few classes, not knowing Logan was the reason. Logan would wait until the teacher wasn't looking and throw things at him, or call him a fag to make the other kids laugh at him. Just thinking about it on his way into the building was making his ears burn. And then there it was, a wonderful thought. An amazing thought. He knew a way to make Logan go away, and make sure he NEVER came back. No more two-faced, a friend at home, tormentor at school.

Alex bet he could get a new game system out of this!

✳✳✳✳✳

By the end of the day, Alex had a plan in his head. He knew once the bus thinned out a bit after dropping kids off, Logan would go back to normal. Then it was only a matter of convincing him to come out to the woods with him. He knew Logan well enough, so he knew how to set his bait.

Alex quickly switched seats next to Logan as the bus bounced along taking them home. "Hey! What are you doing this weekend?"

"I dunno, why?" Logan asked suspiciously.

"Wanna see something really cool?" Alex asked happily, looking for all the world like whatever sins had occurred this morning at school were now forgiven.

"Like what?"

"I found a snapping turtle nest in the creek!"

"Nuh, uh!"

"Yeah, it's upstream from where we normally go, wanna see it?" Alex asked earnestly.

"Why aren't you asking Sean to go?" Suspicions clouded Logan's face.

"His parents want him to do some family thing, so he can't go. So, you wanna see it?"

"Yeah, I guess. That'd be cool," Logan said, trying to hide any enthusiasm for the plan.

"Cool, I'll meet you at one on Mill Road on Saturday, it'll be easier to get to where it is by going through the woods than going all the way down the creek!"

"Alright, cool."

They met on Mill Road halfway down the hill from Logan's house. Logan didn't live on Nazareth Road, the one with the bridge, or on Miles Run, Alex's own road. Alex had figured that if he made it closer to Logan's house, he'd be easier to entice out. But now that it was Saturday and the day was blazing hot, Alex was happy for choosing this road anyway. The forest was MUCH deeper here, so their way should be significantly cooler for it.

"You sure you know the way, man?" Logan demanded.

"Sure, I do. It's a valley, isn't it? The creek runs along the route all the way, except for the little bit of woods we need to go through here, right?" Alex replied in a happy-go-lucky voice.

He was almost positive he could find the creek from here, Logan didn't need to know he'd never gone to it this way before.

They entered the woods and the welcoming shade. Less welcome were the mosquitoes. This close to where the creek started, the ground got marshy in spots, a natural breeding ground for the horrible insects. Even with this added obstacle before them, they were boys, and it would take more than that to deter them from an adventure. In no time at all, they found a swampy area marking the spring that the creek flowed from.

"Are you sure you know where the nest is?" Logan demanded again.

"You worry as much as my mom. It's just this way," Alex replied.

As they rounded a corner in the now deepening stream, Alex could feel his breath catch in his throat. Maybe he shouldn't do this, maybe he should just tell Logan he forgot. Then again, maybe Logan could have stopped hitting him every day in school for the last year, too. Making this jerk go away would make everybody's lives better. He punched on everybody. Alex couldn't even imagine Logan's own parents loved him much as mean as he was. Not to mention there was the possibility of a new game system in this for him, to be fair.

"You getting a new game system this year?" Alex asked as they got closer.

"Naw, I got one when they came out last month. It's pretty awesome," Logan said in a boasting tone, "not like that hunk of crap you have."

"Yeah, I really wish I could have one too," Alex said wistfully and a little over-loud as they neared the hole.

"Sucks to be you." Logan grunted, stepping over a rock, "Your dad should get a better job."

That comment hardened Alex's resolve, Logan really was a jerk. "It's in that hole in the bank, you can just see it when you get in front," Alex told him, pointing to the spot.

Logan stomped into the stream and up to the hole muttering, "If you're full of it, I swear, Alex, I will..."

What that was going to be, the world would never know as he suddenly got yanked into the hole, just like Timmy! Just like before, Alex couldn't see by what. There was a horrid snap that came from the hole, and only an animal squeak from Logan like a mouse in a trap.

Then, as before amid the terrifying noises that filled the little area, the voice was gleefully singing out, "Bye, baby bunting, Daddy's gone a-hunting, got myself a young boy skin, wrapped up like the darkest sin!"

As the garbled noises he suspected were Logan being eaten began, the little red trickle came down to the stream to float right away. Alex turned to leave. He didn't feel as scared this time. He'd given the man what he wanted and gotten rid of the person who frightened him most. He just felt a bit numb about the whole thing.

There was a pause in the noise and the voice called out, "Enjoy your new toy, boy. I'll be here when you need me!"

About a month later, Alex was playing one of his new games in the living room when his mom and his dad came in. Both of them had the concerned expression that adults get when they have to explain something to a child that is important enough that they're terrified of getting what they say wrong.

"Pause the game there, kiddo," his dad said, sitting down on the couch and patting the seat next to him.

Alex was good with his parents normally, especially now that they weren't fighting anymore, so he paused it right away and climbed up on the couch next to his father. His mom knelt down in front of him with a concerned look on her face.

"What's up?" Alex asked. The look on his mom's face made him worried; this looked serious.

"Well, buddy," his dad began, "you know how your mom and I had a bit of a rough time recently, right?"

Alex nodded a little more emphatically than he might have meant to.

His dad smiled ruefully at that, and continued, "Well, it may seem silly to you, but adults argue a lot about money. How much you have and how much you owe. Sometimes it can even make you forget how much you love someone or what the money is even for."

"That seems kinda dumb," Alex said with a frown.

"Well, dumb or not, it can get like that. Well, we haven't been having those problems anymore. A bit after I left, I got a pretty major promotion where I work," his dad said.

"It seems better around here, that's for sure," Alex agreed.

"Well, the thing is, honey," his mom interjected, "that kind of comes with a price."

"A price?"

"To make it short, buddy, I'm being transferred. Which is going to come with another raise." Seeing Alex smile at that, his dad put up his hand before continuing, "Do you know what transferred means?"

"Means you're gonna work in another part of the company, right?" Alex knew this one because Sean had told him his dad had been transferred.

"That's right, honey," his mom said, putting her hand on his knee, "but in this case, the other place is somewhere a pretty long distance from here."

"Long story short, buddy, we're going to be moving."

Alex just stared at them, he couldn't believe what he had just heard. He just couldn't fathom it. Move? But they owned this house, this was their house! Every memory they'd ever had as a family had happened here! He had HIS friends here and HIS creek here! He went to school and came home HERE! He didn't want to MOVE! He wouldn't be able to hang out with Sean anymore!

That thought made his bottom lip begin to tremble. Sean was his best friend! Sean was who he did everything with! He even took Sean down to his creek! That was when the tears started rolling down his face, and little whimpers began to escape him.

He felt his dad's arm on his shoulder, and he slammed his face into his father's side and began to sob. He sensed his mom had gotten on to the couch with them and felt her hugging him as well. They didn't try to explain it to him right now or try and get him excited about the prospect. That was sensible, he was too shocked to listen. They just held him, and his dad kept saying, "Don't worry, it'll be better than ever," until eventually he had cried himself out and fallen asleep in his parent's worried, loving arms.

They told him all the things you tell kids in this situation. *You'll make new friends. It's not that far, maybe we can still visit. Wait until you see the new house, it's great!* Parents mean well when they say these things, and they really are sincere, but kids know better on this one. Every kid knows that the new kid is a dork for half a year, parents forget about visiting the old neighborhood within a month, and the new house won't have all of YOUR memories in it. Kids try not to hold it against them, they know their parents are trying. They may forgive them eventually, but they still don't believe a word of it.

Alex was just determined to spend the time he had left hanging out with Sean as much as possible. Their mutual friend Dan often came along. Alex suspected that when he left for good, Dan would be Sean's new best friend. This created a bit of resentment, but only a bit. He knew there was nothing either Dan or Sean could do about him moving, but you couldn't help but feel like you were being tossed aside in this situation.

Still, they had some time until both houses closed and the packing was finished, and they were both determined to make the most of it. They tossed around the football, went on bike rides, usually much longer than they would have admitted to their parents, and just generally tried to ignore the looming end of their friendship. It wasn't fair, they had both agreed, and they were also both powerless to prevent it.

Sean had been bugging him to show him the whole creek for the last week now. Well, not the whole creek obviously, that would involve going all the way to the lake, that would take forever. But their version of all the creek, all that was in the distance they were allowed to travel. Alex kept trying to beg off of it. He didn't think much about what had happened there, and he often didn't even believe anything HAD happened there anymore. Kids have a way of scabbing memories like that over, especially if they know they did something wrong. But he knew he didn't want to walk down the whole creek like that, he knew that.

He also knew Sean had a point, he was leaving and Sean was staying. Alex was the only kid in the neighborhood who really knew the creek that well. All of its twists and turns, its deep pools and tiny little waterfalls, he knew them all like the back of his hand. If he didn't show them to somebody, a valuable childhood resource would be lost. Sean had kept at him, and eventually, Alex relented.

They started way up by a different bridge, one that crossed to go up to Honeyford Farms. The little country road that crossed had only one destination, but in a weird, quirky right of way. The road up until it crossed the bridge was considered a public thoroughfare, with houses along it. After the bridge, it was just a driveway. This was handy because the deep pools directly under the bridge were one of the only spots on the creek that made for good fishing.

The boys clambered down the path on the side of the rail-beam bridge and started on their hike. At first, they didn't talk much. Knowing that Alex was passing on this wealth of childhood knowledge about the creek gave the whole thing an air of solemnity. But boys are boys, and soon the conversation started. It started where it often did, video games. Sean's parents had relented and gotten him the same system for his birthday that Alex had gotten recently. They played together online now in the evening as well as outside during the day, and both of them had decided they didn't like it if another gamer would join their game.

"Well, that's something cool," said Sean.

"Huh? What's that?" asked Alex, stepping over a rock by the side of the creek.

"Well, we'll still be able to play online, right?" his friend said with absolute sincerity.

"Hey," Alex mused thoughtfully, "hey, that is true!"

It might not be the same as spending lazy summer days together outside, but that was still something.

That broke the gloom between them a bit. The trip stopped being so much of a somber passing of the torch and became what they had both missed since the pronouncement of doom, a fun day together. They skipped rocks at the spots where there was enough unbroken water. They hunted down crayfish under rocks. They pointed out little shoals of minnows darting in the water this way and that. They yelled to make echoes in the tunnel under the bridge past Alex's house.

They were both in the creek, side by side, jumping over stones, arguing about their favorite football teams when Alex saw it. He hadn't been thinking about why he hadn't been coming down here! He was just hanging out with his friend. Maybe it wouldn't come unless called, maybe he should say something?

"Sean!" he began, but just as he said it, a huge hand came out and snatched Sean from where he stood. It was hairy with long fingers that ended in terrifying claws and most importantly, it disappeared into the hole almost as fast as it flashed out, carrying Sean with it.

Alex didn't even think, he lunged at the hole to get his friend back. Splashing through the water, he screamed as he went, "I didn't make a wish! You can't take him! Give him back!"

His face had just reached the hole in the bank when one enormous clawed finger and thumb stuck out briefly and flicked him away. The force was enormous, sending him to land on the opposite bank in a lump.

He lay there stunned and gasping for breath while from out of the hole the voice chortled and sang, "What are little boys made of? What are little boys made of? Blood and guts and meat that I munch! And such are little boys made of!"

After a painful eternity, Alex was able to pick his head up and turn toward the hole. The horrid place that had taken his friend. He tried to hold out hope that the monster would listen, but he could already see the telltale red trickle that said he was too late. He got unsteadily to his feet and lunged back toward the hole, bellowing, "He was my friend! I didn't bring him for that!"

The voice from inside cackled gleefully and said, "Well, you should have told me in advance, we could have had a lovely afternoon tea!"

At this, it laughed gleefully in its ugly, crackling voice.

"I'd get thee home with ye, boy!" it finally said. "Unless I decide I'm of a mind for seconds! But I do owe ye a wish I do, so say what it is and begone home!"

Alex's poor little mind was racing with everything that had happened, but finally, he said, "I hope nobody ever finds out what happened here!"

"Done!"

"Honey, that was Sean's mom. Weren't the two of you together today?" his mom asked after she hung up the phone.

"Huh? Naw, he never showed up," Alex didn't even look up from his game as he lied. The thing was, some part of him believed it. It was just too much for him, and he was already blurring it in his mind. And now, since he had made his wish, in some way, it was true now.

"Are you sure? She seemed pretty convinced he had plans with you today."

"We did, he just never showed up."

This had been the third disappearance of a child in the neighborhood in a year, it triggered a massive search. Alex was no longer allowed to go out unattended to play while they packed up the family's belongings. But with Sean gone, he didn't really want to anyway. His parents wrote this off to understandable worry about his friend.

Just when the search was winding down, they discovered that Larry Amberson who lived by himself in the house he'd inherited from his parents had a MASSIVE collection of child pornography on his computer. It was just a coincidence that one of those pictures was of Timothy Stetz, missing. From there, it was a short walk to a confession, even though no bodies were ever recovered.

But that helped put distance in Alex's mind. It was evil Larry Amberson who had done it, everybody knew that! Since that was more believable than what he had thought he'd known, little Alex had decided to know that, too.

After that, moving put even more distance between Alex and that summer.

Alex would grow up to do all the things boys do. First girlfriend, first dance, High School football good enough to get a scholarship, college, first job in his field, first apartment. He was at this phase in his life now, a handsome enough young man, muscular with an option for stocky further down the road if he didn't keep working out.

He was driving almost aimlessly at the moment. In the passenger seat of his moderately sporty Scion was his on-again, off-again, sort-of girlfriend Tanya. She was a good-looking blond, a buxom chest on a petite body with high cheekbones and flashing blue eyes. She was also shallow, vain, and temperamental as all hell. Which was why she still had her own apartment as well. It was also the reason they were driving aimlessly through the remaining countryside of suburban southeast New York. They had originally planned to go to the lake, but at the last minute, she decided she'd get seasick if they rented a boat.

Suddenly, he pulled the car off the road. "Holy cow!" he exclaimed.

"What is it?" Tanya demanded petulantly.

"I grew up around here, I haven't been here since we moved when I was a kid!" he blurted excitedly.

"Well, that's cool, I guess," she said, slightly mollified.

Alex drummed his fingers on the steering wheel for a second, and then said emphatically, "We got our boots and nothing to do, we're going on a hike!"

"A hike? Where?" she said, sitting upright in surprise.

"There's a creek that runs behind the houses! I haven't seen it since I was a kid! I know a place to park," he said, pulling the car back onto the road.

Just like there had always been, there was a scuffed, gravel-covered pull-off right in front of the bridge before it became the property of the farm. Alex pulled his car over, parked it, and hopped out enthusiastically. Tanya got out with significantly less verve.

"Are you sure you want to do this?" she complained.

"You bet I do!" enthused Alex. "It's all coming back to me!"

And it was. It was ALL coming back to him as they splashed into the little creek. It seemed so small now, and so much larger in the memory of his childhood. It was still beautiful, just smaller. It hadn't changed at all in that way.

It was a beautiful afternoon and here was his little creek again! Yes, it was all coming back to him indeed.... and he had MUCH better wishes to make these days.

First Appeared in "Devolution Z" August 2016

Every town I've lived in that wasn't a major city has had a town character. Everyone knows the person, has stories about them, etc. etc. For a few years, there was one where I live now, very much like the character described here. He fascinated me enough that I wrote a story about him.

Holding the Line

Nobody knew the sacrifice. Nobody could know what he did to keep them safe. It had to remain that way forever. One must suffer, so that others can go through life, never knowing how close the abyss is.

They called him The Line Man. Nobody knew why, but when everybody calls somebody something, it soon becomes impossible to track down the root of it. It just becomes something everybody does or everybody says. Logic has long since left the building on it. There are a million Skeeters out there that have no idea why they became Skeeter. They just go about their lives that way. Look at any popular phrase, there may be a reason for why you would even want a stiff upper lip, but nobody remembers what it is.

Line Man was a small-statured person. He looked old. It was hard to tell how elderly, but the impression of age was definitely there. It was hard to tell how old because of the hooded jacket he always wore no matter the time of year. If it was ninety degrees in the shade, he was still wearing it. No one had a clue what he looked like without it. The only features that you could see clearly in the depths under his hood were a large hooked nose that stuck out like a beak and deep-sunken, glinting eyes bathed in shadows. His features seemed almost rat or weasel-like, at least what you could see of them hidden in the depths of his hood.

Line Man was a town oddity. Well, considering it was a small town and he was renowned past that even better, it would be more accurate to say he was a regional oddity. Everybody knew of him and everybody called him the Line Man. He was a feature of the town no matter how hot, no matter the time of day. In his hooded attire, he would just walk up and down the rural highway with its wide berm through Bashford going to the store and back almost daily.

Occasionally and randomly, his gloved fist would get thrust into the air and pointed back down. It would just happen. He didn't turn, he didn't look at anything or anyone. He wasn't responding to any possible stimulus you could see, he just did it. A human curiosity wandering the hills of Appalachia in the snow, the rain, and the blistering heat. Always with his hooded jacket and his gloves and often with the pouring rain dripping into those haunted, crazed, deep-sunken eyes of his.

Bashford was far from being a real town. It was just a place that had grown up and out of the two-lane highway and now squatted on both sides of it. No real sidewalks, no city hall, it was just random shops with huge ancient parking lots that joined together one after the other. Much of it was neglected. Places built during the boom times still open by the grace of God. Nobody was spending any money to repair their parking lots, that was for sure. Half of them were just gravel on top of potholes now. There were a few vacant storefronts, but usually, the empty ones were younger buildings put up by some optimist who thought the town needed a motorcycle shop, or another bank, or a professional building the town clearly thought that it hadn't needed at all. The older buildings were still operational, just old and worn, often being run by the same families that dealt out medications and hardware as had done for generations now. Not all of them were even the things you'd expect that people needed here like they needed the drug store. For whatever reason, an appliance store that had opened when there were only two brands of black and white TVs available was still there, probably with the same TVs. It was hard to see through the dusty windows to tell though.

One thing Bashford did have was a small shopping center. The only things in it that stayed consistently open were the supermarket and the call center that had its own separate building connected by a parking lot. People would open up something next to the supermarket and often, by the time the residents realized the shop was there, it was already closing. It all sat in a little bit of flat space, a premium feature in Appalachia, below the town cemetery where generations of residents had been deposited on the rolling hill. The cemetery had created its own cottage industry burying former residents, people who had moved away for work but couldn't bear to have their final resting place be anywhere but in their beloved mountains and would leave the request in their wills.

The call center was why Andy Potts knew about the Line Man at all. The company that ran it was a national one, and they had needed someone to transfer to management there. Andy's family was from the area. He had found a lovely little house really cheap on a hill outside of Malvern, one of the many little towns in the region, so he had agreed to take the position. He didn't have a wife and kids to worry about, and he'd always been curious to see where his roots were. The money would have been good for Texas, where he was living at the time. For the Appalachian region, it was a king's ransom. It was a wonderful opportunity to stockpile some cash while reconnecting with his family's roots.

He first saw the Line Man, at least enough to note him, driving home from work one steaming hot afternoon. He had the air conditioner absolutely cranked in his little Escape, the Ford AC turning the compartment into a veritable arctic wasteland. There the man was, just patiently trudging along, carrying a couple of bags from the store. It must have been at least 90 degrees out there, and the man was wearing a jacket? With a hood, no less? Wearing gloves? Andy was staring so intently he felt the gravel on the shoulder under his tires and had to jerk it back onto the road.

After that, Andy noticed him relatively often. Always the same no matter the weather, just trudging along. Not speaking to anyone, not looking at anyone, randomly throwing a gloved hand into the air. Nobody else seemed to notice him either. Nobody disturbed the clearly already disturbed man as the Line Man wandered through the town like a hooded and shriveled specter.

The thing that finally drove Andy to even ask around at work was an attempt to interact with the man. It had been pouring rain, just coming down in waves. A storm must have gotten caught coming across the bigger mountains that surrounded Bashford and had stalled over the town now, unable to get up the strength to force its way over the next mountain. Just sitting there, unleashing its load of water where it was. Andy saw the man humping along, a dim figure in the pouring rain. There was no mistaking him though, even with the poor visibility. Once Andy got closer, the gloved hands made it clear who it was. Andy made a snap decision, pulling the car over off the side of the road, and slowed down. The little man went farther into the parking lot they were crossing but made no move to acknowledge Andy or his car.

Andy rolled down the window, and shouted out, "Hey, it's coming down in buckets! You need a ride?"

For just a moment, the man flicked his eyes in Andy's direction. Those deep-sunken eyes grew wide for only a moment and then narrowed. With not so much as a word, the little man sped up, splashing through puddles, refusing to acknowledge Andy anymore but trudging all the faster.

"C'mon, I don't mean you no harm. But you're gonna catch your death of cold in this!" Andy shouted.

Without even turning to look at him, a cracked elderly voice came from inside the hooded jacket to say only two words, "Go away!"

Andy just sat there, his foot on the brake, completely flummoxed by the repudiation and rebuke delivered in those two words by the odd man. Coming to his senses, he just shrugged and said almost to himself, "Your funeral, buddy," before releasing the brake and letting the car pull back onto the road. He drove by the man slowly as he went by, but the man didn't even spare him a glance, staring straight ahead again before Andy just stepped on the gas and drove away into the pouring sheets of rain.

It had roused his curiosity enough to make him ask around at that point, just too weird to ignore. One day there were a few bodies sitting around in the leader lounge on break. Andy looked around, mentally checking who was in here today. He didn't want to seem like an out-of-it doofus for mentioning something everybody else took for granted. He was looking for someone he was pally with to ask.

Having decided that this crew was safe enough, he turned to the one team lead, Billy, who was watching some amazingly terrible daytime TV on the big screen. "Hey, can I ask you something?"

"Aww gee, Andy, and I was hopin' to find out if the Judge finally found a plaintive she liked," Billy winked, turning to look at him. "What can I do ya for?"

"I gotta know. What's the deal with the weird old guy you see walking down the highway?"

"What weird guy? I ain't never seen no weird old guy," Billy declared.

Seeing Andy's worried expression, he laughed and said, "You're talking about Line Man, everybody knows Line Man!"

"So, you've talked to him?" Andy asked incredulously.

"OK, let me rephrase that, everybody knows of Line Man, how 'bout that? Naw, he won't talk to a damned soul. My cousin works as a cashier at the Kroger, guy never says a word. Puts his stuff on the conveyor, pays in cash, leaves," Billy replied.

Ronnie, an LO3 who had started to eavesdrop joined in, adding, "Yeah, but the old weirdo is harmless."

"Yeah, that's true enough, I suppose. No crime to not talk to nobody after all," Billy agreed.

"Where does he even live?" asked Andy.

"Don't even rightly know, really," Ronnie said, looking thoughtful, "never really thought about it. I guess up one of them little dirt roads that run off the highway and up into the hills somewhere."

"Hey, people!" Billy called out.

The room got quiet except for the TV as everybody turned to look. "Any of y'all know where Line Man lives?"

There was a susurration as people discussed it among themselves until one of the new Level 4's, Andy thought his name was Hunter, said, "I think he's got a place in the holler below Flat Top, but I don't know anybody that's ever been there, so I could be full of it."

"Well, there ya go, Hunter's full of it," said Billy, turning back to Andy. "Any particular reason you asked?"

"Well, you have to admit it's weird," Andy said, a little embarrassed by the fuss.

"That he is, buddy, that he is."

Andy kept tabs on Line Man after that. He wouldn't say he was obsessed with him, but he was curious. It was a boring ride to work alone anyway, and the weird old man broke up the monotony. He would find himself speculating on things, like where the guy got his clothes, did he ever wash them (they always seemed to have a sheen of human grease, compacted sweat, oils, and road grime), did he have family here, things like that.

Andy found himself turning to speculating on where the old man lived. From asking around he ascertained that he most definitely did not live in town, but that in and of itself gave no ideas. There were run down shacks tucked all over the hills from various boom times. For all he or anyone knew, the old man could just be squatting in one of them. Maybe only a cot to sleep on in a building that was one strong wind away from collapsing entirely.

Andy made a point now of marking off in his mind the farthest points from the store he'd ever seen the man, hoping to narrow it down some. But that's the problem with what starts as a completely harmless idle speculation if the answers are not soon forthcoming. Our curiosity, unsated, starts to get the best of us. Andy became intent on finding out where the old man resided. If he had stopped to think about it, or if he had more than casual friends, someone who was close enough to demand of him, "Why do you even care?" it might have ended there. But a single man living alone in the wilderness of Appalachia probably has entirely too much free time. The true perils of boredom and isolation are what we get into when we have nobody to bounce our flights of fancy off of.

Eventually, his curiosity reached a fever pitch, and Andy took to slowing down on those rare occasions when there wasn't anyone behind him, near Line Man's last known position. Creeping along at twenty-five in a fifty-five, with half an eye on his rear view. Trying to see any kind of driveway leading off that might lead to the old man's abode.

One afternoon, his persistence was finally rewarded. It might have been a driveway once, but on the day that he spotted it near twilight, all that was visible was a single straight and well-worn trail going off into the woods. The trees loomed this close to the road. They were already linking their limbs over the spot where the trail started, so even if it hadn't been twilight, it still would have been dark. If it wasn't for the fact that the woods opened up farther back, offering a better view of the trail, he would have never been sure if he'd even seen it.

Now that Andy thought he knew where the old guy was holed up, he wasn't even sure what he should do about it. The guy didn't want to talk to him, or anyone else for that matter. Andy had offered to give him a ride in the pouring rain, and the old man wouldn't even say anything to him except to tell him to go away. The thing was, he was almost considered a town possession and treasure, something the people in the area felt vaguely proud of. A lot of areas are like that, some town oddball everybody has a story about him or her, usually greatly exaggerated for effect. They were part of the very fabric of the area they resided in. They give an area ambiance and character. It's what keeps a small town from being another "blink and you'll miss it" drive-through on the highways of America. Andy wanted the whole story, including how the Line Man lived.

Maybe the guy was living in some old shack about to fall down? All alone out there in the woods somewhere. Somebody ought to know exactly where he was if only to tell social services. He seemed pretty old, and the elderly were usually subject to health checks by the authorities. It was practically his duty to check on the old guy. He became convinced it was in everybody's best interest if SOMEBODY checked on the old man's living arrangements.

Truly amazing the little lies we tell ourselves so we can do what we wanted to do in the first place.

Andy found himself now making up excuses to go through Bashford on his days off. Looking for and hoping to catch sight of the Line Man on his way TO the store, when Andy knew he'd have more time to go look at his residence. Andy had no idea how long it would take him to get back there, but if worse came to worst, he could always bolt down the mountainside and come out in Bashford eventually, so he wasn't worried about getting lost. One of the major advantages of a mountain, if you know what's down from you, you always have a good direction to go.

Parking the car and locking it up, he hurried along the highway back to the trail. Cars whipped by him, buffeting him with winds as he walked, and forcing him to go farther and farther away from the road for safety. He was practically walking in the ditch by the time he reached his destination. Looking at it now, it was clear that it HAD formerly been a driveway. He could see two tracks a vehicle's width and some gravel peeking through the leaf mold and the weeds that had grown up. Curiously, though, of the two tracks, only one showed any sign of being used recently. A thin line of packed dirt heading resolutely straight up the side of the mountain at an angle.

Now he was sure that this was the way, he set his own feet to the path. After a short distance, the trees pulled away a bit, creating some open sky above him and allowing some light to filter down. The way had become encroached by wildflowers and grass. Queen Anne's Lace and wild sweet pea dangled lazily into the remains of the roadway, the white and purple flowers lending an almost pleasant feel to the whole affair.

The trail made its way around a bend and led into a wooded hollow in the side of the mountain itself, a gouge left from some previous geological disturbance of some kind or another. Andy thought he could see a doorway where the trail was leading in the distance, but not the whole house because of the heavy forestation in the way.

When he got closer, he was not greeted with the rambled-down shack of his expectations. Rather, what came more and more into view as he approached the wooded copse that held the house was some grand leftover of a bygone era of prosperity in the region. Most amazing of all, the house itself was in fine condition. Painted a dark gray, it practically blended into the woods that housed it. Now up close, it looked in nicer condition than his own house in Malvern really. Upkeep must be all the old weirdo did with his days. Maybe the Line Man wasn't even the owner, but some really weird custodian of the place. Maybe he had been a worker on one of the nearby rail lines and had signed on as a custodian in exchange for room and board for his retirement. It would explain the name at any rate. It happened, a property would change hands a dozen times over the years. For all Andy knew, some out-of-state coal concern now owned the place in a parcel land deal and had the little man on the payroll without ever having clapped eyes on him.

But if that was the case? Why was there only that little trail leading up to the place? There had been a road, and it had been let gone to seed. You'd think if it was some out-of-town owner, they'd have come out to check on occasion, right? This additional mystery only drove Andy's curiosity even further than it had been, if that was possible. Before it had just been simple nosiness; now, he had to see how this strange old man lived out here away from the entire world.

Andy climbed onto the large porch that curved around to the side of the house, gaping at the scroll-work painted a dark green, stunned by its intricate curls. This was where a little man in greasy jeans and a hooded coat lived? All by himself? The mere concept boggled the mind. He stood at the door trying to peer in through the etched and frosted glass to see if he could see anything inside.

Andy knocked lightly on the main door, still thinking there must be someone else in this beautiful house, it couldn't be JUST the Line Man living here. The knocking was met with silence and the creaking of the porch boards as he shifted back and forth. Andy gave it a few moments, and then knocked again.

Still nothing.

Now, he was at a loss for what to do. Well, not really, nobody is really at a total loss that often, they are just weighing options. Andy was more in a position where the thing he really wanted to do was his last option, but he had to tell himself the lie that it wasn't what he had wanted to do all along so he had to check off the other options first. He also certainly couldn't acknowledge that he also had the option to just leave and go back to the car. But once Andy had gone through the mental hoops of making his actions justifiable to his own self-image of "not being nosy," he tried the door.

The ornate brass knob turned easily in his grasp, and the door swung inside, smoothly. It made not so much as a squeak as it opened. There were no lights lit of any kind; he hadn't even thought to look to see if there was any electricity running to the place. It was hard to see in the gloom that the woods created inside, but what he could see was just as ornate and well-kept as the exterior had been. The entire thing was like stepping back in time to visit a very rich uncle at the turn of the twentieth century.

"Hello?" Andy called out, not having any idea whatsoever what he'd do if someone answered. Thankfully, the house remained silent. He stepped into the place, his hiking boots only making the gentlest of noises on the hardwood floor of the entranceway. Now that Andy was inside, he was faced with a decision: he had four directions to choose from, all of them immaculately decorated in a continued period fashion for the late 1800s. It reminded him of a mansion tour he'd taken once. He could check either of the rooms to either side of the entrance, go down the hallway deeper into the first floor, or climb the stairs.

After considering it, he decided on the stairs. He had no idea how long the old man would be gone, or if he himself would ever be able to work up the nerve again to come back here. If he wanted to see what the rooms looked like upstairs, he'd have to hurry and look now. The other rooms on this floor he could look at if the Line Man hadn't returned by then, and hope for a back door to slip out of undetected.

Andy climbed the stairs slowly and carefully. It was foolish, he kept telling himself, there was clearly no one in the house, but he couldn't stop himself. When Andy reached the second floor, the light that oozed through the trees above had an easier way into the hall coming through the large bay window at either end.

There was another floor above, but he suspected it was only attic space, as the stairs going up terminated in a closed, dark oak door. Andy was content enough to explore this floor, expecting that he might find the old man's bedroom. Seeing that would give him some idea if the old man had just started squatting the building as he found it, the Line Man was just the weird caretaker, or, and this seemed inconceivable yet still a possibility, he might even be the actual owner.

Each door that he walked past Andy would try, but all of them seemed locked. They had probably been locked when the house had been closed up and vacated, however, many years ago. But he was still confident that one of them would open into the Line Man's living quarters here. It became repetitive and automatic, and as soon as it did, a doorknob finally turned in his hand!

Andy lightly pushed the door open. The room inside was almost pitch black. Obviously, the curtains to it were drawn closed. Andy could just make out the outline of a large four-poster bed, a dresser, and a nightstand in the gloom. The dresser only because it was close to the door he'd just swung open.

Now, he tried to remember if he had seen a lamp at all downstairs, or if maybe he could find a light switch in here. He groped around hopelessly in the dark, hoping against hope for a switch to come to his hand. The doorway let in light to the room, but the musty gloom inside seemed almost to swallow it up.

Andy had just turned to go back downstairs to look for a lamp when he heard the front door click open again. It was followed by sure and confident footsteps coming inside. Not someone sneaking in as Andy had, but the measured easy tread of someone who belonged here. The Line Man was back already!

Andy went as quickly and quietly as he could to the large window at the end of the hall and looked out, hoping to escape. No good at all! It was a sheer drop to the ground from here! Maybe he could find something behind the drapes in the room that was open. He stepped back into that room while still trying desperately to not let the floorboards creak from his weight.

That's when he heard the cracked elderly voice yell from below, "COME ON OUT, BOY! I KNOW YOU'RE HERE!"

Andy froze. He had no idea what to do! The old man hadn't actually SEEN him yet unless maybe he'd doubled back and had been coming behind him the whole time. Maybe it was actually the police? Maybe they'd seen him park, and decided to follow him out here? But the voice seemed old and not like one of the young jarheads that counted as the local police force here. Those were mainly state police and not locals anyway.

"Come on down, boy, and take your medicine!" the voice called from the bottom of the steps again. "I know you're there, and you know I'm between you and the door, no point in dragging things out! I don't intend to hurt you none!"

Well, there it was. There was only one open room he'd been able to find, and it was pitch dark, and probably the old man's own bedroom. Most importantly, the old man was at the stairs, between him and the door. His shoulders slumped, and he turned and walked back down the hall. It was just an old man; how bad could it be?

As he got to the top of the stairs, he looked down into the sunken, shining eyes of the Line Man, staring straight up the stairs at him from beneath his hood. "Oh, it's you! I wasn't sure, I thought it might be some local rapscallions intruding on my home and hearth. Well, you might as well get down here, and save me having to go up after ye!" he cackled, grinning at Andy.

Andy saw that he had no choice, so he slowly made his way down the stairs to where the old man waited. The old man's face was split into an insane look of glee, but he made no move that seemed to be a threat. Andy could see no weapon on the old man that might be used to ward off an invader upon his home. It didn't matter, though, every step down the stairs filled Andy with dread! A little-boy dread, that even adult men have the moment they've been caught going about the mischief that lies in the little-boy nature at the heart of a man.

When he finally reached the ground floor, the old man looked him in the eye and said, "I couldn't be sure, but now I am. Your mother was a Hypes, was she not?"

"What? Umm yeah, I think that's right, why? I mean, I'm sorry I broke into your house... well, not broke, I mean the door was open," Andy stammered.

"No, that's alright, it's fine, you done come to where you need to be, young Hypes, that's for true. Saved me the bother of having to track you down and bring you here. Thought I'd have to drag off some young'un from one of the old families afore you came home, and here you are just a-settin' in my house, now don't that just beat all?" the old man smiled happily.

"What in the hell are you talking about?" Andy demanded, attempting to sidle around the old man to give himself a clear pass at the door.

"You don't know it yet, young Hypes, but y'all got a duty to do in this house! And I aims to see that ya do it!"

With that, the Line Man poked a bony, glove-encased finger straight into the center of Andy's chest. Andy couldn't say why, but it staggered him for a second. The Line Man didn't possibly look strong enough to rock Andy that easily. Then, it terrified him. He thrust the old man aside and bolted out the open front door.

He ran through the high weeds as fast as he could, stumbling once, but never looking back. Not that it mattered, as he heard the old man call over his shoulder, making no move to pursue, "Run as fast as you can, young Hypes! But you'll be back askin' a long ton worth of questions! You mark my words, young Hypes! You'll be comin' back fer yer birthright and no mistake!"

*****

29

Andy practically collapsed once he got back to his own house. The old man hadn't hurt him and hadn't called the police on him, so Andy should look at it as "got away clean." But somehow it didn't feel that way at all. Somehow, even back here at his own house, he still felt as trapped as he did when the old man had walked in on him snooping. Time to calm down a bit, jeez, he got caught by the town crazy person poking around the house. It wasn't even like he knew it had been his before, he could just say that he'd thought it was abandoned when he found it. Who was going to believe the Line Man anyway? Andy was in management at one of the largest employers in the area for god's sake, the old guy wandered around town on 90-degree days in a hooded jacket!

No, to hell with that, time to calm down, grab a beer out of the fridge, and consider dinner. He went out to his kitchen and pulled some Chinese out of the fridge that he was sure had a few days left before it went funny. A beer and a nuked bowl of Mai Fun in his hands, he headed back out to the living room. Setting them down on a table, he kicked on the TV and sat down, to hopefully go from completely spazzed to calmed down and maybe a bit fuzzed.

A bowl of noodles and pork and two beers later, he finally began to feel human again. The show didn't matter much, something involving cars and people building them on what used to be a channel that showed documentaries about nature. All that mattered at this point was feeling normal again. Everything about today was bizarre and creepy and left him off-kilter. It was stupid, but it wasn't the kind of thing that occurred to everyone, every day, so he could feasibly excuse himself for being thrown by it.

Later, he figured he might get a shower just to complete his journey back to normal. Andy went to his bedroom and tossed his shirt and pants into the hamper, quickly following it with his socks and underwear. The bathroom was old, set directly off the bedroom. He'd surmised that the house was old enough that it had just been added on when the plumbing had been installed. Most of the houses in the area that weren't the former coal owner's mansions seemed to have been built in portions. The American Dream on the DIY installment plan.

The hot steam wafted up out of the old claw-foot tub, filling the room with clouds. One of the first things he had done after closing on the house was installing a new hot water heater. Winter nights could get cold up in these hills; a hot, HOT shower was worth its weight in gold after shoveling the drive. Andy wiped the mirror clean with a towel and looked at his reflection to see if he could avoid shaving for another day. That was when he saw it.

A black dot, on his chest, right where the old man had poked him with his finger. It sat, not a bruise, although still the right contour of his chest, but not his chest. The hair there was gone, and as he gaped at it, he could see it was perfectly smooth there now. Like a material in his chest not made of him at all! But as he touched it, it still felt like something was resisting, like something had been grafted into the spot.

It had to be a stain of some kind, the old man must have had some chemicals on his hands or something. Lord knew he never took those damned gloves off. They could have anything on them, anything at all. It didn't hurt, at least there was that, it didn't feel anything. Even when he poked at it, he didn't really feel it.

Carefully, he climbed into the shower. He was sure whatever it was, whatever had happened, he'd just scrub it off with some soap and water. For all he knew, he had something on his hands. He didn't remember if he'd looked at his shirt to notice some kind of stain. He'd have to make a point to look at it tomorrow to make sure it didn't get in with the rest of the laundry just in case.

Soaping up the shower scrub, he went right for the spot. But no matter how hard he scrubbed, he couldn't get any of it to budge. Not even a flash of the pink flesh underneath! There must BE pink flesh underneath, right? He scrubbed harder, and then harder still, in a panic now. He only stopped when he was forced to stop, when the skin around the hole in his skin had gotten raw enough that a few spots began to bleed.

What in the HELL had that old coot done to him?

He got out of the shower and dried himself off, trying to think. He reached a single conclusion; the old son of a bitch knew what he'd done. That's why he was crowing about him having to come back! Of course, Andy would, just to find out what the old lunatic had put on him! And Andy knew where he was all right, he knew where the Line Man was at, right now. He was up in that damned house of his, probably laughing about it. Taking some sick glee in whatever party prank he'd managed to do to him.

Screw this! He went to the hamper and pulled his clothes back out and thrust them on. The old bastard could fix this or suffer the beating of his weird little life! He even thought for a moment about bringing his gun but decided not to. Even as weird and crazy as the old man clearly was, a homicide was a homicide, and he didn't want his own life to go south that way. If he didn't fix it, instead Andy could haul him off to the local cops, and the Line Man could tell THEM what he'd done. Andy noted there was no stain on his shirt, the weirdo must have treated his finger with some chemical or another, not some ink, but something that would only react to skin.

Andy would find out as soon as he got up there.

Andy had already started driving down the driveway itself before he forced himself to stop and walk the rest of the way. There was no point in tearing out the bottom of the car just because he was in a hurry. Andy had a little flashlight he'd gotten from a box store at some point in the car, so he grabbed that. No point in tripping in the rutted former drive either. A broken ankle would seriously ruin the intimidation he wanted to achieve.

As he got closer to the house, stomping through the dark wildflowers, Andy could see through the misty mountain night two lights were lit on the house's porch. It seemed like the old nut was expecting him back sure enough and wanted to make sure Andy knew that he'd be taking guests tonight. For some reason, this made Andy even madder, like the old weirdo was playing with him. Like he thought Andy was a local kid who would fall for his mumbo-jumbo about duty, or be impressed that he knew his mom's last name.

"Come on out of there, you crazy freak!" Andy yelled as he yanked the door open.

He heard the man's cracked voice calling from up above, "Ain't no need to be yellin' so! I knew you wuz comin'. I'm up here in the attic, a-waitin' for y'all to get here!"

"What do you want? Look, I'm sorry about coming into your house!" Andy yelled up the steps.

It was quiet for a second before the Line Man called back down, "I tol' you before, I ain't even mad, y'all come on up and I'll explain it. Lamp's right there by the door, bring it with to light your way!"

Andy was thrown for a moment. He'd come up screaming like a madman himself, and the old man didn't sound the least bit perturbed by it. For all the elderly thing could know, Andy could be here to cause him violence, and yet, the Line Man sounded happy to see him! Andy stood there for a second, just staring at the lamp on the stand by the door, unsure of himself now.

While the house creaked in the night as it settled, he made his decision. He'd come here to find out what the old fool had done to his chest, and Andy wasn't going to be given that information standing down here in the front hall, now was he? He seized the oil lamp from where it stood on the nightstand and began his way up the ancient wooden steps.

He reached the steps to the attic, he could see it outlined by what he could only suppose was lamp light as well, but closed. Andy hesitated once again, unsure of himself, until the cackling voice called down, "Well, come on up, you didn't come all this way to have yourself a gander at the attic door, now did you?"

He reached the top of the stairs and flung the door open, hoping to ruin any plans the Line Man had of maybe ambushing him as he entered. He needn't have worried, Andy didn't even see him. Directly in front of him, under the ancient bows of this elderly house, there were candles laid out for light. They guttered from the force of the wind caused by the doors opening, but none were extinguished from it.

But that was not the strange part. Well, certainly not the strangest; that honor went to how the shadows danced in every other part of the large and airy attic, but absolutely none moved at all on the wall behind the candle.! Where there should be light and flickering shadows on the wall, there was nothing, absolute nothing! Andy could see that the candles were laid out in front of it, in what was clearly marked off as a pattern that he didn't recognize, yet the shadows flickered and wandered about the attic everywhere but on the wall behind the candles.

The Line Man spoke out of the darkness, "Strange, ain't it?"

Andy whirled to where he had thought the voice was coming from, but to his astonishment, he could see no one. No one, that is, until the Line Man raised his head to stare at him, and even then, only the wrinkled dirty old face, and nothing else.

The Line Man stepped forward, and Andy gaped when it was revealed that the reason he had not seen him was the Line Man's entire body was every bit as black as the gaping mark on Andy's own chest. Every bit as black as the hole on the wall! The naked old man did not show where something was, but only showed where nothing existed at all! Absolute darkness, which the light of the candles did not reflect off of. The only way Andy could even tell where the man's body was was that he could see the shadows dancing behind the old man as he stretched out his arms and stepped toward him.

"So, a welcome home to the ol' Lord of the Manse, I be supposin'?"

Andy recovered from his astonishment enough to blurt, "I don't know what in the HELL you are talking about, you monster!"

The old man stopped and smiled at that before saying, "Well, monster I may be, but it's a monster you're becomin'."

Now it was Andy's turn to step toward the man, suddenly no longer afraid or in awe, but suddenly furious again. "What did you DO to me?"

"I ain't done nuthin' to you but bring out your birthright, boy!" the old man smiled happily. "Don't y'all know that you're the rightful heir and master to Flattop House?"

"I've never been told anything like that, I just know my family hails from here at one point. I don't own this house, you old fool!" Some part of Andy was relieved now, thinking to himself that this was all a case of mistaken identity. He could talk it out, and have whatever the old man had done undone just as easily!

"Oh, but I'm afraid you do, young sir!" The old man peered intently at Andy and then continued, "Your, I'm guessing, great-great-grandfather built this house around about, oh, 1893, young Hypes. I've just been holding it down and keepin' the Line."

"When did you start doing this job for my family?" Andy demanded incredulously.

"Say, around 1898."

"You really are nuts, you know that? You may be old but you're not—"

"140 years old?" the Line Man said, cutting him off. "I'll give ya that, I might be 143 by now, but my beauty regimen hides it well. But I've just about had it, doin' the work, too old, too worn out. Not enough of the real me left to do it anymore, all of it sucked away into the black as I fought with it! Now I can give it back to you. It was your family's job in the first damned place, but your damned great-great-grandpappy ran out on me and left me holding the bag on this damned place!"

"Alright, that does it! Just fix what the hell you did to my chest and let me get the hell OUT of this nut house!" Andy snarled.

"Can't be doin' that," the Line Man said quietly.

"Of course, you can, you did it to yourself! Now you've done it to me! Now UN do it, God damn it!"

"Don't be takin' the Lord's name in vain, boy, this ain't his fault!"

Oddly, Andy felt weirdly chagrined by the rebuke, it felt like a splash of cold water on his face. "I didn't realize you were religious, I apologize." He had lived in the area long enough to understand the strong religious nature of many residents and to know this was something you apologized for automatically if called out on it. Andy had just responded instinctively.

"If Ezekiel had paid things like that more mind, neither one of us would be in the mess we're in," Line Man said, slightly mollified.

"What mess are you talking about?" Andy demanded, again feeling his frustrations bubble back up.

"Your ancestor, boy! He messed with things ought to be left be. He made a bunch of money in coal, built this house, and suddenly since he was all big and rich now, he thought he needed to be a man of learnin'! Took hisself up north and bought all kinds of books from libraries and stores up there. Just bought 'em willy nilly and stacked 'em up on shelves. Some of those books shoulda' stayed on up North, I reckon. It might be odd for a man to be readin' old romances, but it would have been better by far than what he decided himself to get to readin'. Then he started doin' more but readin'," the old man subsided for a moment.

"Like what?" Andy asked quietly, his curiosity overwhelming him for a moment.

"He started comin' up here and doing things out of the books! He said if it worked out, we'd all be rich forever! Said we'd be like gods! Said the things would help him! More the fool me I didn't light out of here to get a preacher there and then! One day he comes down white as a sheet, didn't eat no breakfast, just grabbed me to get me away from the other servants, and tol' me, 'Shamus, I haves to go, but afore I do, I need you to promise to do things for me, otherwise there will be terrible consequences for everyone, anywhere near here!' Now, I used to be a soldier afore I become his handyman, I know sometimes you have to do things you'd rather not for the good of everyone, so I agreed."

"I'm sorry for you, but I still don't know what this has to do with me at all! I just work at a call center for the love of all that's holy! I had nothing to do with what some, now turned to dust, ancestor of mine did," Andy declared, his voice subdued, but with some of the anger coming back.

"Now that's where you're wrong, boy, would that you weren't, cause, believe me, I ain't got nuthin' 'gainst you personally," the old man said quietly. "Your ultimate sire, he opened something. See that black spot? It's a hole, leading to a place where things dwell, and I do mean things. Whatever shape they have, they steal from our world, and if left to themselves, they'd steal the whole place, just to feel the one thing we got they ain't, the warm glow of life and substance! They look for holes in the world that can lead them between their existence and ours. Holes like Ezekiel Hypes opened up that night. I stayed here the entire time since, performing the rites, making the chants, keeping them at bay. Now I'm spent, and one of the families that was here when it happened, the old families of these mountains, is going to have to hold the line until somebody figures out how to close it up. It has to be one of us, those that were here when it happened."

The old man stepped forward a bit himself so he was almost face to face with Andy now, his face the only part dancing in the flickering candlelight, the only part of him that reflected anything at all, and continued, "It takes some of you back into that hole, to hold the line. Ain't but nuthin' left o' me but my heid, now is there? I ain't got much time left, young Hypes. I was gonna have to grab some poor innocent who ain't done a thing to anybody, didn't even do the crime of helping Ezekiel to open this pit into the abyss, and who should walk in? Why, a Hypes his own self! When I thumped you, boy, I passed the mantle! It's now your job! I'll show you afore I go, but that hole is all yours now, 'bout damned time a Hypes took care of what he done!"

That snapped Andy out of whatever reverie this whole weird scene had created in him. He backed away, "Oh no, no way in HELL! I'm leaving here, you old weirdo, and I'd like to see you stop me!"

With that, Andy turned and fled down the steps, his feet pounding on the ancient wood as he went, yelling back over his shoulder, "I am leaving here, you got that! Don't follow me, and if you ever try to talk to me again, I swear to god I'll run you down with the car! Nobody is going to miss you!"

He was bounding down the stairs, desperate to get out of this house, out of this weird. Get back to his car, get back to his house. He could have a doctor look at the thing on his chest, hopefully it wasn't cancerous. It was just some chemical the old freak got into, that was it! Everything he thought to himself while he fled, he didn't believe, though he just wanted it to be true. He could feel the malevolence of the hole, the black inky dark in the attic itself, lurking away behind him. Its longing and want! But it wasn't his problem, he just wanted to see where his family came from by coming to these mountains, and there was no sin in that. He'd seen it now, and he'd seen plenty!

Andy lunged through the front door and down off the porch. He stumbled a bit, recovered, and got ready to run for his car and freedom. That was when the lights pinned him to the spot. Suddenly, the entire wood and field in front of the house were illuminated by flashlights brightly blinding him.

"Who's there? Get out of my way, I have to leave!" Andy yelled hoarsely, his breath coming in gasps. He could hear behind him the cackling laugh of the Line Man up in the attic, driving on Andy's own panic with his laughter.

One of the lights extinguished itself and a figure came forward to where he could see it. It was Billy! "I'm sorry, Andy, I can't let you do that," he said calmly.

Andy looked at Billy, uncomprehending, and then blurted out, "Billy, you gotta help me, man, that old guy is crazy! You gotta get me out of here!"

"No, Andy. I am sorry but you have to go back there and do your job, buddy. My family has been in these hills a long time, and I got kids, you don't. I gotta care for my kin, Andy, I can't let you leave."

Andy looked down, and saw that his coworker had a gun in his hand. Oh, to hell with these crazy people! He was out of here! He drew himself up to bull past what he had thought was his friend. That was when he heard the series of coffin-nail clicks, of dozens of guns being cocked at once.

"If it's any consolation, Andy, I really am awful sorry," Billy said quietly.

From behind him, Andy heard the gleeful voice of the Line Man, "Well, if you're done, why don't you get yourself back on up here, and I can get started showing you what you need to do! Come and claim your patrimony, boy!"

In the town of Bashford, once a day, a man trudges along next to the rural highway that runs through town. He's carrying groceries from the local supermarket. He talks to no one, he looks at no one, and all of the locals do the same to him.

Nobody knew the sacrifice. Nobody knew what he did to keep them safe. It had to remain that way forever. One must suffer, so that others can go through life, never knowing how close the abyss is.

First Appeared in Schlock! Issues 277-278

I've noted before, I really don't like writing for specialty calls. If for whatever reason the piece you write doesn't fit the editor's vision, well, you're stuck with a very hard to place piece of writing. Generally, I write enough that when submission calls go out, I have something that will work. But when Douglas Draa mentioned he wanted to do a Witches Annual for Weirdbook, it set off an idea. Glad I followed through on it, this piece ended up finishing 3rd Critters, Preditors And Editors Readers Poll for 2017.

Last of the Ashiptu

He was positive one of the reasons that he had worked this hard in life was to avoid life's little annoyances. You struggle to climb the corporate ladder, you have no time for close friends, you put off having a family, all for a reason. He was the youngest company President on the market right now. Companies vied for his services, even though none of them were sure if he was worth it, but a good hype man is better than all of the background checks on earth. He made damned sure that he was in every magazine out there, selling the wondrous product of himself. But the point was, you did all of that to achieve something, to be able to afford to not have the little blasts and bothers that made other people so miserable with their lives.

This week, though, he had been "other people" all week. Today, it had been the ticket and a flat tire.

He didn't HAVE to drive, he could be limo-ed. He certainly had the money, but he LIKED to drive. He bought cars because he liked to drive them. At least normally. Today, he was positive he had paid the meter, he was positive he hadn't been in the Design Center very long, he was sure of all of that. He was also just as sure of the ticket waiting for him on the Mercedes when he got there.

39

Not to mention the flat tire. It had just been that kind of a week.

He climbed into the car to consider his options. He could call Triple-A, but they wouldn't be here for forever. He had a meeting to get to, and he really couldn't wait. He considered fixing it himself for a few moments, he'd changed a tire before, for the love of God. As he stepped out of the car to consider it, a cab whipped by at roughly the speed of sound just then. The whole car rocked from the wind of its passage. Nix that. He decided that he'd just drive on the flat, and deal with replacing the whole rim later. Maybe he'd send some gopher down to change it while he was in meetings. Slowly, he pulled the car out into traffic.

That was when the bike messenger ploughed directly into the door. It had just been that kind of week.

As he pulled into his parking garage, the guy in the booth leaned out, "Hey, you know your tire's flat?"

He just sighed and said, "Thank you for pointing that out," and limped it slowly to his spot.

Williams Bryant, 34, single, moderate height, blond, blue-eyed, hot-shit executive. President of SZN Holdings, second only to CEO Aran Nagi, and his chosen successor. Every year someone made an offer to buy him off to their company, and every year Williams stayed put. In other words, he was living the good life. His politics were strictly mercenary, his music tastes a weird hodgepodge of rap and rock that he listened to in college.

It was in his senior year of college that his mentor and boss Nagi found him. He didn't know why the successful Arab man had taken him under his wing (it would turn out Aran was Iranian, his family having fled to America with all of its money mere months before the Islamic revolution). But here and now, he thought he saw it: Aran needed an American just as soulless and driven as he was, a kindred spirit in his new land. It was hard to argue, life had one goal and one measure, money. At first, it had just been simple laziness. Life was easier if you had money. But now, it was score-keeping.

But wasn't everything? Women, cars, houses, having them was boring. Getting them was part of the fun. The real fun began after you'd gotten them. Knowing that someone out there was gnashing their teeth with jealousy, that was the joy. You might not drive the 1970 Ferrari even once a year, and it might not even be your favorite car, but you kept it anyway. Just knowing that some poor sap out there couldn't have it kept you warm at night, just as it kept him up.

It was one of the reasons he remained unmarried, never owning anything that could take itself away from him. It was a frame of mind Aran would have done well to consider himself. There was a party one night and Aran had left it to go deep-sea fishing in the middle of the night with some of his friends. Which is a privilege of having enough wealth. You can go deep-sea fishing no matter how late or drunk you are, and if there's trouble, policemen exist to make that trouble go away for you. Will had begged off, citing his own intake of alcohol which he had exaggerated.

Which left him alone with Noora. Noora, who he had secretly lusted over for the five years since he had been Aran's best man. Aran had married her because he thought his fortune should have a physical heir, and she had been from a prominent Iraqi family that he had business dealings with, so she was easy to acquire. She was also gorgeous, her dark hair framing a strong yet feminine face that showed fortitude and beauty at the same time, and eyes you could practically swim in. Will, as he was known to close associates, couldn't have helped himself if he had tried. And he hadn't tried.

And while Aran fished, or most likely passed out below deck, Will, his trusted partner, wooed his wife. It had taken Will hours, plying her with alcohol and lies. He found what she was lacking in Aran, and found a way to provide it for her. Her marriage was a loveless, passionless arrangement, so first, he flattered her with compliments, and then he gave her lust and passion. Will acquired her for one night, the same way he acquired everything. Once he had her, her only value would be to hurt Aran, and strangely, he felt bad about that, so he was willing to let it go.

Both of them agreed to pretend it never happened by morning and to never speak of it again. She for fear of her situation, and he out of a desire to not cuckold his mentor. That was five months ago.

Will spent his time in the executive elevator getting more bad news. Word of the takeover he had organized on a rival had somehow leaked out to the press. This was going to cost; the shareholders had mounted a vigorous defense of the food maker, which left him few options. He could either mount an expensive campaign to force it through, every second of which was going to cost them profit when they dismantled the damn thing, or he could sell out of it now while the stock prices were up, which would make him look weak to their competition.

Either way, he was boned when he'd have to explain it to Aran.

Every single day this week had been like this, every day and in every way. One of his cars had gone in for a tune-up and was still in the garage as the mechanic hunted for the rare parts it would need for a transmission rebuild. At his California house, his caretaker had called to tell him that a very, very expensive chandelier was now being swept up and that he, the caretaker, had needed stitches. This, of course, just upped his insurance on that place. He'd have paid outright for the doctor's visit for the guy, but since the man had been bleeding out at the time, he'd ended up taking a ride in an ambulance. He'd met a girl at a very exclusive club a few nights ago, and he thought he was moments from closing the deal with her until her boyfriend showed up, the ex-heavyweight champion.

It felt personal.

Which was stupid, he knew. Life didn't operate that way, but it didn't help his feelings for the knowing of it.

Will sat at his desk, trying to get his head straight before this meeting. He clicked on to Facebook. He kept a fake page on there just for friends. You just don't keep a page under your own name to goof off on Facebook or Twitter, where everything you say can and will go right to the press. He was just about to close it out when he noticed a message request. The profile had no picture with it, from someone named Agnes Sampson. He didn't know anyone by that name, so it was weird to see it on his private profile. He didn't bother to open it, he didn't have to. It only consisted of one word, "Ezeru."

For some reason, Will was weirded out by it. He had no idea what it meant and didn't have the time to look it up before his meeting with some of the underlings from a newly acquired energy concern. He found himself not even listening to the meeting, really just nodding at the appropriate moments, while they were going through projections.

Until something caught Will's attention. "Wait, what was that last thing?"

"We're hung up getting a clearance on a set of fracking pods?" the nervous looking exec repeated.

"Why in the hell are we hung up, I thought for sure we BOUGHT the seats for the local reps there?" he demanded, irate and heated.

"The local didn't stay bought, Will, he went to the press with water concerns," the other fidgeted.

"Why in the HELL did our bought-and-paid-for state rep do that?" Williams demanded.

"Apparently one of our other pods cost his cousin his home, and he developed a conscience and a spin because of it."

"Jesus CHRIST!"

It had just been that kind of a week.

It was Thursday. It was his last meeting for the week, and Will was getting out of here before anything else could go wrong. Especially before Aran found out about the pod going south on them. They'd get the land eventually, and the clearances, but this was going to devour their profit margin for a while. He sure as hell didn't want to be here to explain it.

Will told his secretary Ellen to not forward him anything until Sunday night unless it involved an actual fire. Even then she was to consider if there was a possibility that it would go out on its own. He needed a weekend away. Will wasn't sure where, but it was going to be nowhere near New York City. THIS was the kind of problem money could solve.

Will was already in the parking garage when he remembered that he hadn't left instructions to have the flat repaired. Will had choices here. He could have an assistant get another car, and then have this one delivered. He could also call a repairman. But none of it seemed right, part of owning cars is the manliness of tinkering with them. The entire day seemed powerless, at least he could handle this on his own.

A text buzzed him as he walked. Taking out his phone, he looked down. "Unknown Number." But he could see what it said. It said, "Ezeru."

He almost broke a knuckle changing the flat tire.

*****

Will got to his condo early that day and grabbed a bottle out of his beer fridge. Almost everything in there cost more per bottle than a case of normal beer. Will sometimes doubted it tasted any better, but appearances needed maintaining. He couldn't allow a guest to go in there and find something plain, it wouldn't look right.

He had called in a meal (Will kept a chef on retainer) and went to his study. Will wanted to check his messages and watch some TV. After he ate, he'd figure out where he was going this weekend other than that magical place, "anywhere but here," that people often dream of. One thing he had going: Will didn't have to dream, he just needed to make arrangements.

He turned on the TV, but kept the volume low. Some football, he didn't really need volume for it. The announcers annoyed him half the time anyway, just talking to fill space mostly. They'd contradict each other one play to the next. "Boy, I love the way this secondary never gives up," the next play going for a fifty-yard touchdown with nobody anywhere near the receiver, "You just CAN'T give up on a play like that in this league!"

Will sat down on the couch and opened up his tablet and his beer. Time to clear out his messages in his private email. Will had a private email almost nobody knew, but even with spam blockers working their magic, it would still fill up amazingly quick if he didn't stay on top of it. It filled up to the point where you had to be careful you didn't accidentally delete something you actually wanted, so he was dutifully scanning his way down.

One of the emails was labeled "Ezeru," he deleted it without opening it. Someone was fucking with him. It was either that, or he'd gotten on the weirdest mailing list. He wasn't having it, not tonight, not ever. Whoever it was would sooner or later figure out that they weren't getting to him, and when they tried to goad him further, they'd slip up and let on who they were. When that happened, Will would ruin that prick!

When he went to swing his legs up onto the couch in annoyance at the whole thing, there was a thunk and a bubbling hiss. Will looked down to watch his white carpet begin to soak up about fifty dollars' worth of beer that he'd just knocked off the table. Thankfully, he had a lot more; his plans for the rest of the night included more anyway. Time to eat dinner and drink himself to sleep. Tomorrow would be another day. The rest of the night went fuzzy soon after.

The next morning Will got up slowly, and carefully, thanking all things holy he had remembered to darken the windows before he had passed out last night. He hadn't drunk that much, and he wasn't old enough for a hangover to be an automatic consequence of drinking, but light hurt regardless. If the windows had been letting in full sunlight right now, that would have been considerably worse.

Coffee, the smell of the Jamaican Blue, already filled the kitchen as he wandered in, truly magical. It presented the hopes that the day would not be as awful as he'd suspected when he had opened his eyes. Coffee, a couple of hits off the oxygen tank he kept for just such an emergency, ibuprofen, and some eggs, and maybe things would be fine.

Will sent down an order for his breakfast and toddled off to his study, steaming mug in hand. Flicking on his tablet, he opened up a news page. It was amazing that in a world where they had part ownership of one of the major networks, there would still be news he hadn't heard about already. But god bless the world, it still found a way to be surprising. God damn it, their little paid-for state rep had made the news whining about poisoned drinking water. Time to get the local papers to publish some dirt on him. If he'd sold out to Will's people, there had to be enough of it, and if what they had wasn't sufficient, it was amazing what people would swear to for the right amount of money.

Annoyed, he flipped open his email and started scanning through and deleting. He almost deleted one marked "IMPORTANT" because everyone knows that nothing that is actually important is actually marked that way in the message line. But he took the check off of it when he saw who it was from, Noora Nagi. After hitting it with quick scan and finding there weren't any viruses, he opened it. *I understand that you are having bad luck lately. I think I know why. Meet me at the Great Falls in Patterson at 7 tonight, and I will explain. Please do not tell anyone. Aran might get angry, you understand. -Noora, P.S. Do not call for the same reason.*

Will's brain had twitched to full awake now. Any lazy easing into consciousness had vanished and he was now on full alert. He kept re-reading the message like it would suddenly crack under his scrutiny and relay its hidden meaning. But it remained inscrutable as ever. Did Aran know? Was that it? Was Aran just trying to make his life a living hell now? Get Will to quit on his own without a public scandal? Make his deals look so bad that his value went down? What if it wasn't that, what if it was someone else, and someone was trying to blackmail Noora? What if nobody knew at all and she just wanted to talk to him about his guilt and was using office scuttlebutt about his recent string of bad days as an excuse? Will could already concede the only way he would get an answer now was to meet her. Will answered the email back asking if she could just call him or text him back to tell him whatever was so important, but he didn't expect an answer. He wasn't getting away today, at least not far away.

After breakfast, he researched what he could on Noora Nagi, trophy wife. Most of what Will found he already knew, she came from a well-known family after all. As far as he could tell digging through, Noora's family had been in some prominence as long as there were records to track. Normally not the type to fall in with a con artist like Aran, they probably would have looked down on him for his family fleeing, but the US invasion had screwed with their own holdings significantly. They knew they needed friends in the US to put their portfolio back together, and Aran would do just that. All very, very mercenary.

With nothing in there to prepare him anymore for the meeting than he already was, Will went and got a shower. He would spend the day puttering around the place and be sure to get to Patterson early. Will was actually not completely dreading it, he'd always wanted to see the falls themselves. It might be weird circumstances, but he'd see them today. For all Will knew, this wasn't anything major; she just needed to talk, after all.

In his entire life, Will could only remember coming to Patterson maybe twice, and by limo both times. He'd always been curious to see the falls up close, but never enough to go out of his comfort zone to do it. He was not happy to see all the trash on the streets surrounding parts of the park as he cruised around the park itself. It made him thankful that his Benz was fixed. It was heavily insured and frankly, Benzes were easily replaced.

Will decided to find the most exposed-looking lot he could find and park there. It would at least take some measure of daring to break into his car there. The car itself had enough anti-theft devices they wouldn't be able to drive it off anyway, but maybe location would discourage outright rifling through it for anything stealable. He didn't want to drive back to the city on broken glass, after all.

The day itself felt brisk. Will couldn't help but reason that it was the mist coming off the falls, which he could hear over the noise of the surrounding city and the nearby highway. But there was no denying the pleasant air it gave to the park. Brisk was indeed the word for it. He was almost smiling as he locked up the Benz and strode in down the path. Once inside the gates, he realized the place was actually slightly bigger than he'd been prepared for. Not that much of a worry, though, Noora always dressed spectacularly. An Arab woman dressed at the absolute pinnacle of fashion shouldn't be too hard to spot, even in New Jersey.

In reality, it ended up taking him longer than he expected; she was actually dressed in a Hijab. It was even more striking because he had only seen her ever wear top-of-the-line high fashion before, never anything traditional. "Noora?" he called out hesitantly, still unsure it was her.

She smiled at him, gave a wave, and said, "Will, so good of you to come."

"Well," he said with a shrug, "you did say it was important."

"It is," she nodded. "But first, let us look at the fall. I have had few opportunities to see something like this. Iraq has falls, but traveling to the north for something like sightseeing has been difficult during my life."

With that comment, it seemed like she was shutting him off for now. His need to find out what this was all about had to wait until they had both seen the falls. Considering the urbanization on all sides, he had to admit it was a spectacular thing to have right there. There was a large footbridge across the front of the gorge the falls were in, they walked across side by side. The atmosphere gave it all the feel of two kids on a date.

Once they had crossed the bridge, Noora led them down the steps closer to the falls themselves. The water was oppressively loud now. The noise had become an all-encompassing thing, totally moving past sound into tacit sensation. It was so endless and enormous in its nature that you could feel the pounding. You'd have to practically shout to be heard by the person right next to you, he suspected somehow that this was what Noora had in mind in choosing the place.

She looked over, staring at him with her surprising blue eyes sparkling in her dark face. It was one of the things that had made her so irresistible to him. "So, Will, how much do you know about my family?" An odd question he wasn't expecting.

He rebounded from his surprise quickly. "The basic stuff, established family, used to be loaded, the war wasn't kind to you."

"Yes," she smiled at that, "that's all that really is available without snoops on the ground. But my family goes all the way back to Babylon itself, you can trace the entire lineage all the way back to where records cease to exist."

"That's pretty amazing, really," he actually meant that.

"Let me ask you, Will, do you know what the Ashiptu is?" she asked, looking directly into his eyes.

"No, I mean, why should I?" he asked. The question irritated him in its random nature.

"In ancient times, it was a witch, or a warlock is what your English would call it," Noora said, her face oddly placid and calm as she spoke, despite the volume it took to make oneself heard.

"Oh, OK," he answered, trying to figure out where she was going with this.

"The women in my family have always been treasured, which I suppose as an American you would be incredulous at. We are treasured because we have always had abilities as Ashiptu, and it has brought much wealth to our family over the centuries," she said matter-of-factly.

"You brought me here to tell me you were a witch?"

"No, of course not. Well, not entirely. What I really needed to tell you first is that I'm pregnant."

It took a moment for the full force of the shock to hit Williams. "Wait, what?"

"Before you ask, you are indeed the father, the only one capable of having done it. Which is why, in my rage and upset, I cursed you," she said, staring placidly into the sucking void of the falls.

He grabbed her shoulders and twisted her to face him. "Noora, what in the hell are you talking about?" She stared at his hands for a moment, and remembering himself, he removed them. "Look, I'm sorry but..."

She smiled sadly at him before continuing, "Aran is incapable of it, so that leaves only you, Will. That is what Ezeru means, Will, it is a hex or a curse. You have felt, maybe, like everything you touch lately has gone to hell? It has, and it will only get worse for you, I'm afraid." She looked briefly out over the spray again. "But I realized to my shame that I was being unfair. I know what Aran will do to me when he finds out, and I already heard you refusing to fight to save me inside the walls of my heart. Would you do that, Will? Would you risk your career to be a father and a husband?"

She watched his face carefully, examining it until she was sure she was seeing the denial that she had expected. His hangdog look of "But I can't" spoke louder to her than if he had opened his mouth. "I know, but it is still unfair and wrong to put the Ezeru upon you, it is out of your hands. So, I want to make things right, I want to take the curse away, to offer you the Right of Maqlu."

Something about it all exasperated him worse than before, and he just snarled, "Well, do it already!"

"Would that it was that easy. The law of the gods and the world offer one solution. You must plunge into a holy river at a spot of my choosing," she pointed at a spot in the middle of the falls, where it flattened out briefly before the water's final plunge into the river, "and I chose there."

"Are you out of your mind?" he practically screamed. "What in the hell am I saying, you're talking about magic and curses, of course you're out of your mind! No way am I doing that!"

She smiled as she reached into her purse, a beatific smile, like the one a mother gives a child who is being dangerously foolish. Will looked down and he saw the meaning to the smile. It was given enforcement by the hard lump of murderous steel she drew out. Her mandate had the strength of burning death behind it, she could afford to grin at his childishness.

"I think you will, one way or another. If I shoot you where you stand, you'll fall in. That would most likely be certain death from here. But it does fulfill Maqlu. But if you're careful making your way across the rapids, there is a spot where maybe you climb down, and only get wet and bruised. If I shoot you, I will just tell Aran that you raped me and that I was ashamed and did not want to get in the way of men and business so I said nothing. He thinks all women from the old world are broodmares, good for nothing but getting children upon. He will believe I am so dutiful I would rather hide my shame in silence until I could bear it no longer. Aran will welcome your death."

Williams looked at her. He could see immediately there was no hint of a joke or levity in her face now. She had also somehow moved out of his reach, there would be no grabbing the gun. He didn't know a damned thing about guns except that they made a good wedge issue in a tight election, but he had no doubt it was loaded.

"But why, Noora?"

"Will, I'm doing you a favor, don't you see? If I let it go on, the Ezeru would get worse and worse until it killed you. It is the only way to remove it, this is your only hope now! But you HAVE hope!" Her face actually looked sad and pitying as she spoke.

"Why here?"

"It is beautiful enough to be sacred."

Will looked in the direction she indicated, he realized he didn't have much choice in it. He could just tell someone and have her committed after this, or Aran would. She was only supposed to be a trophy wife, and trophies weren't supposed to wave guns at your partner. Heck, how did he even know she was actually pregnant? For all he knew, she'd just flown off her nut being cooped up by Aran so much. But never antagonize a crazy person with a gun if you had options, even bad options.

Now that Will looked at it, he thought he could indeed see a way down. It looked dangerous, and normally he wouldn't even consider it. But dangerous compared to what? The woman behind him talking about magical powers and waving a loaded pistol around?

Will turned to implore her to think about it when the gun exploded behind him. There was a second noise as the bullet ricocheted off the hard stone next to him. He heard her behind him say, "Please, Will, I'd feel terrible about it, but the next one is going through your thigh."

"SHE'D feel terrible? What about me?" he muttered to himself as he inched toward the water. Getting there wouldn't be AS bad as he'd thought at first, it was dry rock most of the way. But there were spots he'd have to jump or wade. Will was still trying not to think about the crevice-climb down with its slick rocks and pounding water. Thank god he'd dressed casually. That meant he had sneakers on, at least, and the beginning was just light bouldering. Within very little time, he was past the point of any safety. He could hear the roar of the water right below him. Every step was terror now, he wasn't an outdoorsy sort of guy by nature. He liked adventure, but in a clipped-off-to-a-rope sort of way, not a slip-and-die one!

Will could see he was getting close to where he was going to have to risk a jump. He had considered wading but he doubted now up close that he could stay upright in the current. Hopefully, he turned to see if maybe Noora would relent. She was watching him with the gun pointed at him still, with what he was afraid looked like pinpoint accuracy. It dawned on him, wealthy young woman who lived through a war, she could probably hit a fly at fifty yards.

As he turned back to look at the upcoming jump, his right foot suddenly slid out from under him on a patch of algae that made the rock like ice. With no time to stop himself, he only desperately twisted to direct his fall to make sure he didn't plummet in the direction of the rushing water. His shoulder slammed into the hard rock, knocking the wind out of him. His neck whipped in pain at the sudden stop in motion. Will's entire body racked itself in hoarse gasps as he tried to get any air back. Desperately, his mind kept telling him not to move, any move he made that wasn't carefully considered could lead to death. He opened his eyes as he felt the water tugging at his foot, which Will realized had slid into the water.

With utmost care, he got his arms under him and pushed himself up. He was, if anything, maybe a foot farther back from the falls than he had been. As the adrenaline faded, he felt the intense pain of his shoulder where it had slammed into the rock. No time for standing still anymore. If Will sat too long, whatever damage he'd done to himself in the landing would stiffen and he hadn't even hit the hard parts. Dallying now could cost him everything on the climb down. Keep going, get it over with!

Pulling himself the rest of the way upright, he shook his head clear and walked the rest of the way to where he would be forced to jump. There was nothing for it, there was a wide plane of rock on the other side. If he landed partially in the water, he'd have to fall toward the rock and scrabble up. Will took a few steps back and started running as fast as he could and leaped. His heart was in his throat for a moment as he flew over the rushing water beneath him. Will was trying to keep his eyes on the rock ahead and not even glance down. Landing hard, he was forced to stumble a step or two forward, before standing there gasping for air.

In front of him was a wide flat plain of rock that led directly to the ravine that went down. His eyes squinted through the mist that filled the entire thing. There WAS a way, he was sure of it now! It was dangerous, but he could see it clearly! Will risked another glance at Noora and, still seeing no help there, he concentrated on the climb.

He dug in his first footholds and began. The blasting water right next to him now sent up a spray that soaked him almost immediately. He could feel the slick rock, wet, but thankfully blasted free of algae. One hold after another, that was the way! Will grasped for a hold as he lowered himself down again farther, and felt the rock gash his hand. He looked to see blood pouring out down his arm now, washing away in the spray. He had to hurry! Will glanced down and could see there was a pool directly below him now, just a little farther.

Will was going to have to use the hand, no other way. He made it a bit farther down when he felt another stabbing pain in the hand from a rock jabbing into the wound. His hand jerked back automatically. Will felt himself slip. He was going over! Both hands scrambled to regain balance and.....

There was an enormous smack as he hit the water below him, Will heard it as he hit. He felt the water already taking hold of him, spinning him out over another void surrounding him with droplets of water and then slamming again into the river. Under the river. Even in his daze, Will knew that he needed to get to the surface. He fought his way up to the dancing and flickering light above himself, plunging out into the air, gasping, sucking life back into himself.

Will looked up to see that there was Noora standing on another prominence and staring down at him as she stood at the edge.

"There! I fucking did it! Good enough?" His words echoed up the ravine.

She smiled as she stood there, her hands cupped around her abdomen, and Noora smiled at him, looking like an angel now. The way she held her stomach was almost like she was cradling a child, their child.

52

"And now, to FINISH THIS!" Noora yelled, her voice echoing everywhere.

Noora waved at him. He would always remember that she waved a light little happy, jaunty wave like a wife to a husband taking a train ride. She smiled wider, she closed her eyes, and she took one step forward.

The noise when she hit was enormous, it echoed for minutes afterward through the ravine.

He sits in his office, alone, always alone. No boss, or mentor, or friend anymore. That man went mad after his wife's suicide, especially after they told him she was with child. Aran never checked on the genetics of the girl in the womb. This man in the office runs the company now, alone. Alone, with the memory of his tryst with the Ashiptu and the death of his daughter, who would have been the next one.

"If a woman has put a spell upon another man and it is not justified, he upon whom the spell is laid shall go to the holy river; into the holy river shall he plunge. If the holy river declares him innocent and he remains unharmed, the woman who laid the spell shall be put to death. He that plunged into the river shall take possession of the house of the one who laid the spell upon him."- Code of Hammurabi, 2000 BC

First Appeared: "Weirdbook" Annual #1 Witches

This was my first published piece of science fiction, which the wonderful people at Aphelion put out. I don't specifically copy any individual author, but what I'm reading definitely has an effect on what I feel like writing. In this case, blame Roger Zelazny. Actually in a lot of cases you could probably do that, he's always been a favorite.

All the Time in the World to Read Them

He looked down at the woman who occupied his bed, her nude form glistening in the light from earlier activity. She was sleeping heavily, he had assured that. He sighed a little and began to pull on his favorite outfit, starting to slide on his prosthetic arm extensions, clicking them into place and feeling the interface take hold.

He looked down at her, flexing the claws that now extended from him. As soon as he completed his dressing, he would disembowel her with these very claws. It was for her own good really, the locals would do far worse to her after she left here. For being with him. Better to be disemboweled by a sadist deep within a drugged sleep than to be dragged to the town square fully conscious only to be slowly stoned to death or worse.

What started off as a clear-eyed idea of freezing people like him out of society had become an article of religion these days. His name was Edgar Wallace, heir to the vast Wallace fortune, for as much as people even said his name anymore, or for as much use as his money was anymore except to him personally. Funny, the privileged are so blinded to the direction of the wind until the sandstorm is on them.

The last stock market crash had sealed it, even though nobody fully realized it at the time. There had been an increasing series of trends that everybody, including his family's accountants, figured would just die down. People just stopped buying things. More specifically, they stopped buying things from his family's companies. Everybody on the Forbes top fifty list suddenly had a target on their backs, it seemed. If it hadn't led to this for him, Edgar could almost admire the ingenuity of the new economy they created, just to get rid of people like him.

Edgar kept looking at the girl, and not acting, and found himself realizing he was lonely. Well, lonely for somebody who wasn't a member of the ten families, that is. Lonely for something that wasn't pre-programmed for his pleasure. Something spontaneous, something human. He made a decision then, he'd let her sleep it off and then use her again. Maybe Edgar would even talk to her a bit. Another human voice. But he wasn't ready to let her go just yet, that he knew.

He began removing the prosthetic limbs, feeling them disconnect from his senses as the interface was severed. She was dead, she had known it when she had come up to his door. Edgar's money, at least, could still be transferred and turned into credits in certain amounts. They hadn't taken that from him. Of course, there were limits now on anything people bought. No more factory takeovers. His family figured that out after the crash. The obvious solution to people not buying your company's products? Buy companies people didn't know you owned. Unfortunately, the powers that came soon after figured that out too and kyboshed that avenue of power.

Now, though, even talking to one of the remaining fortune's representatives was instant hatred. She had been with him, they would deem her "unclean" by association. That was the new normal. Had the families deserved it? Most likely, but what had the girl done?

Dark thoughts on his mind or not, Edgar's body was not bothered by such trivialities and was demanding food, so he wandered out of his bed-chamber and went downstairs through tastefully decorated, Victorian-styled hallways and stairs and to his kitchen area. After pressing in his breakfast order, he turned on the tri-d to check in with how the rest of the world was turning.

At first, it was the same boring news, different day, but it gave him something to watch while he ate. As Edgar listened with half an ear, one item caught his interest: Hallison had finally died. Hallison was the only other scion of one of the families that still lived on Earth. The rest had their own terraformed planets as remote and isolated as possible. Well, if nothing else, that gave him a plan for what to do with his day.

Any time one of the heads of one of the families died, it made the news. In this case, the crazy old coot had no heirs, so his fortune would end up being split among an approved-by-him list of charities eventually. Lord only knows what those would be, the man had been a drooling nutter toward the end,. Edgar had begged off from seeing him personally for years now.

But that meant that invariably the AMOUNT of Hallison's fortune would be reported, and that meant the natives would be restless for a few weeks. They could keep Edgar a virtual prisoner in his keep, but that couldn't keep him from having some fun playing with them.

Edgar finished his breakfast and went up to the bubble that mounted his compound. It was clear to view through, giving him a commanding view of the Arizona mesas, but it was built out of a material that could withstand a nuke strike. The People's government might have been able to freeze the families out of the corporate world, but they still had an anything-goes attitude if you could prove it was for "personal use," which made sense in a way. The amount of money those families had at this point, even if it just sat in a bank, accrued so much interest it was the only way short of mass murder to get any of their money back into the economy. As of yet, the governments of man had not developed the stomach for a new Bastille Day, bless them.

His father had built Home before Edgar was born, and it was unbreachable by any conventional method. But still, the locals tried. As the terraforming revolution happened, there weren't exactly the best and the brightest left in the more inhospitable areas of the Earth, and resentment of him ran high. The girl in his bed was a prime example of how low they could still go. In a society that doesn't allow anyone to fall below subsistence, who gives their daughter over for a death sentence just for a wad of cash? From someone everyone professes to loathe, no less?

Getting up into the bubble that stuck out on top of the roof of Home, Edgar turned on what he called "the party lights." Club lighting, and music. Loud. Real, real loud. Hey, if they were going to resent him, let them think he had everything to resent, right? Edgar went back down, leaving them on. As he descended the steps, Edgar smiled when rewarded with a loud, shuddering noise as something, undeniably explosive, was absorbed by the bubble's defense screens.

That should hold their attention while he achieved some more amusement at their expense. He went down into the sub-basements. Connecting to them was a network of tunnels, some of which led to the surface in fully concealed openings. He began putting on another one of his tech exoskeletons. Most of them, he had designed personally to, at first glance, look like some of the more "frisky" alien life forms humanity had heard rumors of in its expansion throughout the universe.

This one was a favorite. Claws that had flexing links that extended a full foot from the eight digits on each hand, a fully functional tail, and a head full of teeth. It was almost completely impossible to see him in the suit, and the suit hooked up to his nervous system to give him complete control over it.

Edgar had worked really hard to get rumors into the local celebrity press about his "exotic zoo" for a reason. To be fair, HE DID actually have an exotic zoo in Home, but nothing quite as interesting as the tabloid press had speculated. Always lay your groundwork in advance. Advice to remember.

He clicked on the screens showing the view from the exterior cameras. Edgar knew some locals were hiding out there with blood, his blood, on their minds. The explosion on the bubble was all the proof of that he needed. Now all he had to do was find someone likely that he could play with.

By the time he had gone through the cameras, he came up with about twenty potential choices. Some people must be avid news viewers. Normally there were only ten at a maximum. Of the miscreants, he narrowed it down to six, but two specifically caught his eye. They had unwittingly placed themselves near one of the tunnel entrances and from the looks of them, they did not look like major contributors to society.

Finally, kitted out and ready, Edgar hit the door panel and went into the tunnels. Cold steel the whole way, but not particularly well lit. He knew them by heart, he had played in them as a child. Not that it mattered. The suit's eye visors provided better vision than his own, and a map of the tunnels he could call up. Edgar thrilled at the power he felt in his control within the suit. Physical prowess that no amount of surgery or exercise could possibly provide.

Coming to the exit, he spoke the code to open it. He had no worry about anyone re-opening the door after he stepped out. All of the doors on Home were set to a genetic code scan, which it could read even through the suit, along with a heart rate scan to ensure Edgar wasn't dead or hostage. No one short of his own child could walk into Home, and Edgar had made sure he never sired one of those.

The two men he was stalking were both turned, staring at the bubble and trying to see if all the smoke and noise had meant penetration and damage. One had his rifle trained on it, the other had his pointed toward what, as far as the world knew, was the one and only door to Home. Too easy, but it should be amusing nonetheless. Edgar wasn't out here for real exertion or challenge. Just for chuckles. It might be cruel, but then again, these men were in the middle of a desert, hoping to murder him, so cruel at that point becomes a matter of perspective.

He moved slowly and deliberately behind the first man. Drawing back his arm, Edgar thrust forward with the full strength of the machinery he controlled. A gurgling erupted from the man's mouth and his gun dropped with a crash of plastic and metal. The prosthetic claws burst forth out of his chest, causing a crimson spray.

The other man turned, gun in hand, to see what had happened. Edgar triggered the machinery in the tail, bringing it about in a whipping motion. The other man crashed to the ground, his gun, from the sound of it, breaking on the rocks below them. Edgar advanced then, the first man still dangling from his claws, gore dripping onto the dusty ground. A fully formed horror heading toward the man.

The man was obviously dazed from his fall but had the animal instinct to already be scrambling away. This Edgar stopped by slamming the tail mech over him, slowing him long enough so that he could get one of his great clawed feet to pin the man to the ground. At this point, Edgar took the mangled, dying thing that still bubbled and gurgled and dangled it over the man, blood and spit drooling out of the dying face onto the panicked living one. Slowly and with exaggerated care, he lowered the mutilated man down until the face of the dying one was just above his uninjured compatriot. The prone man made pitiful noises as he tried to back into the ground itself. Finally, Edgar lowered the still barely alive victim to the point where its lips just barely touched the face of his terrified friend.

As suddenly as Edgar began his grizzly amusements, he pulled the almost dead one straight up and whirled his arm so that the body flew down the hillside they were on, leaving a graceful but hideous trail as it arced over the abyss. He immediately released all pressure upon his live friend, chuckling inside as he watched the terrified man scrabble away, finally getting to a half crouch that allowed him to pick himself up the rest of the way. He gaped at the hideous, clawed, and fanged thing before him as it appeared to study him. A low, guttural howl escaped his lips, seeming to well up from deep within him before he turned and fled as fast as he was able down the slope toward civilization miles away.

Wallace was laughing out loud by the time he was returning back to Home. He had rationalized it years ago. These men had been there, maybe for days at a time, hoping and praying with all their might that they might have an opportunity to eradicate the evil they believed he represented. Well, now they had had the opportunity. All anyone can hope for in life is an opportunity. His family had long ago reached a begrudging accommodation about Home and its environs. He asked almost no protection for himself, and they asked almost no questions about what happened here one way or the other. If the one that lived was believed at all, and sane at all when he reached a town and was still stupid enough to report it, Edgar might get a text asking if any of his animals had escaped recently.

Sometime later the girl had awoken, and they were having dinner together. "What I don't understand," she said, "is you'd still be rich. You wouldn't be completely trapped in here if you just did the voluntary fortune reduction, and you'd still never work a day in your life."

"Pride, I suppose," he responded. "Since the old families were given a choice, either reduced wealth, but enough to last that generation from one end to the other, or hold on to every penny, most of them did give it up. If not in the first generation, once they realized how ostracized they were, within one or two. The Wallaces, what we have, we keep. Every red cent."

"But you can't go out, you can't be normal......"

"I suppose you could make a case that the people who accumulated such an incorruptible amount of wealth in the first place, already lived like that, really. Every single picture I've ever seen of my great-great-grandfather in public, there were at least six bodyguards between him and the world. We just became accustomed to it, to the manor born and raised."

"What of it, though," Edgar continued, "if I have an heir one day, let him make the judgment call. I am my father's son, though, better an outcast who will never know want than one of the teeming masses out there, saving their pennies to buy a missile to hurl at my defenses."

"I don't know......."

"Of course you don't, my dear, if you were even as moderately wealthy as is allowed now, you wouldn't be here, would you?"

A scowl flicked across her face, and he added gently to her, "But, I'm quite sure, we could find more pleasant ways to spend the evening than discussing and debating the troubles of the poor pitiful ultra-rich? It's both tedious and redundant. My family and the other nine, well, eight as of today, are the holdouts. We have become, even I will admit, an evolutionary dead end. Hell, we're the only ones left who still own finance that can even be counted in 'dollars' and not just credits. The system gave us a choice, and we chose this, and thus one day, we will be absorbed back into the system, if only by time, like an irritant or a virus. Whatever evil we represented, as far as control of the system was neutralized. We are just remnant. But tonight, there's only you and me. So, shall we adjourn?"

And they did.

Hours later, he had sated himself by using her. After, they had shared wine and held each other. Her wine had contained powerful sedatives; his had not. She was again in a deep sleep, arm splayed out across his bed in the dim warmth of the synthetic candlelight.

Edgar was hungry again. He had not eaten his fill earlier, hoping to forgo a lengthy discussion with her about a point of view that she couldn't possibly understand. Nor did he want to hear her problems and her point of view, which he, frankly, did not want to even consider. They were different people, and he didn't want to play "Empathy the Home Game." She came from a family who had found a way to screw it up, to need money desperately enough to sell her, in a society that refused to let anyone go hungry. He came from a group of people whose pilfered wealth had funded that society's foundation. Well, maybe not his family personally, his forebears had seen to that. Better to die alone than give anything away to a society capable of producing people like her.

Hallison, that fool. Now his entire property would go into a receivership for ten years unless he had specified charities in a will. If no genetic heir turned up, off it would go to the very state the ten families had resisted for all these years. One way or another, Wallace was going to ensure that didn't happen to him. At this point, he was considering one of the women who were advertised on the distant poorer planets to produce his heir. Anything but mating within the ten families. Constant intermarriage between only the families was starting to show problems. But again, anything but just handing it right over to the state, after what his family had gone through to ensure the continuance of the legacy.

He ordered himself a late-night meal. Real steak, medium rare, some rolls, some fries and some real, honest-to-god beer should do nicely. On Earth these days, those were all big-ticket items, but Edgar had the deep pockets to pay. The mec-chef had it done within moments and done to perfection. He picked up his plate and his beer in a chilled glass and sat down to enjoy.

Shame about the girl. She hadn't told him what her family had done to get in such a bind that they were willing to sacrifice her for a payday. Edgar hadn't asked, it was none of his business really. But that reminded him. Before he finished her tomorrow morning, he should finish the transaction. Life had always had a price, all the way back to when there was no money to set prices, just foods and fornication. In this case, the price of hers was 100,000 credits.

He opened up a pad at the table and set about making the transfer card. He'd have it delivered to her family by courier tomorrow. It was what they wanted. One card, 100k, unlimited usage. Which, frankly, once delivered was totally untraceable. Not total idiots, Edgar supposed. They didn't want to pay taxes on their little windfall, the instructions she had arrived with were a little hard-hearted even by his standards.

Edgar punched in his access code. He was about to hit print to create the card when he stopped chewing on his steak for a moment to check the transaction over. That was the moment when he noticed he'd forgotten a zero, so he quickly punched in another.

He swallowed his meat. An instant later, he felt a sudden pain in his throat. Oh my god, oh my god! He couldn't breathe! Edgar tried to yell for help but no sound at all exited his mouth. Clutching at his throat, he lunged out of his seat. Dear lord, his chest hurt. He tried desperately to tighten up his stomach, anything to get the steak to dislodge. The girl! If he could get to the girl! Quickly, quickly! Things were getting dark. He had to.... hurry....to.... the......steps.......He was vaguely aware of hitting the floor, and then, he was aware of nothing. Ever again.

She awoke in the morning. In many ways, nobody was more surprised by it than she was. She knew full well what happened to girls who were sent here, but her family had insisted. They had more than insisted, they had told her bluntly that they would sell her to a whore house that they knew of, otherwise. That wouldn't even begin to cover the gambling debt his father had run up, and for that, she would be turned into one of those walking dead women she saw at the illegal houses. Bruised and beaten, often strung out on drugs, no government supervision or protection in those bottom-of-the-barrel slave trading places. But always a demand, for a place where there were no rules, and the women desperate enough to accept it as their fate. Better one or two nights, and then a quick death.

The house around her was silent. Which she thought odd. But then again, she wasn't expecting to still be alive, so the whole day was odd at its onset. None of the other girls she had heard about had made it to a third night before the body was found in the hills near here. She felt oddly detached about everything as she got up, still naked from the night before.

She left the room and walked to the steps downstairs to the dining room. Upon reaching the landing, she saw him collapsed at the foot of the stairs, hand reaching out to the bottom step. She felt nothing. No screams, no terror, nothing at all. She was expecting to be murdered, and there below her unmoving and cold, was her assumed murderer. Maybe it was the remains of the drugs in her system, or maybe the improbability of this reprieve was so unthinkable that it left her blank. Or possibly, it was knowing that if she went home now, her fate was probably still the whore house or worse, being stoned to death, driven by the fanatical nature of the locals. Her reprieve was in many ways unwelcome. Edgar Wallace had in his power the ability to save her, and Edgar Wallace was not moving on the floor.

Feeling like she was still asleep and dreaming, she went down to his immobile form. Turning him over, there were no doubts left. Protruding tongue, rigid, and blue were not signs of good health. There was no helping him, so she moved on to the kitchen, seeing the half-eaten meal.

Looking over, she saw the screen still open. She saw the cursor blinking over the amount. Languidly, she pressed zero twice, and then print. The hard card ejected from an unseen slot in the tabletop. She stared at it almost unseeing for a second, then snapped it up, and set it back down. If it was to be of any use to her, she would have to find a way out of here. Surely the man had vehicles, some means of egress from this fortress. Something that none of the locals knew of. It was time to get dressed and scout around and make plans for a future, a future she hadn't even considered needing to plan for when she had passed out the night before.

A half an hour later, the front door, the only one readily known to the local population, of the dwelling known as "Home" slammed open. A hoverboard floated out in a slow ghostly manner, carrying a grizzly cargo. The door slid shut immediately after the payload had cleared it.

Slowly, men crept in from all around. A doctor was called in. Soon there was an enormous crowd clustered around. All to confirm that they had seen it. The thing on the board was the body of Edgar Wallace. The monster of the mountain was indeed dead.

Within moments, the thoughts of all there turned to the hoard the beast must have had within its home that it had now vacated along with life itself. Soon they were pressing themselves against the door. Pounding at it. But it seemed that his fortress was just as impenetrable, even if he himself had not proved to be immortal.

*****

A rock wall in the desert. The base of a long hill of rock reaching down to the flatlands themselves. It slides aside silently. A vehicle is in the entrance, custom built and expensive. It looks like something from the Earth's distant past when vehicles ran on CO2-emitting fossil fuels. Built to look like what a student of the time period would call a Bel-Air hot rod. Its engine, though, runs silently, fueled by syn-gas.

The vehicle speeds away, and the wall slides instantly back into place.

The driver's name is Ivy. Ivy de Caudecot, but she is thinking about changing the last name already. It calls attention to itself. She is suddenly very wealthy and suddenly treasures her anonymity. She speeds away into the desert morning, but she will return one day. She is carrying with her the last scion of the vast Wallace fortune, and he will want his patrimony.

First Appeared in "Aphelion" July 2016

My mother got very sick when I was young, and I've only met my actual birth father twice. So I didn't have a lot of adult supervision. This meant going out and being on my own from a pretty young age. Suffice it to say, you collect stories that way, and sometimes it's cleansing to use them as the basis for a horror story.

Sayeth The Lord

The phone rang. Dee ran over to get it. Funny that, she wasn't his girlfriend. It technically was his mom's trailer, but since he said she could stay here while they got it together to move to the city, he never actually talked on his phone. He didn't even answer it anymore. No point, it wasn't for him anyway. If he said anything over the phone at all, it was filtered through her because she was on the other line. He'd just say something, she'd pass it on, and then click back to her conversation.

She talked excitedly into the phone. His manners were good enough, though. He wasn't listening, but trying to pay attention to the TV. That, and Dee talking excitedly about anything signified nothing; she could get violently worked up over the weather. That, in and of itself, explained why she wasn't his girlfriend. He'd experienced enough drama in his life, and she exuded it like perfume. She was probably very exciting to date, but then again, car accidents were very exciting as well.

He heard her finally hang up and looked over at her to tell her to grab him a beer while she was out there. That's when he saw that she was crying heavily. Bullshit drama or not, full-blown waterworks were a rarity from Dee. This was probably a good time to try to attempt to be a decent human being.

"Dee, what's up?" he asked, coming into the kitchen where she just stood there crying. She responded by just sinking into his chest, sobbing away for a while. After letting her cry for a bit, he wanted to break his own unease if anything else, and tried again, "Y'know, I might do a better job of this if I knew exactly WHAT I was comforting here?"

"Jennie....Jennie...." she sobbed at him.

"Jennie what, Dee?" Now this was sounding serious.

"She was.... raped, Jim!" Dee blubbered out.

"OK......Ummm...OK....we're gonna take a moment, you can cry...uhh, take the time you need, and then you can tell me what happened," Jim said, his face suddenly turned to stone in anger. Jennie was a mutual friend, a compatriot in the young adult war against normalcy and complacency. They had all been planning to move up to the city together. Jim's Mom's was sort of a way station to secure free rent while saving up, but Jennie had gotten a boyfriend and moved up there ahead of them. But that was sort of like an advanced force in a war, they were all still in the same army.

Something about the steadiness of his voice seemed to snap Dee out of it. "It's....it's OK." She pulled away a little bit but kept his chest in easy weeping range just in case it would be needed again. "Some guys broke into the squat with guns.... they think they were from the crack house down the block...they made Arnie watch while......" and it was back to crying. But now Jim knew the important facts of it.

After giving her a minute, he called out, "Jerry, do me a favor?"

Jerry was staring at the whole thing in mute horror, letting Jim handle the comforting. "Yeah?"

"Take Dee out for a little wander around to calm down a little bit, and then we'll get our crap together to go get Jennie, OK? We'll get there in an hour and a half, easy."

After they had stepped out into the field and were likely out of earshot, he went to find something to punch. It turned out to be the flimsy door to the trailer's heater. He slammed his fist against it with a hammer blow. The force of the blow went right through the flimsy fiberboard that passed for trailer construction and his fist crunched a bit against the metal of the heater itself. His mom would be pissed about that, but the door was just for show anyway, and at least it wasn't a window this time.

"Ow," he said quietly.

Jim drove them to the city, not even because he really wanted to, but Dee was a mess and Jerry couldn't drive, so that left him. He didn't have a license, but then again, he was the least likely to wreck the car at the moment. Dee sat next to him up front. He occasionally patted her leg in what he hoped was a reassuring manner. Life had already gotten enough shots in on him, he was really good at looking like nothing was wrong at all while the crisis was still ongoing. Crying was for when the fire had been reduced to steam, not for when it was still blazing away in the night. The world needs people like that to operate, god only knows what people like that need. Nobody asks.

Sometimes it made him seem cold or distant, but those who knew Jim best knew that it was a damned thankful thing that he kept things so tightly wound. The heater door was a testament to when he let that unwind a little bit. Chilliness was his public service. Jim was wound especially tight right now, but, again, you'd have to know him. Jim hadn't flipped off or called a single other driver an asshole, and Jerry was getting kind of worried about that.

As the lights of the tunnel whipped by them, his voice came from the back seat of the elderly Caprice wagon, "Dude, you OK?"

"You'll have to speak up, I can't hear you over the wind!" Jim said loudly. He was being a dick, he knew he was, he heard him. But the wind whistling through the taped-up, busted side window gave him an excuse. The last time they had been in the city, someone had helped themselves to the elderly roach of a car's stereo, which just goes to show that no matter how close to garbage something is, somebody somewhere is still willing to steal it.

With that, Jim reached down and turned up the volume on the little mini-thing they had to play tunes with. Portable meant hideable, but of course, it also meant shitty sound quality. Jim Carroll scratchily called out into the tunnel as they plunged along, "Every night I have the same dream, the other night I had a strange dream."

It took forever to find a parking spot. It always did, and as always, it was forever away from where they wanted to be. A city with over ten million people involves walking a lot. Dee was going off to find Jennie, who was staying with a friend. Jerry, who used to stay at the same squat where Jennie had lived was to go pick up Jennie's stuff and check on Arnie, her boyfriend. That part would probably be brief; Arnie had probably already wrapped himself in a needle of self-pity. As long as Arnie was alive, they could consider him "checked on."

Jim gave them a time to all meet back at the car and watched them go. He had given them some vague story about finding somebody to keep half an eye on Arnie after they left. Jerry had said he could find somebody at the squat but agreed when Jim pointed out that if anybody at the squat was competent in finding their ass with both hands and a map, the three of them wouldn't even be here picking Jennie up right now.

After they had all gotten out of the car, he locked it up for as much as it mattered with the window and all. They might steal a stereo out of a Caprice but the vehicle itself was probably safe. Too big to be worth the trouble. If you couldn't sell it on a blanket laid out on a sidewalk, why bother? He gave them a time to meet back at the car for about three hours from now, which should be plenty of time. Dee said a quick bye and hurried off, so he set into a loping city pace next to Jerry.

Neither of them talked much, there really wasn't much to say. Both of them were locked into their own heads with their own worries and anger. Expressing it right now wasn't going to happen. There weren't any women present, they didn't need to express anything, they were both pissed and upset, and each of them knew it. Why spoil it by talking? Young men use their vocal skills mainly for arguments, picking up girls, and dumb jokes. Not the time, not the place.

At some point, Jerry was going north and Jim wasn't. "OK," Jerry said, "I'll see you in a bit."

"Yep," he replied, stone-faced, "see you back at the car." He watched Jerry go for a while and then kept walking down East the way he had been heading. They had useful things they needed to do, so did he. He wanted to get a good look at the place these bastards had come from.

It was getting past dusk by now, winter hours, so the streets were all pretty dimly lit. After a few blocks, Jim turned north himself. His intention was to zig-zag up to where he could get a good look without Jerry seeing him heading that way. It was dangerous but necessary. Jerry wasn't much of a fighter, so why get him into it? Finally, when he was paralleling a block south, he saw what he needed: a hole in the row line where a house had been torn down or burned down at some point.

He cut through the gaping hole, avoiding the crazily twisted and dangling fire escape of one of the more rotted buildings as he kept to the shadows. Jim looked around, and sure enough, connected to what had been the common yard area was another missing tooth in the jaw of the skyline. It should be right in line of sight with the crack house itself, so he headed over to have a look at the building from the shadows.

The place was a trainwreck, no real surprise there. Kind of a shame because it might have been a nice area once, old steps and old brick. It must have been pretty once. Now it was dirty and covered in spray paint. Most notable though was the wound over the whole facade, the metal front door. Its purpose was pretty obvious, even a farm boy could figure it out: "We sell drugs in here, and you only come inside of here if we let you. Put your money through the slot, and crack pops out, thank you, come again, and you will." So, he wasn't going to get a good look at the inside tonight, that was for sure. But he was seeing enough of the outside to make some decisions. Two soldiers of the operation, who, he was pretty sure, were carrying something very lethal in their bulky jackets, were standing nonchalantly outside. The nonchalant routine was as much laziness as an attempt to seem unobtrusive. No cop in his right mind who ever wanted to see retirement would come anywhere near this block.

There was no point in reporting the attack, no one was ever going to investigate it. If Jennie had even called out, no one would have come to her aid. No one that valued their skin. All of the houses still in good enough shape to have tenants were barred tight, nobody was out on the street. The animal instinct to hide when flight wasn't available had taken root here.

He heard something knock over a can in the lot behind him. Jim whipped around quickly to see a sunken corpse of a human lunging toward him. The man had his hand in the pocket of his horrid thrift store, disco-era, brown leather jacket, and that hand was thrust forward to indicate he was packing something in it.

The remains of a man were startled to see him whirl around like that, but rallied, "Give me your wallet, white boy, call it a tax for trespassing."

"Ain't got a wallet on me, man," he replied, his face staying completely deadpan.

"Bullshit, you got money on you. You here for the same thing I am," the man rasped in desperation, reaching out with his free hands to pat at Jim's pants pockets.

"Look, dude, you're wasting your time here, I'll even empty out my coat pockets," Jim said. The crackhead wasn't even looking at him now, as he was frantically pulling Jim's pants pockets out and checking the thigh pockets of his BDU's.

It might have made some difference in what happened next. Jim got his left hand wrapped around the knife that was in his inside coat pocket, and stepped quickly to one side. As he did, he took out the knife and stabbed down hard on the arm whose hand was wedged so threateningly inside the coat pocket. The man started to yowl in shock and pain until Jim brought his other elbow slamming down into his nose with an awful crunching noise.

You could see that the smashing of his nose had stunned the shuffling human remains into silence. Jim levered hard on his knife, wrenching the man's hand out of his coat pocket. It was empty. He slapped at the pocket itself to make sure it was empty as well and wrenched the knife out of his would-be assailant's arm. Released as it were, whatever frenetic energy had been driving him completely drained away and the mugger-in-training collapsed on the ground.

Jim looked at him for a second and then drove his boot into his ribs hard enough to lift the desiccated body up off the ground. "That is for bluffing on an empty hand, fuck face!" he said as he started sprinting back for the car. The crackhead had made enough noise to grab someone's attention, no point in being anywhere near him if anyone got curious enough to check. It didn't matter, he'd seen what he had needed, no point wearing out his welcome.

After he had gone a few blocks and no uproar or pursuit had happened, he slowed down to a casual walk. He had a lot of time to kill so he stopped at a bodega and bought a 40 ouncer and a hip bottle of vodka for after they got back home. If the crackhead had checked his jacket pockets first, then he might have found the money Jim had on him. Oh well, he probably did the poor wreck a favor. A nice stay in the hospital right about now might end up saving the guy's life, and trying to mug people in this neighborhood with no weapon would certainly be the end of it. Most of the denizens of this neighborhood weren't as forgiving.

Jerry finally rolled up looking a little sullen. "So, how'd it go?" Jim asked.

"He was nodding out when I got up there. A couple of people said they'd keep an eye on him, but junkies watching over a depressed junkie?" he shrugged his shoulders.

"Wanna get a slice? We probably got a little bit," he asked.

"No point in being hungry and pissed off, I guess," said Jerry as they set off.

They were leaning against the car about a half an hour later when Dee came down the street, with Jennie in tow. Jerry and Jim didn't say anything but just hugged her for a minute. Eventually, Jim broke off and opened the back door to the car and said, "Let's get you home. You're safe now."

The girls were ensconced in his room now, he'd set up camp in the living room with Jerry. They weren't talking much, nothing to say. The TV was turned up, mainly so they couldn't hear the girls talking in his room. It was only a trailer; with those thin walls, privacy was strictly an illusion you sold to yourself. Jennie needed comforting of a non-threatening variety, and neither of them qualified nearly so much as the childhood friend she'd come to this part of the world with.

Jennie and Dee had come to this industrialized part of the east coast hub of cities from an Okie ass-backward, central-state town. One of the itty bitty little cities that centered around coal or something, maybe steel, who knew? Whatever the people had done there, they didn't do it anymore, that's all he knew. Mainly they seemed to collect welfare checks and bitch about the Government on the way to the unemployment office. Jim had gone out there with them once. The girls hadn't wanted that and had their eyes set on a nice east coast Sid-and-Nancy fantasy.

But for right now, tonight, there was one thing he could do here, and only here, something he'd lose when he left. Something he'd always been afraid to try before now. But sometimes, the night calls out for vengeance, and he felt ready to listen just this once.

"I'm goin' for a walk out back, I need to think a bit," he announced. With that, he popped the back door, jumped onto the oil tank for the heater, and down into the long grass. The property hadn't been cut for hay again this year, so it was up, dead and dry. It whipped along his legs as he walked through the empty property. His mom and aunt had both

71

inherited when Great Grandma Dandridge died, so now they had a bunch of empty land they had no plans for and taxes that took all of the spending money away. Oh well, not that it mattered, it wasn't like his mom spent what little money they had wisely anyway. They'd be just as broke in a bigger town.

His great grandmother had walked him back here once when he was a kid, while the adults were all talking around the TV. She was old, and he was young during that visit. Nobody really pays a lot of attention to either. Both the immature and the elderly are believed to have the same complete lack of intellect, and it was assumed they would be happier not having their minds cluttered by what the adults were discussing. Pretty insulting on both counts, but people are like that.

The moon was high and full. It made the dead hay in the field practically look white, it almost seemed to glow. It was a long walk to where he was going on the property. It was a good walk though, away from everyone else, his mom hiding in her room or out watching TV with Jerry, Dee, and Jennie locked in his room, away from everyone with their sadness. He almost felt a level of peace here and now.

But he wasn't here for peace, that was for sure. The trees of the hedgerow were starting to loom up and made the entire area look dark and foreboding. It didn't matter much, he knew right where he was going. He'd been here before. It didn't take him long to find the little stream that hid in the trees. All he had to do was follow it down the hill. Just like he had done the first time. All those years ago.

He walked past garbage that had been dumped here for generations, no trash pickup this far in the country. If it didn't burn, it got hauled out here to the fence line. He moved a couple of large sheets of old tin roofing as he got close. The rusty sheets were hiding the same thing that they were hiding all those years ago.

The Shrine.

Of course, shrine connotates something holy. Instead, he could tell even when the old lady first took him here, this was quite the opposite. She was a good woman, old and worn out, which kind of made her look like a witch. Old farm women always look like that, and she was in her late 80s by then. But she had this as her secret out here. Maybe she was a witch, but she didn't act like one most of the time. She taught him how to play solitaire too, and that wasn't very burning-at-a-stake worthy. His little kid memories just rebelled at the thought of her being some kind of witch, despite this. Then again, that side of the family had been here since the 1700s. Maybe the way you stick around that long IS having something tucked out in the woods like this. In case of emergencies and all. She wasn't sure what the real nature of the god was that owned this shrine, she'd said it was best not to ask too many questions sometimes. She did say, though, that if it was being used for revenge, the intended victim would fall by their own greatest weapon. Maybe the dark god of the alcove fancied irony. Maybe when this was over, he'd look up what gods rolled that way.

Jim looked at it, a dark-on-dark alcove on the side of the stream bank, hidden by refuse normally and uninteresting to most, even if it wasn't. Who looks hard for a trickle of a stream on a hillside, and another piece of garbage sticking up past the dead washing machine and the ancient bike frame? There was some kind of dark statue hidden in its dark recesses. He hadn't looked too carefully at it when she'd brought him out here as a kid, and now under the trees, he couldn't see what it was that lurked in there even if he wanted to. He was pretty sure he didn't want to exactly know now. As long as this worked, it could look like Bozo the freaking Clown for all he cared.

He'd brought along a packet of herbs. She had said it hadn't really mattered too much what kind, but like old people do, she rattled off a list of the type she liked. The elderly do that, "any kind of soap will do, but PERSONALLY...." But those were easy enough to come by. He had kept some stashed away in the trailer for years, just in case anyway. His mom probably thought it was weed. Or maybe, she'd been taken out here too, and was willing to ignore it. He set the herbs in a little cup in front of the alcove and then lit them. The smoke was sweet smelling, inciting a homey feeling, oddly enough. After that, he lit two candles on either side of the alcove, which still didn't provide enough light to see what lurked in there. Thank someone for small blessings.

Well, here Jim was then. Was this important enough to put the stain and tarnish on his soul? Once he started the chant, there was no turning back. He'd have that black mark to work off no matter what because intent would certainly be there. He had never even considered it before really, maybe in a temper-tantrum sort of way, but not really. No matter what kind of bad things had happened, he had never sat here before, with the candles lit and the herbs in the cup.

But one thing was clear as the night air to him, there ought to be some vengeance in this world against men who rape teenage girls. Maybe he couldn't be there for everyone that suffered. Certainly, he couldn't do anything for every victim, every little girl suffering the misery caused by another's capricious lusts and cruelties and greed upon their body. But Jennie was his friend. He could damned well do something about this one.

He started to chant.

Corruption expands, rust, slime, and rot.

Fear takes control; let's see what we've got?

Fight or flight, my dears, which shall it be?

It looked to be a slow night. Most of the drones and hangers-on had left for the night. Other than customers at the door, there wasn't much to look after. Willy was out front tonight, Jamaal was supposed to be as well, but fuck that, it was cold out. Nobody in their right mind would try anything anyway, and Big D barely even came down from the top floor anymore, so he'd never know.

Jamaal was sitting down on the shitty couch with Terry watching TV. That and the hotplates on the third floor was all that was allowed to be plugged in by the workers. Any of the scumbags using a room had best not be plugging shit in. D could plug in whatever he wanted in his own private room. But too much power being drawn might red-light the pencil pushers downtown. Once paperwork became involved, they might have to increase their bribes. Hooking into the grid for free did have downsides.

There was a knock on the door, which meant a customer. He sighed and got up from the Batman re-run they were watching and went to see how much they wanted. He loved corny old TV shows and old horror movies, so the distraction was not welcome. While he was away down the hall, Terry thought he heard some kind of cracking noise from inside the wall. But nothing dimmed, and the TV was still on, so he figured it was just rats. He passed out some vials through the slot and took the money.

Then he swore he smelled smoke. If one of those crackheads upstairs had set something on fire, swear to god!

It was just as Jamaal came back down the hallway that the wall cracked away. Revealing billowing flames behind it! The whole room seemed to shimmer for a second, like a haze had fallen over everything and then just lifted up. That's when he saw something leap out of the couch. Where Terry had been.

Something out of his childhood nightmares!

It looked like one of the vampires that used to give him nightmares as a kid after he'd watched Blade when he was told by his mom he wasn't allowed to. All fangs and pointed ears and shiny skin. It snarled at him menacingly. Then it started toward him like lightning. Those things were always fast in the movies.

Jamaal screamed and fired multiple rounds from the Glock he always had drawn when he went to the door. He screamed again and holstered the Glock and slung his Semi-auto into his hand and ran for the door.

When he got there, he tugged on it, screaming, but no matter how hard he pulled it wouldn't open. Jamaal threw back the slot and looked out. Standing right outside was another one of the monsters waiting for him. My god, what was happening here? Why was this happening? He had to warn D, but first, he slipped the muzzle of the semi-auto through the slot and opened fire at the thing. He didn't bother to check on it, the fire was billowing out of the room where the first one had been. He had to warn D.

Up the stairs to the boss, that was the important part now. The boss would know what to do!

The haze seemed to be on Jamaal's eyes. Everywhere he looked now, things looked hazy and wavy, almost like looking through glass with a slight warp on it. He must have gotten something in his eyes from the fire. Get to the big man and get him out of here on the fire escape, that was the important part.

He reached the second floor where all the crackheads they let in the building "lived," if you could call what they did living. He heard moans. Man, he'd heard something like this in the movies too! Jamaal stood real still and quiet on the steps for a second and listened. He thought for sure he heard shuffling over the sound of the fire below. Something moving through all the garbage that collected on this floor from their "tenants."

That's when he saw the first one leaning out of the doorway moaning and looking at him.

Its flesh was rotting off, its clothes were rotting off. You could see bone sticking through in places. Soon all of the doorways leading out into the hall were filled with one or two struggling to get past the first one. Oh crap! He knew this one too! Zombies! What in the hell was happening here? This was like every nightmare he'd had as a kid, but real!

But he knew how to deal with them, he'd seen enough films, aim for the head. He started firing quick bursts at head height. It was with no small degree of satisfaction that he saw them drop one by one. As he worked his way up the last set of steps, fumbling in his pocket for the keys to the big man's floor, he kept up a steady stream of lead to return these horrors to the grave.

Denzel was scared out of his mind now. He'd heard the gunfire in HIS building. First on the ground floor, and now it was on the stairs leading up here. He was pretty sure somebody was finally making a move on him. You get a little bit of money and some other son of a bitch gets jealous, you had a hard time sleeping at night worrying about it. That's always the way. Well, they weren't getting through that door. And if their asses did, he had enough firepower to take out an army. He had a car stashed that no motherfucker in his right mind would be dumb enough to mess with. Once he was sure it was clear, he was out of here, with his money and his guns and a plan to start over. But for right now, he was scared they might be coming for him.

There was someone at the door now. Denzel could hear the key in the lock and thought they must have gotten it off one of his soldiers. He waited now with his gun pointed right at the doorway as he heard the jingling of the keys and the fall of the tumblers. His finger was twitching uncontrollably, waiting to pull down hard on the trigger under it, and sweat was pouring down his face. It sure was hot in here for some reason.

The door swung open, and just as he feared. There stood the thing Denzel was afraid of most in life. Manny from uptown, finally looking to put him out of business for good. Just like Manny had stood there in every nightmare he'd had for the last six months. But it wasn't going to happen today. He let his finger do what it had wanted to do so badly and then the shotgun erupted. In the echoes left by the blast, he heard a body falling down the steps.

He approached the doorway cautiously; just because one of them was down, that was no reason to assume there wasn't more of them out there. When Denzel got to the door, he felt the flames, smelled the smoke, and finally saw the tongues of fire leaping up the stairwell toward him.

No way out there, and what he really needed was a way out now.

He had the only window in the place with metal grates and a key. It led out to the fire escape and the courtyard below. They'd bricked up every other window that went to it. Escape was at the top of his mind right now. He ran over to the window, popped the lock, and yanked it open. Climbing out onto the windowsill, he could see the bottom floors now. Fire was gushing out of the windows where it had burnt through.

It was now or never, so he grabbed a duffle bag of money and jumped down onto the fire escape. Almost immediately after his feet landed on the grating, he heard a loud series of snaps, and then the whole construction lurched sideways. The fire escape, it was pulling free of the building! Panic seized him by his throat, and instinct took over. He lunged back at the windowsill. It was slightly out of his reach by now. No choice, no chance, had to jump for it. His whole body tensed, and he leaped.

His left hand caught the edge of the sill for a second. He was just swinging his other arm over to grab it with both hands, his arm slowed by the weight of the bag. Then that second ended. Gravity, having discovered what he was about, unleashed her dreadful fury upon him, and he plummeted! His head bounced a couple of times on his flight off the remains of the fire escape, so he was probably dead already when it finally came to a crashing end in a pile of trash behind the building.

With one thing and another, his body wouldn't actually be discovered for weeks. The last body to be recovered and identified. Between the fire and all the people with bullet holes in them, the coroner and the police were too busy to start searching for bodies out back.

The police had already pulled up front by now, which meant reporters weren't far behind them, and soon enough there would be fire trucks. Fire trucks always came last in this neighborhood; they didn't show up until the police made the area safe to work. For those people now coming out of their houses, who actually paid rent to live there,

there were now clear looks of relief on their faces, despite the flames and the worry about their own buildings catching.

Better one evening of worrying about things than a lifetime of fearing for your life.

Jim drove into town while everyone was still asleep. He wasn't a morning person at all, but he hadn't bothered to sleep that night. Smokes don't buy themselves and all, so everybody would be happy to see he'd picked some up. The rolling country soon turned to town, and town to city again. You get far enough from the big city, the distance between farmland and moderate city was brief. You can go from 100,000 souls working and dying within inches of each other, to cows within a few miles.

Finally, he parked the elderly wreck and walked off to the local newsstand. It wasn't a big city one, with the papers all splayed out in front and a little window to a confined and claustrophobic booth. This far out, it was a little hole-in-the-wall store, with racks of magazines and gum.

He asked for a couple of packs of butts and then looked down at the day's papers on a rack in front of the cash register. There, piled up, was one of the city's tabloids. The headline screamed, "DRUG HOUSE HORROR SCENE!" Jim picked one up and looked at it, then he smiled. He picked another one up for Jennie and put them on the counter.

"You gonna read 'em or pay for 'em?" asked the gruff old-timer working the cash register.

He happily plunked down the money.

"What d'ya think happened?" asked the old man.

"Maybe they finally saw the bogeyman in the mirror?" he said, smiling.

Everything has a price in life; sometimes, you're happy to pay it.

First Appeared in "Schlock!" #298

This was my first novelette. God bless Trever Denyer for taking on the task of editing it and printing it, since I also didn't have any editing software at the time. Thanks for seeing something.

The Fire That Remembers

It was dark now.

That was good.

Pig liked the dark. Dark places and loud noises.

If it was dark, he wasn't any uglier than anyone else. If it was loud, you couldn't hear him talk. No one knew why he had come to this place at this time. Nobody knew much about his life before he had come. He was just there. He made no sense, unexplained. Nobody even knew why in the hell he was called Pig.

An anomaly.

He was a constant test to people's tolerance and patience.

A hardcore punk kid with a horrific speech impediment.

The speech impediment was probably the least of his issues though. That wasn't WHAT the problem with Pig was, but it served as the base and home of the problem. Hardcore punk rock kids have a tendency to want to out-tolerate each other, if for nothing else than to prove to themselves that they weren't their asshole parents. There were lots of people with physical disfigurements in the scene, and according to the police, and the church, and social services, the whole group of these street kids had a mental one.

But Pig was.......

He leered at women. He told horrible homophobic and sexist jokes, and not even the funny ones you laugh at despite yourself. He smelled funny. He was almost useless in a fight. He was all around slovenly. Everyone suspected he stole stuff, but nobody wanted to confront him about it. But what were you going to do? Have yourself be seen in public berating a kid with a speech impediment? All of your instincts wanted to root for him, to forgive him, to apologize for him, and he always left you wondering why in the hell you had bothered.

Pig, while he might have been short on book learning, had animal cunning to beat the band, and he exploited the hell out of the situation. A lot of people with speech issues, people give up on them early. Schools do that, parents, jobs. But they aren't stupid, they just have a hard time talking. Pig wasn't stupid, but if you wanted to think he was, he was happy to let you. You would let your guard down, and he'd leave with your house in his pockets. A decidedly unpleasant human being had found a way to turn tolerance in on itself, to carve out a niche he could survive in. Life will find a way, and people with impediments are allowed to be assholes too, just like everyone else. Maybe you could say since life had dealt him a hard hand, he deserved extra tolerance, but he was indiscriminate, using and abusing friend and foe alike.

In that world, he had found his own corner of it, and it was dark and pathetic. Like everything else in his life, it was something other people had finished with. Most of this "lifestyle" centered around the building he was sleeping in. It was enormous. Enormous and abandoned. The city didn't want to tear it down because it was historic, but at the same time, they couldn't find a developer to bring it back to its former glory. It's not uncommon in a major city. Part of the property value comes from the history, all of the neglect comes from the cost of refurbishing it, so it just falls through a giant crack. An absentee landlord situation on a grander scale, with location, location, location.

Like all old buildings, it had a checkered past, of course. It's something people living in cities learn to ignore and live with. No matter how nice your apartment is, somebody died there once. It's part of life, the ghost stories and horror stories in the country of "And he died in this very room!" mean nothing with millions of people filtering in and out all the time. Funny that in the country one person's death will be a horror story for the next century, but the same death in the city is barely likely to make the city papers.

Still.

There was a reason it became abandoned, even if forty years before, it had been the city Stock Exchange building, rivaling even mighty New York City. It caused a boom overall of local college graduates who could now easily stay in the city and work here, instead of moving far away to New York or London or Tokyo. That had ended due to a mysterious and fatal fire. The damage had been exactly in that middle ground. Not enough to tear the building down, leaving hope of better days to come, but enough that nobody stepped up to pay for it.

And every stop before that, every couple of generations, another tragedy or horror there, but so what?

Every elderly building has stories like that, so it hadn't made this one unique. Homicides, jumpers, fires, it's just the flow of the city. Nobody thinks much of it really, nobody even pays much attention to the people directly in front of them in a city. Ghost stories run a distant last place in things of interest, not becoming one ranks much higher. Most major cities have been in place for centuries. Londoners routinely lose Kings, so your penny-ante quadruple homicide isn't going to last more than a news cycle.

Then, there was the recent history, which, while sad in its way, at least wasn't gruesome. First, the ground floor had been partially refurbished, a couple of stores on one part of the ground floor, a swanky attempt at a nightclub in the other. Nightclubs are not a good long-term investment, so no ghost story needed for why it closed. You can be packed one week, and the next you're giving out fliers for free admittance. The week after that, you're putting up plywood over the windows. The city, though, had never noticed that they had left the power on in the nightclub. Nobody was in there, so the drain on power was so small that nobody in control noticed. That, and it would have taken sending someone out to kill it from inside the basement. City workers can find a million things they'd rather be doing than wandering around dank abandoned sub-basements looking for a power cut-off switch.

That failed business venture would lead to someone like Pig being master of an entire major building, in a major city. Its next great adventure would be as a squat for the local punk scene. Squats, for those that don't know, are a variant on the theme of "squatter's rights" which most countries have if it's abandoned long enough. And someone else can use it; at least, they can try. The punk scene in almost every major city has one or ten of them. Victory Squat would quickly become legendary. It had lights, a disco floor, freezers that had been left when the place was abruptly closed, and floor after floor of creepy, dusty, empty upper floors to explore in a drunken haze. Pig would come there sometimes during those glory days. Sometimes they'd let him sleep there, sometimes they'd suggest he should get the hell out.

Squats always lead to trouble with the law, it's just a rule of their existence. Even though nobody wants something, the mere concept of somebody having that trash for nothing leads to some kind of magical resentment on the part of authorities, neighbors, and city planners. "We didn't even know we wanted it until you had it!" has been the unofficial battle cry of many an authority figure. This time, the city sent a worker, and this time, the worker did go into the basement and that worker cut the power.

The party officially ended.

Except for Pig.

For him, this was the greatest victory of all. He owned the squat! They wouldn't let him sleep there half the time, but now, he owned the whole place! So what if it didn't have lights, he could get candles and little convenience store flashlights, right? People had heard of this place, they still wanted to come here, and then they'd talk to him. Just because the guys who'd been running it before had moved on was no reason for him to as well. Quite the opposite really. Just like they had scooped up someone else's trash, their discarding it didn't mean it didn't have value. Just because they didn't want it now with the lights out didn't mean it was valueless. Pig valued it quite a bit.

Suddenly he had a social life he didn't have to beg for, for once in his life.

The problem with trying to be happy with someone else's castoffs is, soon enough, it wasn't enough. People still acted like they were doing him a favor by coming here. They left most of the time. They just came in here to get high and then left, just like any other crack house, any other junkie flop. Girls, girls only stayed with him if they were runaways or so high they couldn't think to leave. Then they left the next morning and avoided him around the city if they could. He was the king of an empire of filth, he knew it, somewhere deep inside of himself.

*****

82

It was probably sometime around then, he started to hear the whisper. The first time Pig heard it was when he was going through the basement alone. The easiest way into the building was the broken lock out back in the alleyway, so he used that whenever possible. You came in there, you entered a hallway that led to the still active businesses, but a door that was supposed to be locked to the left that led into the squat itself, they had taped the lock permanently open. Every once in a while, some wit would find a way to bar the outside door from the inside, but most of the time, if you wiggled the door just right, you walked on in.

Pig was walking slowly and carefully through the basement. You wanted to be careful doing this. There was piping and rusted machinery all over the place, and the metal stairs were often slippery, not to mention the feel of rust under your feet in the dark automatically felt unstable. If you fell, no one would ever be finding you, nobody was even going to look. But it was still preferable to the other way in, climbing up over the steel sheeting outside and then inching along to the large metal shutter that was broken.

The first time Pig heard it, it was just a whisper. A hint of noise there in the vast darkness. He wrote it off as the wind somehow getting down there. It made him move quicker, and Pig was thrilled to come out onto the first floor finally after twisting his way through the sub-basements, which could be a maze if you didn't know your way. Just because you had a logical explanation handy didn't mean you believed it there in the dark by yourself.

He didn't pay it much mind though; it was a spooky place when you were in there by yourself anyway. The place was large and dead even with you in it, your alive couldn't fill up that much of a tomb. Wind did move through the upper floors as well, maybe it found its way down below. Pig certainly never heard anything when he wasn't in the building, so it wasn't like he was crazy.

Then one day after hanging out downtown, he was coming back late, through the back by himself like always. He had a flashlight in his pocket but was using a candle to spare his batteries. As he moved along, the only sound was the clanking noises of his Doc Martens on the steel steps. In the flickering light almost dancing with the shadows the candle created, a disembodied whisper said, "Euuuugggggeeennnnneee."

He dropped the candle.

Pig considered his options there in the dark. Finally, as he fumbled in his pocket for the flashlight, he said, "Dat ain't muh name, ain't nobody call me dat!" He just said it instinctively the way he always reacted to his real name.

The wind in the basement went in little puffs that almost sounded like a chuckle, and then the voice said, "Very well... if you prefer.... Pig."

"Whose der?" he asked, turning on the flashlight and aiming it around the basement in sweeping loops.

"A............friend," the ghostly voice replied.

"What da hell you want?" Pig demanded as he grabbed the candle off the step where it had landed.

"I wannnt you to think about.... what do YOU really want...." the voice almost intoned, and then it was gone. Pig could feel it, like it had been an oppressive force, and now, it had left him! He wasn't taking any chances though, he bolted for the upstairs, and its perceived safety.

For the next few days, he said the hell with it and stayed out late, so he could just come in by the shutters without anyone seeing him instead of using the back way. But, try as he might to put the whole thing out of his mind, Pig kept thinking about what he REALLY wanted. It was the kind of question that nags at a person. Whatever Pig wanted, it was more than just the control of a dead empty building, that was for sure.

He had a new problem as well, he worried constantly about his mental health. He'd met people who heard voices on the streets, nutters all of them. Pig felt fine when he avoided the basement though, even better when he was out of the building altogether. Crazy people didn't just turn off being crazy, did they?

It didn't matter what he worried. At the end of the day, he didn't really have any other place to stay, and no other way to be popular. So like a little kid who runs away from home, he always returned to his life, such as it was, at Victory Squat. Like anyone who doesn't have much of anything, when he was in the building, Pig fantasized about getting what he really wanted in life. A seed had been planted by that question. He would picture himself, rich, a music star, with all the girls he could manage. He might have been an odd bird to look at and talk to, but his fantasies were as normal and American as apple pie.

He was going through the basement again, thinking whatever weirdness had happened before hadn't been anything at all; of course, the fact that he was thinking that meant Pig had doubts. But everyone knew if you're low on sleep or you've been drinking, acid you took ages ago can come back on you, and he'd ingested enough of that over the years. But today he was sober when the whispering began again. He was ready for it this time. "What da hell you want now?" he blustered.

"Come....down.... here," the voice whispered.

He thought about it for a while, common sense said to keep moving, maybe even at a light jog. But he'd had days of fantasizing about the question of what he really wanted and was willing to look on the hope that it might be there. Teenagers can be big kids, and little kids get into vans for candy. So, he turned back and went to the landing where another set of stairs led to a lower level of the basement.

"Where are you?" Pig asked, flicking his flashlight all over the place.

"Come to.... the boiler...."

"Which thing's the boiler?" Pig asked, his flashlight never stopping its sweeps to and fro.

As if in answer there was a pulse of a glow in a far corner, "Here....come...here."

Pig carefully made his way toward what indeed was the remains of an old boiler. There was a glow, though, coming from the grate, which was impossible, the thing was covered in dust. But impossible or not, the area was lit by the glow of the thing.

"So, I came down, let me see you!" Pig said as he stood there.

"I am here, it is the fault of your eyes that you are one that cannot see me. That may one day change, but today is not the day," the voice said. And now it clearly said; it was no longer the airy whisper it had been, but a clear masculine voice that came to him now.

Pig wasn't really sure what his next move here was, it's not the kind of thing even the cleverest of people prepared for. In some ways he had an easier time thinking through this than a clever person would have. A clever person would have started asking too many questions. In Pig's thinking, this was easy, something that could talk, that had some kind of power since it was making the furnace glow, had mentioned wishes. Problem solved.

He could think of one question though. "Who is you?"

There was a moment of silence, and then the furnace pulsed again. "I'm not...sure anymore. I have been here, for very long, with my friends to keep me company." There was another pause and then it continued, "But my friends, they leave eventually, and then I need.... new friends."

"So... you want me to be yer friend?" Pig asked with a confused expression on his face.

The voice chuckled and then said, "I don't think you'd want to.... yet, at least. But I do want you to make sure I HAVE friends."

Pig's face twisted in thought and then he said, "Well, I bring people in here all da times!"

"Yes, Pig, you do, but if you ever want to see what fantasies look like in real life, you'll make sure that some of them don't.... leave....me."

Soon after that, Pig tried to see if he could get another place to stay. Whatever it was hadn't come out and said it, but he was pretty sure what it had meant. Maybe he hadn't understood, he didn't understand a lot of things, but a homicidal building? Well, maybe he could beg up less murderous crash space.

"C'mon man, jus lemmee crash in the attic, man, you got a whole building, wut you care 'bout the attic for anyway?" he said to his companion.

"Dude, I told you before, I don't own the place, man," said the dread-locked young squatter Pig was scurrying along trying to keep up with.

"But de like you, you could ask," Pig implored.

"I did, Pig, and it's not me, man, heck, it ain't even you, they've just decided they don't want anyone new at the house for a while, man. It's a community, man, the community makes the rules, and that's what they decided," said his friend. "But hey, to make it up, I can hit you a couple of blotters of acid at cost, huh?"

"Nah, man, thanks, but no thanks. I gotta see if I can catch Jerry," Pig said, scuttling away.

Jerry was no help either, and that night, with nowhere else presenting itself, Pig found himself once again working his way through the basement of Victory Squat.

"Boy........" the voice came suddenly now, "thank you for my new.......friend...."

"What de hell you talking 'bout," said Pig angrily.

"One of your guests......has decided....to stay with me," the voice intoned. "When you find her......I will show you how....to make sure no one.... knows."

And then it was gone.

Pig fled upstairs, confused. What could it have been talking about? He might have had suspicions about what the voice had meant earlier about "friends," sure, but he hadn't DONE anything. He entered the main hall of the former disco still confused, before something caught the corner of his eye in one of the large side rooms at the outskirts of his flashlight's beam.

Someone was lying there. He flashed the light on them, but they didn't move. That didn't MEAN anything though, they could be asleep. People crashed here all the time. Slowly, he crept over to the person. Finally, the light played on the face. It was a girl he had seen in here a few times and around town, Ally or something, he couldn't remember. Finally, with his hand shaking, he reached out and shook her.

She didn't respond.

His mind was racing now, terror gripped him. He washed the light all over her, trying to see any sign of life at all. That was when he saw the needle and the works, the needle jutting out of her arm like an accusation. His heart sank.

Just to be sure, he watched her chest for a while, to see if that moved at all. Nothing moved except the flashlight in his trembling hand, certainly not her chest. What was he going to do now? If they found a body in here, no matter how or why, they were going to blame him. People always blamed him for things.

Then Pig remembered, the voice had said she was here and said to bring her to it.

So he did, what choice did he have?

"How did you know?" Pig said toward where the voice always came.

"I said, boy.... I have.... a new friend...." the voice said. It sounded almost smug about the whole thing, if that was possible for a disembodied voice.

"What you want now?" Pig asked.

"Put the meat.... into the boiler....and I....will make it go away."

Pig was trying to avoid the squat again for a while, but he checked in on the place every day. He blamed himself for the girl's death to a degree. He'd been trying to get out of the place and look what happened while he was out. Now, somebody might find out: they'd miss her, they'd know where she was going, they would blame him. No body or not, they'd blame him all right.

But the more he lingered around conversations when people were hanging out, the more he noticed something very important. Nobody missed her at all. They asked after her, SURE, but they didn't MISS her. Everyone assumed she was just "someplace else." Rumor was doing all of the work of protecting Pig FOR Pig, it was amazing. She was all kinds of places. She split for New York, her parents had put her away, the cops had arrested her, even, she went to Europe. But the thing was, nobody wondered, and nobody worried that she wasn't HERE. For all the tough street kid posturing, they were little kids at heart. Nobody died, they just went "somewhere else."

He almost began to feel offended on her behalf. These people were supposed to be her FRIENDS, was it all THAT shallow? "Hey, see you later, unless I don't, who cares?" He'd never really had friends before, but watching this reaction Pig almost wanted to scream, "Don't any of you people even CARE where Ally is?" Common sense and self-preservation leapt in at that point of course, but still, the emotion was there.

The reality of having no home grabbed him by the collar eventually. No matter how hard he tried, Victory would drag him back. He had nothing to fear, nobody would look for the girl here, nobody was looking for her at all. Which made it time to go back home.

"Where have you been.... boy?"

"I go out sometimes, you a building, you don't own me," Pig snapped in frustration.

"True...."

"Anyway, you promised miracles, and dis place is as cold and black as it always is," said Pig sullenly as he began up the stairs.

"I think.... maybe...the wind will not blow through the shutters so much anymore.... your wellbeing...it is important," said the voice in a tone that said it had made a prediction.

Life returned to as normal as it ever got. The voice seemed content to leave him alone for the moment. You'd be surprised at how quickly tragedy is forgotten in circumstances like this. You live meal to meal, you have few routines, everything becomes an endless "now." So, the past vanishes almost before the dust settles and the blood dries. Frankly, he barely knew the girl. His hidden outrage at the indifference of others to her demise aside, she wasn't all that important to him either.

If anything, the place seemed to have gotten more popular. People still had a tendency to leave or crash out in different rooms than Pig, but he was beginning to feel that reflected popularity it gave him again. Which led him to be up in the loft alone, with Renee. The loft was a recent construction from the attempt at turning the ground floor into a club. It was poorly made, and as poorly conceived, but the carpet-covered steps up at least created the illusion of privacy in the otherwise open club area.

A bunch of them had gone up there, everyone else had been dosed out of their minds on acid. They'd been melting candles onto the steps to watch the trails as it dripped. Everyone else had left, saying something about going to one of the city's historic graveyards. Renee had stayed. In all honesty, she was just too drunk and tripping to really want to attempt moving much at all when everyone had taken off. But Pig had put together a different math. She could have left, she could have gone somewhere else in the building. She hadn't, it was just the two of them. In simple. teenage-boy logic, the equation came to a simple and easily reached solution. It was his lucky night.

He was kissing her neck (well, slobbering on it more, teenage boys are rare who don't), his hand trying to dart under her t-shirt. Sure, she kept pulling her shirt back down, but it was only a matter of persistence really, at least in his mind. She wasn't saying anything, but that was fine. He wasn't very interested in talking.

It would be hard to say what Renee's feelings would have been about Pig's feverish advances if she had been in her right mind, but she was pretty far from it. All she was really thinking about was how much she really wanted to concentrate on the candle, and something kept distracting her.

Finally, she decided she had had enough, all she was getting here was distraction. "I gotta go," she said abruptly, getting unsteadily to her feet.

"What you talkin' 'bout, girl, we were going to do it," snarled Pig, getting up after her.

"Were we? Well, now I guess we're not," she giggled, going over to the stairs.

"Well, get out of here, you teasing bitch!" Pig snarled and shoved her hard in the square of her back. She stumbled forward, then she teetered for a second there on the top step. While she was failing a test with gravity, her foot hit the wax that had been dripped there earlier, leaving gravity to claim its victory at that point. First, her head pounded off the top step and she began a fast set of sickening thuds down the steps. Pig heard her hit the far wall below, an echoing final thud.

And then, the entire building was silent. Like a tomb. Pig couldn't even breathe for a second, he was so shocked by what had just happened. Slowly, with trepidation, he moved over to the top of the stairs. Pig looked down at her. Her body was twisted awkwardly, and her neck looked far beyond awkward.

He crept down the steps to where her body lay, every creak of the plywood steps adding to his fears. Looking at her, there was no point in checking for breathing now. Nobody's head could be turned in that direction and be "all right," it just wasn't possible. A medical degree was not required for this diagnosis.

He wasn't even thinking now, he carefully went upstairs and blew out the candle, then came back down with his flashlight in his hand, operating on auto-pilot. As soon as his feet hit the ancient marble of the first floor proper, he bolted. He flew downstairs and was pounding down the steel steps, only thinking about pounding back up on the other side of the basement and fleeing.

That's when he heard the voice that stopped him in his tracks, "Thank you, for my.... new friend...now.... bring me the meat."

He had slept in the building, he really didn't know what else to do. He'd been here for some time, but he still slept out in the large front rooms where people who were only partying and crashing usually slept. There were large plywood blocks lining the walls for benches. He hadn't even tried to bring in a full bed yet, even though you saw them all the time left out in the trash. They had been manufactured for clubgoers to sit on when the place had been in operation. They were long and wider than a normal bench, so clubgoers could take advantage of the dark to do more than sit. It might have been because he still didn't feel like the place was his, or that it allowed him to keep an eye on where people congregated when they came in here, but that's where he slept.

When he woke, Pig kept his eyes shut for the longest time, trying to assimilate the nightmare of what happened the night before with his waking hours. Some mornings are like that, you don't have to quest for what happened last night, it was right at the front of your brain waiting for you. After a bit though, something was irritating him. It was so bright, he hadn't slept outside, he knew that, so why....

He opened his eyes to a little miracle.... the power was back on. The long hallway, the side rooms, the stairway that led into the gutted upper rooms all lit up again. Just like it had been when this had been the most famous squat in the city.

And it was all his now. Just like it had been, but all his now.

His mind raced trying to consider his options. It was hard plowing for him, he had multiple thoughts to organize. But one thing rang out in his mind loud and clear, every person who died here made here all the better for him. The wind didn't blow, the lights were back on, miracles all.

He saw the others hanging out later that day in a park they sometimes frequented. The air in the park felt clean and clear, which is really what parks are there for, to break up the smoggy monotony of the city itself. His visitors from last night looked worse for wear, which worked to a degree for him, less likely to think of any questions, let alone ask them. "Hey," he said with forced cheerfulness, "anybody seen Renee?"

"Naw, man," said one of them, Bobby he thought his name was, "we thought she stayed at Victory last night."

"No, no, man, she split right after you guys," he said with that weird, wide grin he would get all the time for no reason.

"Wow...where'd she go?" asked another one of them, Terri he thought her name was.

"Dunno," he lied, "said sumthin' 'bout goin' to some graveyard I never heard of."

"Man, she should've joined us," said Bobby, "we all went to Saint Vincent's eventually."

"Dunno, man, she was.... she was real mad at you," said Pig, still with that smile.

"Why was she mad at me?" asked Bobby, his face flashing concern.

"She said you ditched her at the squat, man." Pig was immensely happy at how this tale was spinning for him now.

"That's bullshit, man, we told her we were taking off, man," Bobby said angrily.

"Don get mad at me, man, I's just tellin' you what she said," Pig said, putting his hands up and flashing his most disarming mongoloid smile, "shame she left when did!"

"Why's that?" Bobby asked sullenly.

"I was gonna do her all over de place," Pig quickly followed that with a booming laugh and shoved Bobby's shoulder to indicate he was kidding. "Naw, man, de lights come back on!" he said happily.

"No kidding?" asked Terri, coming back to the conversation from wherever her mind had been floating.

"I thought the city turned them off?" said Bobby.

"I don't know WHY de back, but de back alright, hurt my eyes when I woke up," said Pig, grinning away like a kid who finally told a big secret.

But it wasn't a secret as much as a happy surprise, one that he wanted everyone to hear.

He'd gotten a wish; Victory Squat was back in business.

Except that it wasn't, not really.

There were more people, sure. There was more beer, there were more drugs, there were more girls. But it wasn't the same. People weren't staying there, and actually squatting it for starters. People, multiple people, called this place home not too long ago when the lights had been on the first time. The band had broken up when the old place had closed.

When the power had been killed, they'd all found other places to live. Nobody was going to push Pig out, but...nobody wanted to live with Pig. The guys who had been here were personalities, Pig was just Pig.

He had a party hideout, not a squat, a grown-up version of a tree house, and not even really grown up. Nobody was fixing things up. Nobody was organizing things, nobody was doing anything but getting high, and either passing out or moving on at the end of the night. Maybe he couldn't get them to love him, or even really like him, but he knew a way to make the place good enough that they'd want to stay.

Every time someone died, the place got nicer. Pig had figured out a pattern, there was no denying it. How that worked into what he wished for he didn't know, maybe getting your wish granted meant making things happen in a way that allowed for it, one thing having to happen after another to get to where he wanted. But the nicer it got here, the more people there would be, that must be part of some greater plan. Maybe he'd get discovered because of the squat or something? He'd ask whatever it was down in the basement, but, really, he didn't like talking to the thing anymore than he had to. It was one thing to have an arrangement together, that wasn't call to get pally about the whole thing.

He didn't think this time he could risk killing any of the kids that were coming to the place. Yes, they didn't do a good job of keeping track of each other, but this was becoming where they were expecting one another. It might not be a home, but it was rapidly becoming a popular hangout. Not SO popular that people wouldn't notice a new hanger-on, but popular enough that if somebody disappeared, this was where they would be expected to turn up. Maybe the gossip mill would cover his tracks again, maybe it wouldn't, but taking risks now was just foolish. Two dead scene girls had had some connection with the place already, even Pig knew he didn't want to risk a third.

He needed someone that people cared even less about than street punks.

But that's the nice thing about a city, if you've got your head together enough to understand the concept, then there is ALWAYS somebody that everybody cares about less than you. He just needed to get out there and find them and lure them back to Victory.

*****

He had some money for a change, so that helped. More people at Victory meant partying. Partying meant various intoxicants and almost all of those were illegal. People didn't only need a place to partake of those party favors, they wanted a safe place for money and enjoyment to trade hands. Even someone who might be considered a bit slow-witted could find a way to dip into that well, and Pig certainly did. The way he figured, money was always a headstart if you needed anything, even a new playmate to make the building happy. He wasn't sure HOW it was going to help, but he knew it would. Money equals opportunity no matter what you wanted.

He was out walking, and he was doing it alone. It wasn't like Pig had a hard time arranging solitude even in a city of millions, call it a blessing. He didn't want to think about it that way, but Pig was hunting. Nobody was supposed to be in the place tonight, it wasn't a night when people were going to show up anyway. Tuesdays exist for people to either sober up, or nurse their addictions in pitiful privacy. Nobody wants to see someone lit up on a Tuesday, you have to consider your own abuses that way.

"Hey, baby.... you lonely?" came a voice out of the dark.

Pig stopped and looked over to where the voice had come from. The voice belonged to a young-ish woman, you had to say young-ish because she looked like a trainwreck, just not an old trainwreck. Indeterminate age almost might have done it. Pig smiled, and replied, "Maybe I am, you lonely too?"

"For twenty bucks we could keep each other company," she said. She didn't even seem a little bit worried that he might be a cop, the natural slur to his voice to her translated as drunk, so maybe she could roll him afterward for whatever money was in his wallet. Beggars couldn't be choosers. It was getting late and this could turn out to be work with a bonus.

"I got a place near here, if you don't mind squats," he said.

The girl really had stopped minding much of anything as long as she got paid for it. They walked off together, two predators in the night.

"You don't live in a basement, do you?" the girl said, looking down the steel steps in front of her.

"Naw, de part I live in used to be a nightclub back in de day, but you gotta go down to go up," Pig said disarmingly with a grin.

The girl shrugged, this was going better than a lot of things she'd done and had done to her. As she was coming down hard, she only hoped she could get this over with before she started feeling really sick. Just as they were reaching the landing, Pig called out, "Hole up jus' a sec, here, take dis candle for a sec, I should go back and check the door, you ain't careful you get thieves. I'll be right back." That sounded good, if he was worried about thieves, he wasn't thinking of her as one.

With that he ran back up the stairs, his feet clomping away up the stairs. The girl stared down the steps that led to the lower basement. Something about the large looming pieces of mechanical equipment caught her interest there in the flickering candlelight. It made the pipes look like reaching arms, or a spider waiting to encircle and envelop.

Her reverie was probably why she didn't so much as turn around as she heard Pig clomping down the steps coming back to where she was. When his boot drove into the small of her back with a cracking noise, she hadn't so much as tensed even a little. There was something pathetic about how far she flew. She had so little mass to her the kick sent her arcing over the abyss above the basement and then plummeting down. She landed with an enormous boom as her head struck a piece of machinery followed by various clanks and clunks as her remains bounced the rest of the way down to the floor.

"You're mine now, Eugene!" the voiced cried in the darkness, sounding exultant. "But that isn't so bad, I like a man who's willing to commit to dreams." The light in the furnace unnoticeable a moment before flared brightly. "You've done well, with her pain and the chemicals gone, this one.... had a remarkable mind. She might.... even forgive you one day once she understands how you've freed her. But for now, let us dispose of the remains. Tomorrow, I recommend you wander around the building some, and don't go out. You might be.... unnerved, and prone to.... mistakes. And I do so want to protect you, Eugene."

The next day Pig woke around noon, at least that was his best guess. He could see the sun coming into the hallway from the double front doors. They had never barred them since they opened into a major city street, it would have been wasted money. But they were tinted enough as to make it difficult to see anything inside the building itself.

With the power back on, the bar refrigerators were working again, and since he had money he'd stocked up a little bit. Wednesdays were almost as unpopular as Tuesdays. There was some beer, and some cold cuts in there, so he wandered over and drug out a 40 ouncer for breakfast, such as it was.

It took little time at all for nature to call. Pig avoided using the toilets in the building since the water was turned off, better to piss from one of the upper floor's broken windows into the courtyard. But by this point nature wasn't calling, it was yelling loudly. He could always pour some water in the toilet later; after all, they'd had enough times with no running water as a kid. He knew how to deal with that.

After he had stood there for a while admiring the tiling, he leaned back and zipped up. Instinctively, without thinking, he reached out and pulled the handle. The eruption of the flush startled him, he had flushed without thinking but it working had snapped him back immediately. The water in the building was supposed to be off. He watched it swirl for a minute and listened to it refilling. Curious to test the situation further, he went over to the sink and turned it on. The pipes groaned for a minute, but soon enough, rusty colored water rushed out into the sink.

Now he was beginning to wonder. Did the building have any other surprises for him? He had come to think of the voice as the building itself at this point, and maybe it had more than just this to give him for last night.

He had the rest of the day to kill and had never really looked around the false basements before this, so he decided to explore a bit to fill the day. The club and stores had actually built up the over the original first floor some to create the marble-floored atmosphere, and it had created a floor of little rooms and nooks and crannies. They weren't really part of the basement, and since it had been altered, it wasn't really part of the first floor either, a hidden netherworld of twists and turns.

It was time to do some checking around to see if the unexplored parts at ground level had any other surprises for his day. Maybe Pig shouldn't get greedy on getting gifts from the building, but this time he had killed on purpose for it, he figured that owed him something extra. The one thing he wasn't feeling at this point was any guilt, Pig just wanted his rewards for services rendered.

He crept along the hallways beer in one hand, flashlight in the other. No one appeared to have been down here since the day the club itself closed. He passed by an old walk-in cooler, even if it worked at all he wasn't interested in opening that door. He'd done some demolition work one time and they had to clean out an old meat locker. The smell was ungodly. He didn't KNOW anything had been left in there, but this area seemed left in a rush, and he wasn't fool enough to find out just to settle curiosity.

He hadn't gone very far, but already this area had begun to take on a maze-like quality, reminding him why he had never come down here before. Still, Pig felt that he could find his way back, there was only so much building here after all. He was looking down one end of a hallway junction when he saw it.

A light.

There down toward the end of the hall, light was seeping out under the bottom of a door. He approached it slowly and carefully, trying not to make any noise. It was silly on its face, but for all Pig knew this somehow opened up into one of the first-floor businesses that were still open. The hallway itself looked manky and heavily undisturbed, but that was no excuse to give one of those storefronts their excuse to call the cops to complain.

His hand was sweaty as he turned the doorknob. It turned freely. It was unlocked, so that should mean it wasn't a store. Nothing possibly, though, could have prepared him for what he saw as the door swung slowly open. It was a forgotten and unused-in-decades privacy VIP lounge barely visible in the light of the single lamp that was on. Pig just stood there and stared. Finally, he stopped gaping to turn the rest of the lights on, flooding the glamour room in a tastefully subdued glow. He had never dreamed of being IN a place this nice in his entire life, let alone having it for his OWN, but the building had delivered more than just flushing toilets and lights this time. This was SWANK. Couches, a bar, everything he could dream of, even a TV.

Now this could get him some respect out of people! Everybody would want to be friends with a guy who controlled a place like THIS!

He'd have to be careful about who he brought down here, Pig considered as he set down his beer and started exploring his new domain. He had to, his friends trashed stuff, and this was HIS. The old crew hadn't found this part, Pig had. They hadn't.... well, they hadn't...they hadn't worked as HARD as he had to make this place better. No way he was inviting just anybody down here, just for them to use him and make fun of him behind his back. No way, this was awesome, this was special and this was ALL HIS!

He went behind the well-proportioned bar and grabbed a bottle off the shelf that looked expensive and began to contemplate his new kingdom.

What he lacked in leadership qualities, he made up for with cunning and judging people. He had surprisingly solid instincts as far as who he could trust. Some of the guys Pig had been working with, and frankly skimming from in passing along little packets of heaven, quickly made up his security force. Some of the others, though, got politely and firmly frozen out. His hand-picked crew now had a place to operate free from the prying eyes of customers, and he gained even more money from the improvement of circumstance. Even with criminal activities, it takes money to make money and giving Pig some to ensure this kind of privacy was money well spent.

They installed a new lock on the door and made sure that only he and his lead connection Jerry had the key. Jerry wouldn't even let him crash at his place not that long ago, but now he relied on Pig, and he relied on having that key. Jerry didn't live here, Jerry didn't watch the place all the time; Pig did.

Pig had also stopped by a local sporting goods store for some added security of his own in the form of a Louisville Slugger. He had thought about a gun but decided against it. Guns caused immediate heat from the police, and right now he had everything going his way. Why jeopardize it? Anything a baseball bat couldn't handle was probably above his head anyway. He also kept a boot knife in case something happened in tight quarters, but he frequently would just leave that in the lounge itself. The nice thing about a bat, you almost never had to use it, people just needed to know the implied threat was there. A knife, once you pulled it, you almost HAD to use it now, you had escalated the situation to life or death now.

Still, it didn't feel like enough. Pig had new clothes, he had food when he was hungry, he had any booze he wanted, he had drugs, he even occasionally had women. But he wasn't happy. He wasn't miserable, that was for sure, not by a long shot, but something was missing. This still wasn't IT, what he had hoped for. He wanted to be a famous musician who had DONE something, not an unknown small-time drug dealer.

He tried scrabbling down lyrics in a notebook he hid under the one couch. The problem with that was nobody wanted to let him sing in their band because of his voice. Pig was even afraid to show anybody what he wrote. He had gotten a couple of guys to bring guitars over, but then everybody would get stoned or drunk and nothing would come of it.

His stomach was full but his soul was empty. He didn't even feel bad for what he'd done to get all of this. It had gotten him a better life at the cost of people who had nothing, the American way really. There might be some feelings in the lyrics he was writing, but nobody was going to know about it the way things were going. It was almost like the building was holding him back while it sustained him.

Maybe that was the problem, maybe he just hadn't done enough.

The building was still mainly empty some nights. Maybe he needed to do more.

He started wandering the streets near the building on Tuesdays and Wednesdays after he locked up the room. Pig doubted he'd find another girl as desperate as the one who was keeping the building company now, but you never could tell, you get lucky sometimes. He'd almost institutionalized Tuesday as being an "everybody go away" night, saying things about needing a day to clean up.

After a few weeks of it, though, he was getting increasingly desperate. Pig couldn't harvest somebody coming to the building to hang out before; with the money coming in, he really couldn't risk it now. He instinctively dodged another bum lurching out to ask him for a cigarette, or money or something, it seemed like they were everywhere. It got to the point you didn't even notice them, you just moved away by instinct driven by your peripheral vision.

You didn't even notice them....

Bingo!

He would have to wait until next week, to make sure everything was set up just right, and to be sure the building would be empty, but there was his salvation right there. Nobody notices bums, nobody cares about them, and they are all so desperate they will take almost any perceived help. Most of them were completely out of their wits. Whatever wits you start with, the street knocks them right out of you.

Just as simple as that.

The week went by like molasses fresh from a refrigerator. Pig could feel he was getting closer every time to what he wanted. The building and him, they had an arrangement. Pig was amazed he hadn't considered this way before, the city was rampant with a hearty population of invisible people just there for the taking, and he would keep taking until he had what he wanted, as simple as that. Nobody could complain too much if the streets got cleaner and less depressing for their walk to the subway.

Finally, Tuesday came around again. He made a point of leaving the baseball bat inside of the door. In retrospect, he'd gotten lucky with the girl. Just kicking her down the stairs like that might not have worked and then he would have had to have gone down there and finished her quickly in case she started screaming. He was pretty sure you couldn't hear anything outside, but when you're trying to finish off a screaming bitch with a broken back, it's not the time to find out about any pipes leading right to the sidewalk.

And then the hunt was on. The streets in the entire downtown area clear out fast at night except for the main drags which mainly slow down. New York has sections that "never sleep" but most cities don't operate like that. The businessmen who work here finish their day, and either go home to the suburbs or to get slammed at a local "pub" where well-heeled executives get every bit as shit-faced as the gutter trash they look down on. All that separates the two is a suburban upbringing and a first-class, paid-in-full education. At the end of the day of hustling at doing things people really wished they wouldn't, they both get completely slammed in a den populated by their own kind. It all comes down to the cut of your jib and the price of the drinks.

But what he was looking for was to cut an easy kill off of a different pack of animals. These were all weak and wounded and old, it was just a matter of finding one that piqued his interest. He started cutting back alleys, that's where they slept a lot of the time. The ones who risked the city grates for the heat and steam coming up also ran a risk of getting roughed up and slammed in jail by police in a bad mood. They might even just get assaulted right out in the open, beaten up by kids who often roamed at night venting their youthful frustration and aggression. But there were entire mobs, a ragged army tucked away, in side alleys and back streets, where there were barely any lights, and barely any traffic.

He wanted specifically to find one isolated and alone, coming on them in a group might be too risky. Pig knew what he wanted one for, he didn't need to confront a mob of the shambling wrecks. As he was working his way back to Victory, Pig found the deer driven away from the herd. Sleeping tucked partway into a walkway between two buildings. Better yet, there were a couple of empty bottles in brown paper bags stacked near it. It was reminiscent of a fairy-tale creature, a rubbish heap carrying everything it owned on its back. You wouldn't have been surprised to see mushrooms and small trees sprouting out of the moldering pile of clothes that engulfed it.

Pig looked at it carefully a moment. He was guessing this was a man, but with that much grime and the bulky figure, it was hard to tell. Finally, he decided, this was the one, and it was now or never. If we stop to consider most of our vile acts too long, we won't do them, and then where would history be? Pig crouched down next to it on the balls of his feet and gave a shove.

"Whophhtt?" a male voice sputtered, eyes snapping open.

"Hey, hey, it's cool, just checkin' on ya," Pig said, rolling back on his heels.

The man's confused, wild eyes stared at him for a moment, and then his gruff voice asked, "Are you an angel?"

This took Pig aback for a moment. Some small part of him winced at it, but then he smiled and said, "Yeah, sure, you want something to eat, a safe place to sleep? I got a place, it ain't far from here."

"You ARE an angel!" the desiccated old man exclaimed, pulling himself upright.

It was hard not to get impatient, walking the shambling bum back to the squat. He wore layers upon layers of clothing, you could tell he didn't eat much when he did eat, and Pig had woken him up. He kept muttering to himself, "Got me an angel!" the entire time which almost drove Pig to insanity! Still, he wanted to get him back, and get this over with as fast as possible. Pig was dressed pretty nice, him walking with what was society's refuse had to look suspicious.

His conscience was not exactly pleased with him either. Pig kept telling himself he had to do this, and the crackhead had worked out better for her after all, and what did this guy have to look forward to, freezing to death? But the way the guy (Sparky was his name, and Pig did NOT want to know that) kept trying to talk to him, or lapsing into muttering about angels, was starting to get to him.

By the time they reached the door of the squat itself, Pig had come to absolutely loathe Sparky. His mind was becoming so fevered, he kept suspecting that the man KNEW what he was up to! That this had become some secret con, to make fun of Pig for not recognizing a con. He'd get inside, and all of his buddies from the lounge would be inside now waiting for him. They'd point and laugh. Well, he'd show this old reprobate what funny was once they got inside, that was for damned sure.

"Here, take this flashlight, I might get in trouble for it, but I'm gonna let you sleep in the basement," said Pig.

"You said sumthin'.... 'bout.... food?" muttered Sparky.

"I'll have to go get it once I got you settled in," replied Pig smoothly. But his confused brain was screaming, "You INGRATE! I'm giving you a place to stay and you're complaining about FOOD?" He opened the door and waved the man in, "I'll be right behind you, I gotta make sure the doors locked."

"Oh yeah, right...OK," said Sparky as he began to clump inside. Pig came in behind him and shut the door. As Sparky started going down the steps, Pig's hand reached out to find the baseball bat he had stashed there, letting his fingers curl around it. A smooth movement hiding it behind his back, being careful not to give away its presence by letting it bump into anything.

"Where I go now?" asked Sparky as they reached the landing.

"You just...gotta go...right down.... THERE!" said Pig as he swung the bat with all his might at the man's head. It connected with a horrible sound that managed to sound simultaneously like a rotten fruit being squashed and wood being splintered. The force of the blow sent Sparky tumbling down the steps, and each time his body struck there was a wretched thudding noise that rang and echoed against the cold, rusted steel. Finally, it ended with the body landing boneless on the concrete far below.

"Hello? Who's there?" said a voice in the dark as the door to the upstairs crept open. Then a flashlight swung full through the darkness of the lower basement to catch Pig full in the face. What it illuminated was him standing there holding the bloody bat, and then it swung down, illuminating the shape down below.

"Holy shit!" the now clearly female voice exclaimed. The light disappeared and the door slammed shut.

Pig stood there dumbfounded for a second. As the sound of retreating footsteps could be heard through the door, the slamming of the door echoed through the basement. Then finally he let out a "Holy shit!" of his own and flowed up the stairs after her.

Terri was running blind, she kept forgetting to hold the light out in front of her she was so intent on running. She had been up for just about anything tonight, except for maybe seeing Pig kill a guy. All she was trying to think of was a way of getting out of this place alive now. As far as she knew she was the only person in here, and if Pig was willing to kill one person, he was probably willing to kill two.

She was wondering if she should slow down and catch her bearings, try and think about how to get to the main hall and pop out the shutters, when she heard the basement door slam open. Hell! Rest was for the dead, and that's exactly what she was afraid of. Her feet overrode her brain and took off running through the maze that was Victory's lower levels.

That bitch! What in the hell was she even DOING in here tonight, let alone wandering alone in the basement for the love of God? He told everybody, he wanted the place clear on Tuesdays and Wednesdays. Everybody KNEW that! Those were the rules! It was HIS building, and HE made the rules, damn it!

And she had broken the rules. No point in having rules if you don't enforce them.

He stopped for a second, but then he heard her footsteps echoing in the empty building. Pig took a deep, ragged breath and took off after her. His feet thudding and echoing into the hallway as he pursued her.

*****

Her breathing was coming in gasps when she stopped to wave the flashlight around desperately. Steps, thank god! A way out of this godforsaken pitch-black basement! She didn't recognize these particular steps, but for now up was the right direction. She had to get out, not only was he down here somewhere, following her, but to see she needed the flashlight. If she used the flashlight, he'd see it too, acting like a beacon for her pursuer. At least once she got to where there was SOME light she'd be able to consider hiding or using reflected street lights through the window instead of the flashlight.

She paused a minute, looking up at the stairs. They were ornate but dusty and rusty. Plaster had fallen down here or there in chunks leaving a white powder coating on everything except the cobwebs that strung along the rails. It got through to her a bit that she had no idea where these steps went, but they HAD to connect somewhere that led to glorious, wonderful OUT of here.

There was a loud boom in the distance. Terri wasn't sure what it was, but she wasn't going to wait around to ask at this point. She made a decision and began pounding up the stairs.

Right now, Pig was just following the sound of Terri. She was wearing boots and running scared, so all he had to do was keep on the trail of the noise she was making. He ruminated that it was a bit of a shame. He had hopes of convincing Terri to spend some quality time with him in the lounge one day. She was cute, but not cute enough to ignore that she was a material witness to a murder he had just committed.

The more he considered it now that he had time to think, the surer he was; he was already going to kill her, no reason to develop morals now. Nobody was telling Pig he had to just kill her right away anyway, nobody but the building told him anything now. His grandmother used to always say, "In for a penny, in for a pound." It wasn't until he had gotten older and found out that the pound was English currency that he even had a clue what that meant, but it was appropriate here all right.

Pig came to the steps and saw her footprints in the dust and heard the pounding echoes going up and down the stairwell. He smiled in the dark. It was almost impossible to find your way to the steps leading down into the club from here, unless you knew exactly where you were going. She had just doomed herself to eventually going to the roof.

He'd never done it on the roof before, under the stars. He had a skip in his step now as he began to climb the stairs after her.

Terri was gasping for air when she finally reached the top of the stairs. She'd considered trying to open one of the doors on the lower floors, but she'd only been up here once, and even then, from the main stairs. She remembered that a few of the hallways had been blocked off on the lower levels, but she couldn't remember on which floors. The last thing she needed to do was go bolting down a hallway only to find it was a dead end. She knew there HAD to be a way to the main stairs from the roof though. Hopefully, Pig was far enough behind her, she'd have a chance to find it.

Terri slammed open the door not even bothering to close it and ran out on to the roof. She stopped then for a moment and scanned around for the entrance to the main steps. The problem was immediate: there were numerous things sticking out of the roof obscuring her view from here. Various vents, former antennae installations, etc. She could see the remains of the courtyard in the center, and the overall shape of the building, but she couldn't say exactly what of the numerous protrusions on the building would lead her to where she needed to go.

The building she remembered was shaped perfectly square, with an enormous square courtyard scooping out the middle. First things first, she had to find the main street and work from there. So, since the courtyard was on one side, she started moving toward where she hoped the street would be, but even if it turned out to be the alley behind the building, it would give her an idea of where she was.

As she came to the edge of the roof, Terri looked down and saw the street below. OK, that let her know where she needed to go at least. She started angling across the roof toward what she was guessing would be the way to the main stairs.

That is when Pig joined her on the roof.

"Terri, I'm kinda sorry 'bout dis," panted Pig, staring at her, "but you gots to go, baby girl!"

"I won't tell anyone, Pig, I swear!" Terri yelled as she backed away from him across the roof.

"Now you know that ain't true, girl," Pig said, advancing on her methodically. Unlike Terri, he DID know which set of stairs she'd have to take and exactly where they were, and he was already angling to cut her off. Both of them now were starting to move in the direction of the courtyard steadily.

Pig had gotten to within about five feet of her when he decided to rush her. He had just planned to land on her like in pee wee football, a tackle to bring her down. He still had hopes for some other amusements and having the girl pinned and out of breath would work out fine, so he leaped. He misjudged her height though, catching her in the shoulder as she ducked, which ended up sending him flying over top of her. They both went down, but Pig hit the rooftop significantly harder. Terri had been able to roll with it more.

Clambering back to her feet, she realized that if she went back the way she had come, the way out through the basement was clear now, so she turned to bolt for the stairs she had so recently exited. As she turned to run though, Pig kicked out with his own foot and sent her sprawling down hard again!

She lay there on her face, panting with exertion, tears beginning to stream down her face. She rolled back over to face him. Terror gripped her now as she realized she had almost rolled completely off the roof and into the courtyard! She scrabbled sideways in a panic to get away.

Now that she could look in his direction, she could see that Pig was up on his feet, bat in hand. Any semblance of the dopey good nature that usually marked his demeanor had completely vanished. Simple sanity seemed to be gone now too as he moved to her to finish this. His eyes blazed with fury and frustration.

"I tol' you I'm sorry about this, but now I ain't," Pig said as he raised the bat over his head to bring down a crushing blow. Terri's eyes frantically looked everywhere, looking for something to use as either a shield or a weapon. When nothing presented itself, she did the only thing she could think that was open to her to do, she kicked him.

It wasn't the kick to end all kicks. Powerwise, it was lacking because of her awkward position. But it possessed just enough power that it made Pig stumble sideways. He went to put his foot back down to recover, only to discover that it was floating over open air. He teetered for a second, his arms waving to try and right himself, gravity was not having it. He plummeted out of view.

Terri stared in horror as she saw his fingers briefly grasp hold of the side of the roof, but then they quickly slid away and were gone. Pig didn't even utter a noise he was so shocked as he plummeted down to the overgrown courtyard. His ultimate arrival at his destination created an enormous booming noise that echoed in the empty air.

Slowly, Terri pulled herself to her feet and looked over the edge. She found her flashlight and let it shine down into the gaping mouth that the courtyard looked like in the dark. Finally, the beam caught sight of him, lying there, in a dark expanding pool of what looked like ink in the light of the beam.

Moving on numb legs, and shaking, Terri walked carefully and deliberately to where the main stairs were. As she descended through the building, she looked deeply at everything, taking it all in. She knew she was never going to look at any of this again. Until tonight the place had almost been a second home, but that was over. Finally, after taking a deep shuddering breath, she made her way to the basement to leave.

She shuddered even more deeply when she saw the now cold body of the homeless man, like a pile of rags in the light of her flashlight, a puddle of its own wreathing it. Regrouping herself, she climbed the final metal stairs to the outside world. Before Terri opened the door, she wiped the tears from her face, patted her hair a few times, and stepped out into the night, making a point of letting the door slam behind her as she stepped out to a city that for the first time ever, seemed like the safest place she could be.

No one had noticed the body of the bum, until it had begun to smell. The various dealers that were now using the squat as a base of operations actually did decide to wedge it into the broiler which seemed to make the smell go away. But they didn't realize the end of the good times were already nigh. You would think they would have looked at it as an omen, but bums drop dead in all kinds of places, for all kinds of reasons, and Pig's additional disappearance was, if anything, considered a blessing.

The police took to watching the building closely not long after that, they had heard that a major group of dealers was operating in the area.

They weren't really "major" dealers, but this was right in the center of the city, not some forgotten ghetto, so police had a tendency to pay more attention. You can move tons if you do it in a crappy neighborhood nobody cares about, but move a sheet of acid where a tourist might see, you become a drug lord. Eventually, there was a MASSIVE raid on the place. Jerry and all of the small-timers were scooped up, as well as a couple more major players they had no idea were in their midst. Most of them plea-bargained, went state's evidence, and then suddenly remembered they had nice parents out in the suburbs.

The city actually followed through and showed a bit of initiative at that point. They'd had enough of this huge building being an eyesore. Within weeks they announced a plan, partnering with developers to refurbish this shell of a building completely. Not to mention, going through all of their records related to it, they found a set of proposals by an architect who had perished in the blaze all those years before. The plans had been light-years ahead of their time, it was declared, and using them would be a fitting tribute to a man who had perished in the building all those years before. The city's mayor declared that people would talk about the wonder that this previously unknown architect had designed for years to come.

Pig was standing next to a young boy watching forlornly as his former lounge was being dismantled. "It just isn't fair," he said, all traces of his lisp now gone, "I never did get my dream."

"But, Pig, I didn't really even fully understand your dream before you joined me like this," said the young boy. His name was Elijah, and he was the spirit of Victory Squat. Not a building, but a ghost. He refused to speak about his internment on the grounds in Colonial times much, exactly enough to have it be understood that he had been helped to his demise by outside forces and that he was still pretty mad about the whole thing.

It was he who had spent the last few centuries acquiring friends, letting old ones disappear to their eternal rest while convincing wishmakers through time to create their replacements. "This is James's dream, he worked very hard for it." They both looked at the less substantial figure next to them smiling at the resurrection of the building. "As soon as this is complete, he'll go wherever people go eventually. I hope they don't hold the fire he died in against him. Just like you, he thought I'd be delivering him his wishes directly, the frustration finally made the poor man snap. Seems silly, I always make sure things get better for each of you, and then you all do something to ruin it."

"Still doesn't seem fair, I wanted to be a rock star," said Pig sullenly.

"Well, I didn't know that before, now did I? Even if you had just come out and said it, which you didn't I might add, I wouldn't have really completely UNDERSTOOD it," Elijah said peevishly. "You would have said you wanted money, money to buy things, but now you don't need things. So, stripped of it all, now that I can see your soul, Eugene, I see you want what all of you have wanted since this began, recognition. You wanted the recognition of having done ONE great thing in your life. Now, look!"

As they watched, one of the workmen set down the massive couch on the floor. Moving it had left Pig's notebook of lyrics lying there, revealed. The workman looked at it, then picked it up. He thumbed through it a bit, stopping here or there, his face becoming thoughtful. Then with a shrug of his shoulders, he walked out to set the book next to his lunch and other personal belongings.

"Well, there we are, the wheels are turning for you," said Elijah with a bright smile. "All we need now is for someone to come along who really believes that wishes CAN come true!"

First Appeared In "Hellfire Crossroads" #6

To those lovely people in the 1980s whose response to a boy with blond hair, who was way too young to be hitchhiking, was to not call the cops, but to give him a ride, and sometimes a meal. Thank you.

Last Chances

God, he needed God right now. John claimed he didn't believe in God, but Catholicism digs deep and now would be a great time for God to put in an appearance. The wind and cold buffeted his rail-thin body, knocking him sideways. Sometimes the pain would get so great he would moan slightly. It couldn't be melodramatics since there was no audience, but it felt better to do it. If nothing else it filled the moments, and walking alone on a country road gave him plenty of moments that needed filling. The earlier rains had soaked John to the bone, and now the fall cold had come right behind it with wind and teeth.

At times the wind knocked him into the road, only to let him stumble back to the gravel shoulder. Not that it mattered if he was in the road. John hadn't seen a car in ages, he could walk right down the middle if he really wanted to. No one cared about him in this encroaching dusk on this lonely country road. John made all kinds of accusations of heartlessness to each car that had passed, ignoring his outstretched thumb. As if they could know John's pain and were just choosing to abandon him out here out of spite. He was just a shape looming up in the dusk to their eyes, not a freezing kid aching with increasing desperation. Night was coming on and fast. He'd have to find somewhere to sleep. He had no idea where he was really, John just knew what it looked like on a map, and where it would take him sooner or later. As long as he didn't fall over before he got there.

Eventually, he reached a crossroads. One way continued down into the woods, the other went toward rolling hills and fields as far as he could see. He needed to turn here. John had only been going east to get to where he could go north, and the fields went in the right direction, to the highway north of here. From there he should be able to hitchhike pretty easily.

Food would be great, he thought as he began the Northward portion of his hike. John had a little, but God help him, with his fingers as numb as they were, pulling them out of his pockets to dig through his makeshift pack would only make it worse. At this point John didn't feel like he dared stop anyway, keep moving forward, that was the only way. If he stopped now, he might not be able to will his body further. As far as he could tell, it was only willpower that was moving him.

The clouds from the earlier rains had cleared away a while ago. On the plus side, it meant John could see where he was going by the full moon if he didn't find shelter sooner. But the price to pay for that night vision was the heat-trapping humidity had gone with those clouds, leaving only this biting cold that sapped at his strength if not his will to continue. Even John's will and desire had become a mindless thing. He walked because he had to keep walking, it had become a base state now, no sense to it anymore.

In the distance, John saw lights. The slight roll of the corn fields silhouetted the farm against the night with the moon coming up behind it. A farmstead. He looked at it dumbly for a minute. A house, many of the house lights already out, early though it was. A large barn sat near it, probably the cow barn. But a small distance away from that, an older ramshackle-looking barn, that probably dated back well over a hundred years. The thought clawed its way through the sludge that had become John's thoughts, a barn that most likely nobody used anymore. A place to sleep safely. God was running late, but he'd gotten here eventually.

John turned his leaden feet from the road and started to plod across the cornfields, now crusted over with a light covering of ice, and cleared of its stalks. The clear sky and full moon worked to his favor in avoiding tripping over the protruding stumps. His heavy, tired feet, though, worked against him instead. John still tripped and stumbled as if drunk as he forced himself across the frozen field.

Wide though the field was, it did not last forever, and John reached the rough, unpainted wood barn. It was enormous and dusty, cobwebs hung from the rafters. The tractors in here looked to be older models, not recently used and coated with greasy dust and grime. Bales of hay were stacked heavily on one side, probably good clover hay, but on the other side, it looked to be mainly straw bales. No one would need that until later in the day tomorrow, if at all. This barn was far enough from the main barn that it was entirely possible no one would even come in here at all tomorrow, they most likely had a supply in the main barn stacked in case of snow. Getting back to the road tomorrow would be tricky, but he could run for it, or just say he was cutting across country, farmers rarely complained about that.

Exhaustion began to rear its ugly somnambulant head now. John realized he'd never make it back to the road, even if he wanted to. If he did, it wasn't like he had seen any better options out there. This was going to have to do. John stumbled around the darkened barn for a while trying to find a spot completely out of sight of the door on the straw side. Finding the best spot he could, he rooted his sodden blanket out of his bag. It wasn't completely dry, but it was dry enough. With the blanket and the loose straw he pulled over himself, John didn't get warm per se, but at least the cold had ceased to hurt and bite so much. Finally, after his hands and feet warmed from completely numb to aching painfully, they almost began to feel comfortable if not a bit puffy and sore. His hands free, John dug a candy bar out of his belongings which he devoured ravenously.

It wasn't long after that, in his damp cocoon of straw and blanket, sleep finally claimed him as its own.

John hadn't had a choice really. The school would have killed him if he had stayed much longer. It was less a school than a whole community, and the community was its own community. They weren't forbidden to have contact with the local town, but that was almost impossible. They were only allowed off campus together, and only for a very limited amount of time. John had nowhere to turn for help there.

Self-sustaining, self-enclosed, ripe for abuse.

John's house parent had attacked him, thrown him around, broken some of his few possessions. Somehow that didn't hurt that much. If John's life before the school had been normal, he never would have been there in the first place. He'd been hit before. But the names with the abuse... Here was this man who didn't know him. Had no idea what went on inside of John, shouting vile things like he had a God-given right to do it. Like John was nothing but garbage who somehow owed this raving maniac for his time. That John was nothing, and would never be anything, and should be thankful to have someone around to beat the shit out of him. He had never fit in there before this, and in its own way, that was expected. You move enough, you never do fit in. Now John didn't want to fit in. One of his only possessions left in this world was his sense of dignity, often assaulted, tattered and battered, but still his own, and John would be damned to hell if he'd let this prick take that.

He didn't cry. He didn't curse. John sat staring at his desk as the lunatic's curses trailed away down the large dorm hall. He waited. Until he heard the door slam to Gary's private living quarters. Then he grabbed a blanket, and the few possessions that weren't broken and might be of use. This had been the final straw.

John sat with only a lamp on until midnight. Then, he ran for it.

Tap, tap, tap.... "Hello?" .... tap, tap, tap...... "Boy? Hello?"

Suddenly John was wide awake and terrified, he scrambled back away from the contact with his foot until his back hit a beam. The man who had been tapping his foot looked almost as scared as he did for a second, and then his face creased into a look of concern.

"What chu' doin' here, son? " he asked.

"Sle....sleeping," he mumbled as the sudden rush of adrenaline warred with his lingering exhaustion.

"Naw, son," the man said, smiling kindly, "I mean why on earth are you sleeping in my barn?"

"Tryin' ta hitchhike home....it got so cold last night," he shivered, "nobody was on the road...I just ran out of gas. I'm so sorry! It was the only place I could find!"

"Where are you headed then?" the man asked, standing back upright from leaning over him.

"Philly...I'm from Philly," he said, propping himself up.

"Well, I don't think I can get you that far, but I can probably spare some time and get you as far as the highway," he said, smiling again.

"Get your stuff and come on in and have some breakfast. I can't rightly leave you out here half-frozen and hungry to boot."

The man, his name turned out to be Jimmy, was polite and nice, and thankfully didn't pry too hard, keeping the lies John had to tell to a minimum. But the oatmeal and coffee still felt warm inside him, which put him miles of road and miles of circumstance ahead of where he had been when he fell asleep last night.

Jimmy had the decency to look worried about letting him out near the highway. "You sure you're going to be all right?"

"Sure," John lied, "I can call to have my mom pick me up from here, she'd have never found her way on the back roads."

"Well, if you're sure you're OK, well, be seeing you," and then, Jimmy drove away.

He was able to hitch one more ride soon after that. A family on vacation. John was as polite as possible and kept his hands to himself. They most likely picked him up at all to keep their kids occupied for at least a few miles. They seemed nice enough, but then again, everybody seemed nice enough around strangers. That's where everyone keeps their happy, special face, where everybody who they think is judging them can see it.

It was just outside of the state's ugly capital city that the rains began again. They weren't pouring rains or a light drizzle. This was the type of rain that moved in and stayed. Farmers like to call it a "good soaking rain" and it was doing the job it was named for. Within a half an hour of walking in it, John was drenched. Soaked all the way through, he began to shiver again.

The outwardly directed self-pity set in. He cursed the people in their nice and dry cars as they whipped by him again. It probably all works out, the kind of person that can fly by a soaking wet kid as he shivers by the side of the road probably had a few curses coming to them anyway. Standing by the highway during a cold soaking winter rain was like being hit by everywhere. You can't pull your collar up anymore, the water just drips in anyway, your pants are welded to your skin, nothing but wet, nowhere but cold.

The thought of turning back, of going back, never once crossed his mind, no matter the pain. Better to suffer for a while now than to spend the rest of his life from now until graduation suffering there. If he even made it to graduation, a kid or two every year checked out of school and everywhere else as well. He was determined more than ever to survive this all.

In the westbound lane, he spotted a beautiful old classic car driving the other way. Must be nice. Leather seats, a good heater, taking you to the kind of house cars like that are parked in front of in magazine ads. There was still the business at hand though, walking backward with his thumb out and a pitiful expression on his face. John didn't have to work at that last part anymore, it was coming pretty naturally now.

After a few minutes of miserable backward splashing, in the distance, John could swear coming toward him he could see the car he'd seen disappear going in the other direction. Must have made a wrong turn somewhere was all John could figure. But somewhere in his frozen mind, the thought reared up, *Maybe he's coming back because he feels bad for me.* Children, even teenage boys, even teenage boys with a bruised soul still hold out hope for pity, often it's the only thing they can hope for. The mood broke when an enormous Impala swerved specifically to hit a puddle, spraying him with it. John quickly jerked his head in the direction and let his grief release in a hearty "F-You!"

Common sense told him to not even stick his thumb out as he saw the enormous '40s classic bear down on him. But hope is sometimes more powerful than sense, if anything John stuck it out farther. But he still didn't turn his head back to see if the car stopped, instead he scanned ahead to see what might be coming next. A squeaking noise finally grabbed his attention, the squeal of brakes. Unbelievably, the car had stopped and was sitting idle by the side of the highway a few hundred feet away. John ran for it as well as he was still able to, trying to have a turn of speed in his numb legs.

John reached out for the door handle gingerly. The well-dressed man in his thirties gestured impatiently for him to get in. His own face was a mask of worry, this was a very expensive car, foreign and classic. The door pulled open completely smoothly, not even a creak to show its age.

"Come in, sit down, sit down," the man said equally as impatiently as he had gestured, "the seats are well oiled, I don't think a bit of wet will damage the leather over much."

John sat down carefully and closed the door. He tried subconsciously to make himself as small as possible to touch as little of the car as possible. "You won't break it, boy, it's a very expensive car, I'll grant you, but for the amount of money it costs, it isn't fine china either."

"It's just, I've never been in a car this nice before, sir," John said, starting to feel the ache already as the tension of bearing up to the weather let go.

"Well, to be fair, not many people have ever been in a '47 Bentley, so you aren't alone. Since I can't just call you 'boy' all the time, what's your name by the way?" the man said in a rapid-fire staccato.

"Uh, John, sir," he said, staring straight ahead. You try to make as little eye contact with a ride as possible. If they're a creep of some kind, they always take that as encouragement. You keep your eyes forward and mind your own business, even in someone else's car. If you want to get where you're going with a minimum of fuss, you talk politely when spoken to and keep everything to yourself.

"Well, John, my name is Richard, we've made a start at any rate. Now where are you going on this abysmal afternoon?" the man said, staring at the road, but smiling slightly.

"Ummm Philly, sir," John said in a subdued, cautious voice.

"Richard please, sir is so formal, but yet we make progress. Alright then, what on earth could drag you to the city of brotherly love?" Richard asked, eyes not leaving the road.

"It's where I'm from," John said, also staring straight ahead.

"So, what on earth are you doing all the way out here in the sticks?"

"I was visiting relatives, my mom couldn't come to get me," John lied.

"Oh, and why not?" Richards' eyebrow raised.

"Car broke down, so I offered to hitch," this was at least partly true, the car was the reason his mother had given every time Jon begged for her to come take him away from the school.

"Mm hmm. Well then, I can offer you a ride, and obviously, I am. But if I'm any judge, you could also desperately use some food and dry clothes so let's see about that as well. I may be an old cynic but I don't think I can leave you to freeze or starve to death, or more like, to catch your death of cold," Richard said, smiling and briefly glancing over.

"You don't look that old," replied John in lieu of anything coherent.

"Nice of you to say. To address your other concerns, since you've been on the road a few days I assume you have plenty of concerns or you wouldn't have made it this far. I am neither a pervert who seeks the comfort of little boys nor do I hack them up or in any other way molest them. You look like the thing you need most right now is a friend, and I'm easily bored enough to want the company. Deal?" Richard laughed.

"Can I think about it?" John asked quietly.

"Of course, we have a bit before the exit, I hope you like pot roast, because that is what's in the crock-pot. Maybe today's good deed gets a few sins off my record," Richard drawled, smiling.

Eventually, they turned off the country road they had been on, onto a wooded driveway. Richard had attempted to get conversation going, but John had been as quiet and close to the vest as possible, refusing to be drawn out. His eyes worriedly trying to keep track of where they were, listening for any sign that things were going weird. Charity was already a weird thing to him, something to be viewed with deep suspicion. You could PRAY for help all you wanted, but to just accept it when it came, you had to read the fine print. The man, Richard, looked to be in his mid-thirties, but he didn't have that desperate hunger for confirmation of value and worth that holy rollers seemed to exude. They always looked so in need of a pat on the head and a hearty "Good Boy!" Richard, if anything, just looked mildly amused by everything.

He was far too wealthy to be a kind "good ol' boy" looking to do "the decent thing." John's first ride of the day had fit into that category. A boy from Philadelphia with a mentally ill mother, no father to speak of, who got shipped to a place like the school had learned long ago not to trust the "kindness of strangers." But try as he may he couldn't find any ulterior motive or even a hint of it. For all his suspicion, it still looked as Richard said, "Doing good for the amusement of it."

"It opens up in a second, the trees were planted years ago to give the farmstead itself some privacy," Richard said.

Soon enough he saw what Richard had meant, a brief drive in the woods opened up into rolling farmland. The woods were, if anything, extended natural privacy fencing. The barn was mostly the kind you saw attached to the encroaching horse farms of the area. It had originally been a solid, honest barn, but now it was too clean, too well maintained. There were probably a couple of riding horses attached, but it was mainly to show that the property WAS a farm than to do the solid farm work it had been built for. You couldn't put up a pretentious sign declaring the place to be "Rolling Acres Farm" without an actual barn, it looked silly. It was painted a bright white with red trim. The hexes were like none John had ever seen before during his time in this part of the state, black circles with deep red hex signs, the points sharper looking than normal.

The house itself was another matter entirely. It had started as a stately farm house, like many of the manor homes in this part of the country. But then it had been expanded upon considerably. The original house's shape could still be seen, but only just. Built around it in stone was a vast cavernous expansion, not nearly as simple as the original building.

"Well, here we are, my humble abode," Richard said ironically.

When they got inside, John was in awe. Rather than the plastering that was usual in these old farmsteads, the walls were artfully wood-paneled in what seemed a deep luxurious mahogany. The furnishing was tasteful, antiques all. The entire place exuded old wealth and privilege.

"It started as a farm, on the original land grants dating back to colonial times. It has, of course, been improved upon considerably since then," Richard said, showing the awed boy inside.

"It's beautiful," John breathed.

"Well, I quite like it, so I'm glad you approve," Richard smiled. "But you won't catch your death of cold on my watch, so to business. Your pack you can leave here, or take with you, however you prefer. Up the stairs, second door along the hallway to your right is a bathroom, please use it for its stated purpose, please. There should be a robe inside, please dump your sodden clothing down the laundry chute so they can be cleaned and dried. I should be able to find you actual clothes to wear while I'm caring for your wet things. They may smell strongly of mothballs, I'm afraid. It can't be helped, teenagers in a growth spurt have not seen these walls for years now, but they will at least be clean and dry, so that puts you well ahead already."

"But...."

"Son, you're soaked to the bone, and you've clearly been without a bath for some time. You'll feel better and it will make you better company. I've already decided to help you today, at least we can be orderly about it. While you're bathing, I will see to your clothes, and set out food for you. That will be in the middle room directly ahead. Altruism does not come easy for me, so, please. If it makes you feel better, the bathroom has a lock on it, so up you go," Richard said.

"Well....OK, I guess," said John quietly.

"There we go, go get clean and warm and I'll go take care of seeing you're fed."

John went to the room he'd been told and entered, shutting the door behind him. Turning on the light revealed the bathroom itself. It was decorated in a maroon and black tile pattern. To one side was an ancient claw-footed tub with a large brass shower head above it. Looking at himself in the mirror above the pedestal basin, he had to admit, he was plastered with dirt. The rain hadn't cleaned him as much as packed in the dirt to his skin. He was pale and his hair hung lank and stringy both from the rain and the lack of bathing. If Richard was a pervert, he would certainly have to have very rarefied taste. He walked over to the door and locked it anyway, no point in being stupid. John admitted to himself the very thought of soaking for a while in hot water had an appeal. It had been days of running from nosy police, cold, wet, and in pain. A half an hour of letting hot water get the numb out of his limbs might also help restore some of his numbed sanity.

John turned the tap on the tub and let the water run for a while until he saw steam, then swished his hand under the stream to check the heat. As the tub filled there was a knock on the door and Richard called through the door, "I was right, there were some clothes that should fit, just toss your old ones down the chute, they should be clean and dry in no time."

For a second John listened to the retreating footsteps then unlocked the door and looked out. As promised a pair of slacks, a dress shirt roughly about his size, and a pair of socks sat there. He picked them up and re-locked the door. Oh well, if he had to run for it, it would be better dressed than he had been when he got here. John hung his sopping jacket on the door handle and disrobed, dumping the sodden lump down the chute.

Finally, almost joyously John climbed into the slightly too hot tub. Climbing in had to be done by degrees, he was still so cold, and the water so hot it hurt, but it was the type of pain one withstands bit by bit, just for the promise of pure relaxation that it will bring eventually. Finally, gratefully John sunk below the steaming water. Bliss, everything he'd hoped and prayed to have for days, wrapped up in a warm cocoon of water.

When the water finally started to chill down and he had scrubbed himself thoroughly, John was willing to get out of the tub reluctantly. For the last half an hour, there hadn't been any problems, and he was loathe to give the feeling up. But he still got out dripping water and dried himself off with the towel on the rack. John padded damply over to the pile of clothing he'd been given and put them on. They were formal and a little tight because of his height, but overall comfortable enough.

John thought briefly of putting on his shoes but vetoed it for now; they were practically dripping still. He picked them and his other belongings up, trying desperately to glad-hand them and keep them away from his now clean, dry, and warm self.

John left the bathroom and padded downstairs almost silently on his stocking feet. He looked around the front room where he had first come into the house and re-oriented. Getting his bearings, John then went to the double set of doors under the balcony. Through them was a long hallway going off in either direction, but, sure enough, there was another set of doors directly across from the ones he had just opened.

These opened into an enormous dining room. The only real light was from the fireplace that had a decent fire in it, but with signs of only being recently lit. But considering the recent lighting, the flames were still fitful and it left the far end of the dining room itself bathed in shadows. There was a slight sullen glow coming through what appeared to be a dark red stained-glass window, but that shed no real light at all, it only made for a glowing red spot in the gloom.

The door clicked shut behind him and on the table in front of him was thankfully food. A steaming plate of meat and potatoes and a soda. There was an envelope next to the plate, but at this point John wasn't very interested in reading, realizing how hungry he was. It was just as well that it said "Read After You've Eaten" on it since that was the plan anyway. The steaming pot roast tasted like heaven. He barely remembered to wash it down some with the soda that was with it.

When he'd eaten enough to consider opening the envelope itself, he clawed it open clumsily. It read in a neat and tidy cursive hand-

Dear John,

I write you with the opportunity of a lifetime. I have had this property and this position for many years, trust me on this, I am much older than I appear. A man, to be of any use here, has to be OF a time, not just existing in it, and I am afraid time has long since passed me by. It has reduced my value here, so I am going to be re-assigned somewhere my experience and knowledge will have more usefulness. It is a lucky man, such as I, who gets to pick and train his own successor into a position he has loved but can no longer fulfill. You were not my first choice, to be honest, but I think you will be a much better one by far. The one who you would replace was corrupted already, he had already stolen with glee for the theft rather than need, and took love which was not offered by force. My side of the equation, to be truly effective, needs some virtue in it.

If I were not such a practiced sinner, it would almost make me despair for the youth of the nation. I need someone who has at least some virtue, you cannot understand the way of anything if you have never known it. But you appear to be mainly an innocent still, despite what has happened to you in life. I can offer you now, today, things you have only ever dreamed of in life: wealth, position, a future. How much do you have now? You have prayed for all of this, over and over. Prayers can be heard and answered, here it is.

There is a task you must complete at the far end of this room. When you look upon it, it should be readily apparent what you need to do. Do it quickly, and believe me boy, your ship has come in.

> *-your friend and mentor*
> *Richard*

He re-read the letter twice to make sure he understood the situation. What did he mean by "innocent" anyway? Cynicism wanted to hold his attention, but at his age, you're used to being acted upon by adults. Free will is really something one hasn't fully developed yet. An adult was acting on him, nothing new here, adults acted upon him all the time. They cut his mom's food stamps, they put him in the school in the first place, they locked his mom up sometimes and put him in foster care, they evicted him. Telling kids what to do was just something adults did. But this time, unlike the church, unlike the state, this adult seemed to want to actually help him and was asking, not telling. All he had to do was look. He hadn't done anything but accept some charity, he could always say no.

As he walked down the length of the table, it seemed that the stained glass started to glow brighter, and not just because he was getting closer. The shadows almost seemed to swirl around it like tendrils, an obvious trick of the light he dismissed. Once John got close, he saw that there was some kind of flat surface of stone directly in front of the stained glass. A shape covered most of it, and a sheet covered that, obscuring what it was.

John reached out with a shaking hand, afraid now that whatever this final task was, he wouldn't be strong enough. He thought of himself as lacking fortitude, it had been him whimpering in the cold last night after all. Richard was right, this was what he prayed for, some massive hand coming down and plucking him from his hideous life. He didn't want to lose it now due to frailty. John drew back the sheet itself.

John stared in shock. On the slab was a boy his own age, nude and hairless. He was breathing, unconscious but still alive, breathing shallowly. The light behind the stained glass seemed very bright now, creating all kinds of shadows that almost seemed to be reaching for him! There were five golden knives next to the boy, and five dots on the boy's body, two in the shoulders, two in the hips, and one.... John turned away.

John ran back the length of the room in a panic to the door and wrenched on the handle, but it had locked when he had entered the room. John pounded on it for a moment ineffectually and yelled for Richard. Silence was his only answer, broken only by his own ragged breathing.

Stillness came over him, and he walked back down the length of the table to where the other boy lay unaware of the presence of his would-be murderer and stared down at his face. Even in sleep, it seemed to have a cruel cast to it, it seemed to John. Maybe it was the fire, maybe the light of the stained glass but there seemed to be tendrils of shadow flickering completely around the slab now.

What if he didn't do this? He'd seen so much, could he really believe that Richard was just going to let him waltz right on out of here, no foul, no harm? Nobody even knew he was here! Who would really miss him anyway?

Who would miss him anyway.... Who *would* miss him anyway? His crazy mom? The reprobates she brought home and called his Daddy? Well, maybe they might miss having a target for their drunken temper tantrums, but they certainly wouldn't miss his conversation.

John reached down and picked up one of the knives, weighing it in his hand as he thought. It almost seemed that the stained glass was blazing now, casting a red glow over the entire scene. Why in the hell shouldn't he? What did he have to look forward to even if he left? A few more years at home, and then tossed on the street to fend for himself? Richard was right, this is what he had prayed for secretly, a chance to be something, to have a chance to make his own way one day and succeed. To not have all the cards against him for once, isn't that fair? What was the point in praying for anything if you had to give it up for moral reasons when someone wanted to give it to you?

It seemed to him that out of the corner of his eye, the limbs of shadow tried to embrace him now. This kid was a rapist and a thief, all on his own without any prodding. He'd had his chance, and failed. The kid wasn't on this slab right now by sheer accident. He had been judged and failed. But God, to end a life, a human life, any human life.... He'd never done anything more than shoplift gum and food when it got desperate before this, maybe get in fights at school. This was murder. This was a human being before him.

God would judge. John had called out to God a lot in his young life, when had God ever come to help him? Richard was willing to save him. But still, could he murder? He sighed as the tendrils stroked at his face and arms now lovingly. Could he pay the price for everything he wanted?

The Jaguar purred like a kitten as he pulled it onto the road. God! He was furious, that idiot State Treasurer had actually shot himself! That wasn't the game they were playing here! He was supposed to go to jail in Club Fed, and then come out clean as a whistle saying he found Jesus or some crap. It was supposed to instill the public with sullen distrust in public institutions, not outright horror! People just didn't know how to play the role he wrote for them some days. He wished Richard was around so he could have someone who understood to talk to. Wonder where Richard was these days?

Soon though, the hum of the road eased the tension out of him. The road, it is the one thing that is eternal. From the day back in dusty time when it was a path that said, "This way to water," to the dirt wagon trails, to the country lane, to the superhighway. It is the eternity of man, always going somewhere. It offers up endless vile entertainments, endless temptations, endless opportunities to do the devil's work, and Johnathan Richardson was a man who knew where all the best exits were if you could pay the fee.

First Appeared In "Schlock!" #289

I think at every horror author's career they have a moment of fascination with heaven and hell and, of course, demons. So, yeah, I had a moment. I'm proud to have had this piece be part of a charity anthology to fight addiction, something we lose far too many to.

Damnation by Degrees

Welcome to my little moral tale. Pleased to make your acquaintance. Oh, my name? I'm afraid my real name would be almost unpronounceable to you with that crude mechanism for making the noises you call language, but you can call me Topsy. If you're feeling formal, I also answer to Doctor Topsy. It's an inside joke, but hopefully we clear that up later. Speaking of jokes, I've often said that when he made humans, the all-knowing god must have been admitting a mistake with his first crew of companions and servants, so he dumbed down your design a bit. Thus, you having such difficulty pronouncing what I consider a perfectly commonplace name. Still, it comes in handy, as it keeps me from getting summoned by every Anton, Aleister, and Harry who bumbles his way to the chapter on summoning in whatever book on the dark arts is in his possession.

As a demon, I AM the black arts, and don't like to be interrupted by amateurs, thank you very kindly.

Which of course begs the question, why am I speaking to you? Well because, frankly, I suspect your friends and family think you to be a fool. Oh please, do not be offended. I don't mean that in a drooling imbecile sort of way. Frankly, those people have neither imagination nor intellect to understand what I have to say. I mean it more in a "Head always in the clouds, heart always in a book," dreamer sort of way.

Everyone needs somebody to talk to, after all. It makes all of us, even demons, feel a little better, don't you think? A shoulder to cry on, a friendly ear, the reason bartenders stay employed? I think I've an accurate idea of you. A little bit look-I've-just-bought-a-Lovecraft-shirt with a smidgeon of Lord of the Rings thrown in? Of course you are. No use in denying it; nothing to be ashamed of, anyway. And you make the perfect confidante, for who will believe you about me, should you be inclined to blab? Perfect.

I think that we get bad press. I know, we're DEMONS; what kind of press do we expect? Maybe not bad press as much as unfair. We aren't running around tempting mortals for their souls and tearing apart victims in all kinds of icky, bloody tortures once we've lured them into our grasps! Well, not as often as we used to. Well, a bit, alright I grant, it does come up, but it isn't the overwhelming obsession like your films and books make it out to be.

Prove it, you say? Well, first off, I would point out that here I am, talking to you! You haven't been whisked around straight to hell, have you? You still have all of your appendages still attached, do you not? Please, go do an inventory yourself if you don't believe me, I'll wait... I did not do a thing to THAT! That IS the correct size, and I had nothing to do with the present situation. Don't think you can sucker me into some major corrective surgery for what God neglected that easily!

We have many more diverse interests than that. I could prove it with a couple of stories of my recent fun. Then, maybe you'd see it wasn't all just rending flesh and dastardly drawn up contracts. Why, yes! I could give you a contrast and compare! I could give you two stories, one that is maybe a little more, shall we say, true to our reputation. The other could be the kind of thing I REALLY enjoy, and I could leave it to you, my new friend, to decide which one was the most, shall we say, demonic?

So, what shall it be first? Blood on the walls? Or the kind of evil which warps the soul?

Why did I know you were going to go for the bloody one? Predictable, really. Nothing you people seem to like more than seeing one of your own's blood and viscera flying everywhere. I wonder why you even bother with music. Put out a song and call it "Screams of The Tortured Dying." It would probably sell a million copies. Oh well, I'm nothing if not obliging.

It all started simply enough. I was in my study, you know, studying things…what do you mean 'what things'? Alright, if you must know, I was thumbing through some old Chick Publications comics. I can't help myself; I find those things hilarious. The guy was a special talent, I can tell you that, worth his weight in ichor to us.

Anyway, I was giggling away, when I heard my name spoken on the mortal plane. Most demons can hear if a mortal speaks their name. Of course, your more powerful demons hire lesser infernal folk to hear their name for them. Baphomet would never get anything done if he heard his name every time it was invoked. He keeps an imp handy almost like an answering machine, who goes through the daily mentions, weeding out the casual oaths. I've thought about getting one, but really, my name is so difficult to pronounce, it doesn't seem worth it. When somebody manages to vomit out my name, I want to see what they're about for myself.

Upon hearing my name, I raced to its source and found an area to make my appearance nearby. I entered into the world in a countryside. You don't appear right away next to the speaker; that's bad form. Instead, you try to find an unobtrusive spot near them. It's a shock to see someone just step out of the ether, and it leads to questions. Yes, we have gone for the big appearances for shock and awe, but to be honest, half the time we just use flash pots like any magician. It's cheaper. No, you want a look at the little scoundrel taking your name in vain, it's better to see the situation and plan what you want to do rather than going in tail half-cocked. That and when we manifest, well, it's embarrassing, but there's always a little brimstone. Can't be helped.

Peering out from my hiding spot in the nearby woods, the situation became apparent. What I spied with my evil eye was a middle-aged, overweight man standing next to a relatively nice Mercedes. His face was flushed, his brow tensed in annoyance. In one hand was the mutant hunk of metal that made up part of the Mercedes-Benz jack, his other he was shaking as if injured, and he was yelling forcefully enough to cause a spray of spittle to fly with every eruption of his jowly mouth.

Now, I knew the situation. Someone didn't know how to change a flat on his own car. Perfect! He'd accept any help offered with no second thoughts! A bit of checking my internal GPS gave me an idea of where I was: somewhere in New York State, close enough to the Hudson Valley to give me my cover story! Stepping back to my personal chambers, I grabbed a few things I thought I'd need and slammed them into a svelte designer bag before putting on a glamour for appearances. Slinging a camera around my neck, I popped back where I had been just a moment before.

"Hello?" I called out, stepping near to the edge of brush.

The man lunged backwards, startled, "Oh! Hello! You gave me quite a fright!"

"I'm dreadfully sorry," I said, stepping out into the road, "I heard someone, well, cursing. I was in the area taking photos, and frankly getting myself turned around, so I thought I'd see if I could help. Maybe figure out where I am."

"If you can figure out this blasted jack, you'd be saving my tukus!" the man said with a beaming grin. "Sorry if you heard me, but I assure you, I wasn't cursing." He smiled again and wiped his brow, "A habit I picked up as a child. When I'm especially angry, I just make up a word and bark it loudly. Hopefully, god can forgive me that!"

He certainly could, but I am not in the forgiving business. The opposite, really. Transgressions, even those of an accidental nature such as this, must have consequences. There is no point to having rules if one is not prepared to dish out the punishment which comes with breaking them. I mean that for humans, of course. I break any rule I find inconvenient. I suppose if I found punishing a mortal for speaking my name inconvenient, I could break that one too, but when is that ever going to happen? Oh no, no fun for me please, all full-up here?

I chuckled aloud, and said, "Here's to hoping he doesn't consider intent. Let me take a look at it. Maybe I can save you considerable blast and bother!"

"You do, and I owe you a drink and a meal and a ride back to wherever you got turned around from!" he said with a broad smile on his broad and sweating face.

I had no problem with the jack. It was a Mercedes after all. My tribe had quite a lot to do with their original designs, as it were. Good German engineering. It's a shame we couldn't figure out a way to let the nutter win that war. But the angels got sick of us fixing up his tactical errors and stepped in to counter us. Goody-two-shoes spoiled sports! Oh well, his loss gave people hope back, I suppose, and hope is where damnation is truly made and fermented, after all.

He watched me carefully while I worked. You could tell the man had an inquisitive nature. He wasn't just standing by while some chap labored for him. He was paying attention, learning as he went, so he would never be in such straits ever again. I hadn't the heart to tell him he wouldn't.

"Well, thank goodness for that! I'd have been here all the livelong day if you hadn't come along!" he said, clapping me enthusiastically on the shoulder once I had let the car down.

I turned to look at him, smiling with what for all the world was the smile of a good Samaritan happy in a job well done. He thrust out his hand, "Doctor Richard Farnsworth. Pleased to meet you, sir! And your name is?"

"What a happy coincidence! I'm a Doctor as well, Doctor Topsy, Seth Topsy!" I said while vigorously pumping his extended hand.

"Well, Seth! I do believe I owe you at least a drink, but I'd be delighted if you'd dine with me at my house tonight! I don't get many guests, to be honest. Where are you parked?" The words came in a nervous, yet relieved, rush.

"I'll tell you what," I replied, "if you can give me your address, it'll give me a chance to clean up a bit first."

He wrote his address on the back of a business card, which I noted was a very nice stoneware linen with thermographed type. Very classy. We arranged that we should meet at his house later that very night. I took note of the address as he drove off. He wasn't just any type of doctor, apparently. One needed a wealthy clientele to afford such an elegant spot in the old space-time.

A vanish here, a reappearance there, and I was driving off to the good Doctor's mansion in the woods. I had on a nice enough suit, nice, but not too nice. I was playing the part of a general practitioner, after all. In these 1960s America, your Doctor would be upper-middle class, but not filthy with it. I also wanted to establish myself in the inferior position. I needed him to be trusting of me, and the great and mighty always tend to trust the slightly less successful members of their trade so long as they act like they are content with their lot in life. A corporate lawyer loves the guy playing local-yokel lawyer adjudicating chicken cases. They tend to assume there is some special honor in "not doing it for the money."

To complete my appearance of subservience, I was driving a very nice Oldsmobile, upper-middle class all the way.

I made a point of bringing a special wine and showing up ten minutes early. Early always shows throat, like a dog rolling over and baring its neck to the wolf. He greeted me at the door of his estate himself, which was a surprising gesture, one he explained away, saying, "I only hire servants for special occasions and cleaning, really. I believe a man should know how to cook and take care of himself, without a woman's help, if need be. Anyway, how often do you even have guests out here in the sticks?"

His explanation told me plenty. Firstly, I did not count as a "special occasion." This was fine with me, as I didn't want to be one, and being so would complicate my plans for the evening. Secondly, he told me in no uncertain terms that this was a second home, judging by his wedding ring and the lack of a wife, who I assumed was staying in the city and not, as he put it, "out in the sticks." But most importantly, he told me we'd be alone tonight, just the two of us.

He asked if I minded dining in his study instead of the dining room, explaining the latter was too large for comfort. I happily agreed. A quiet study, two chums dining casually, a perfect situation. Sure enough, when we entered, there was a nice, smaller table away from the fireplace perfect for informal dining. We settled in, and he served. After swallowing a mouthful, I asked, "This is absolutely delicious! You made this yourself?"

"It's good enough, I suppose, but truthfully, half of cooking is just following directions. But I thank you for saying it," Farnsworth said, waving his fork as he spoke. "You said you were a Doctor?"

I decided to take the conversational gambit. "Oh, yes. Nothing glamorous enough to afford the likes of this. Just a small practice in the suburbs." All of this I said in a self-deprecating tone that Farnsworth devoured along with his meal.

"Oh, there is nothing wrong with that!" he declared. "For every single person saved by the likes of me, there must be a hundred who come to you for help."

"Kind of you to say," I smiled.

We conversed quite freely after that. I gave him the manufactured details of my imaginary practice, and he gave me his in kind. It turned out the good doctor was a surgeon and nerve specialist. He was very expensive, a fact he only half-downplayed, eager as he was for more of my fawning, which I gave. During a lull in our conversation, I feigned a need for a bathroom break so I could do some quick off-dimensional sleuthing about the man. By the time I returned, I had a full understanding of Doctor Richard Farnsworth, and my plan was complete in my mind. I'd had a seed of an idea before, but now it was blossoming before my eyes. My wine would have a splendorous effect upon him, being as I had made sure it was at least part ichor.

Ichor should be explained, I suppose. It is the blood of the gods. At least that was the original recipe, but much like plasma for you, my kind has been manufacturing it on our own since forever. What are gods? Well, you could run through your various mythos and come up with dozens of different answers, and all of them would be more or less correct. Suffice it to say that, since the creator stopped talking to anybody and everybody, the role of god has been filled by various individuals from the demon and the angel variety. The best of the best, as it were, or you could say the ones with the biggest egos. I mean, if you were petty. I would never say that, of course, at least not until I was sure of who was listening. Anyway, it turned out that the blood of those A-Grade holy of holies had various abilities in the hands of the mystically inclined. The more mystic, the more abilities. As a demon myself, you don't really get much more mystic, do you? With a few words here and a wave of your hand there, you can make it do all kinds of things. It will heal just about any wound, knit up your skin and muscles just like nothing happened. It can also do some other things.

Like what it did to my host right then.

I heard a shocked gasp escape him. His hand released the glass he had been drinking from with my fine vintage in it. I sighed at wasting even a little ichor as it crashed to the floor beneath his seat.

I tsked, "Such a shame, you know that particular vintage is absolutely impossible to get around here." I smiled my most winning evil smile as I stepped toward the man. "It has amazing properties, don't you think? There you are, unable to move a muscle, yet completely aware. And here is the really fun part: no matter how much pain I cause you, no checking out with a convenient heart attack for you! No, you're going to survive all of it, and you are going to feel all of it! It will be an experience, and make no mistake!"

I could see the shock and question in his eyes, or maybe I only imagined I did. "Your little habit of making up curses has gotten you into quite a spot of bother, Doctor Farnsworth! Did you know that a demon hears its name when it is spoken by a mortal? We can be quite peevish about the whole thing, really! Your habit of hiding your cursing has cursed you very well indeed. Now, where do you keep your tools of your trade? I'm sure you have a private office for those off-the-books procedures nobody likes to talk about. Oh, don't be so coy about it, Farnsworth. You know the ones, the kind which come in the middle of the night and leave your pocketbook flush by morning. Well, no matter, I'm sure I can find it myself. You're indisposed at the moment!"

It didn't take long to find what I needed, and I returned in a trice. "Goodness me!" I said with the happy smile of a child who had just been gifted a balloon. "You did have all KINDS of goodies in your operating theater. If only I had more time, but I have something specific in mind, and one mustn't get distracted from the task at hand!"

I lifted up the fat doctor as though he was a rag doll and placed him on his back on the dinner table. I showed him the scalpel I had acquired for the evening's entertainment. His eyes didn't grow wide, they couldn't, but I could see the terror there anyway. A good demon always knows these things, after all. You need to not look at the eye because even the shape of it can lie to you. No, you need to see beyond the pools of the iris to the depths below, to a place which exists outside of the material plane, for it is in the eye you may catch a glimpse of the higher self, the so-called soul. The soul is bare of artifice and cannot hide its terror, and the pureness of its emotions are ambrosia.

I removed his shirt and his thin undershirt, exposing the lily-white flab of his torso. His skin pimpled reflexively at the cool air striking it. I slapped at his tubby belly and watched it wiggle a bit as a bright red hand print appeared on it. "Good thing we're not trying to cut through all that, eh?" I grinned at him.

Next, I took the scalpel firmly in hand and began. The first cut occurred on the chest, at a diagonal angle near the breastbone. Next, I cut in a long line going up past the shoulder and another at the other end, like a large 'I.' I would take breaks as I cut, so I could watch the man's eyes. It was joyful to see the torment, trapped in there, unable to allow itself the release of screaming. After the first cut, I made a point of picking his head up from the table a little to show him my handiwork. A consummate professional like him would appreciate the view, I thought.

"I wonder if you can even guess what I intend to do? Don't you worry, I won't spoil the surprise! But you know, I think using this professional little blade is spoiling some of the fun, don't you?" I said, the scalpel on the table next to his ear, so he could hear it clink on the table. I held up a serrated steak knife so he could see it. "I think you'll REALLY be able to feel this, don't you think?"

Moving some of the fat out of the way, I could get to work. It was tough going, but I loved every minute of it as I sawed crossways through the muscles of the pectoralis major. Every screaming pain it caused as one after another of the fibrous muscles of the chest fell to the onslaught of the blade's rasping touch. But good things don't last forever, no matter how much we're enjoying ourselves. Time flies, and all that. It was with a forlorn sigh that I pulled the muscle up and let it flop over Farnsworth's shoulder.

"Moving on," I said, sing-song. I smiled at the good doctor, drinking in his beautiful agony, his soul and his brain screaming so loudly it was almost audible to the naked ear. "I'd have let that go on a bit longer, Richard, but you're out of shape. I only had so much muscle to work with. I think we can make this next bit of fun last a little longer if we...use something a bit duller?"

I picked up a butter knife and waved it under his eyes, "A good thing you had a full complement of cutlery at the table, isn't it? I might have rushed all of this and just used the scalpel, and what a shame it would have been to cut short our time together."

I moved some more fat and I saw my goal. A happy little M for Misery there in the armpit, if that's how you chose to look at things. Now, an amateur would cut those where it's the most obvious, wouldn't he? But I, my friend, am not an amateur. I am a doctor, after all; that wasn't mere deception.

I began to draw the butter knife with its tiny serrations across the medial nerve cord. The nerves: the delivery system of so many vital sensations and commands to the brain. Like pain. I had to hold the slippery thing taut with two fingers, gripping it vice-like as I worked.

There was an audible snap as it finally gave way. I did regret that some, it probably would have been much more torturous for him to feel the last shreds of it slowly hacked away, but alas, you can only work with the materials you have at hand.

Next to go was the lateral cord. I humored myself for a moment as I pulled it tight, flicking it with my finger to hear the musical note it would produce. It might not be high art, but it was music to my ears, and we all play our instruments for ourselves, do we not?

I spared my victim another glance. I could scarcely credit it, but there were beads of sweat on the man's puffy face. The pain must have been beyond human description that even with the ichor steadying his vital signs and keeping him from shock or acute myocardial infarction, his body was still producing a sheen of sweat. I smiled again.

"Well, now that we've gotten those two fellows out of the way, we can get a good crack at the posterior cord!"

The pleading and begging in his eyes I saw then, I savor it on nights when I'm bored and despondent.

Finally, it was over. It didn't have to be, to be sure, for there are plenty of other nerves to play with, but it's no good having a plan if you don't intend to keep to it, now is it? I had intended to wipe out the nerves leading to his surgery arm, and I had. Anything else would be overkill and lacking panache.

"I'm going to leave you in a bit, Richard."

I could see a twitch in his eyes.

"Oh, don't worry, I'll be putting you back together. Well, except for the nerves, that is. In fact, you will never, ever, ever be able to speak of this to anyone. But I think it's time for you to go to sleep. I wouldn't want you to actually experience the relief of the end of your torment, after all."

I waved a hand in front of his eyes and let his consciousness drift away. It did not take long to reattach his muscles and close up his skin. Ichor is indeed magical stuff. All I really needed to do was to hold the muscles down and dab it with the stuff to get the bits and pieces to return to their previous, un-ravaged form. But not his nerves; those I left severed.

I was brisk after that. I carried my charge up to his bed and changed him into his pajamas. I tsked at him a bit for his taste in bedclothes, but it wasn't worth waking him to say. Instead, I just tucked him up nice and snug in his bed. I cleaned up any trace of my visit: the blood on the table, my plates. I pocketed the wine. Before I left, I made sure to leave his plates, and the wine he had opened for us before that. I left it empty, of course, drinking it down in just a few mighty droughts. I was setting a scene.

The scene I set that early sixties night? A middle-aged, rich surgeon, with the country house to himself without the wife. He goes to bed after drinking far, far too much wine. When he wakes, he has no feeling nor functionality in his right arm at all. The diagnosis considering his weight would be a snap judgment. A stroke. Most of the tests would say it was one and given him admitting that he had had bad dreams of some kind all that night would go a long way to confirm it. They would put him on medication, he would never have another stroke, a success of modern medicine!

That was fun, wasn't it? A body torn apart, pain and misery so excruciating it would make a man insane! Funnily enough, the phantom memory lurking in Doctor Farnsworth's mind did indeed drive him mad soon enough. He died in an asylum. So that's one way to do evil's work.

The next story isn't nearly as fun, I'll admit, but it's quicker. In the 1980s I went to college at Harvard. What could they have to teach me? Not a thing! I had contributed to much of the older texts, after all. But I needed to be in position. Great things were happening in human history, and somebody needed to be nearby to observe and perhaps influence.

So, I became happy, normal med student, Neil Topsy. It was fun, I had to admit: no responsibilities, no worries, just basically showing up for classes whose topics I knew intimately. I don't think I so much as cracked a book until we got to some of the newest cutting-edge procedures. This gave me plenty of time to hang about and corrupt the morals of a few law students, most of which would go into politics, of course. I was mainly laying down a back story and making the types of friendships I would need later.

My classmates and I went into the workforce after school. I didn't really keep in touch with most of my former "frat brothers." The things they intended to do with their lives were no more interesting to me than what I was pretending to do with mine. Investment bankers seem to come out of the womb corrupted, and since my little nudges down the path of Gordon Gecko had been easy and fast, they were well on their way to making god knows how many people miserable. Even more so for the lawyers.

One day I was having lunch with my friend Kevin. Kevin was in electronics. He had seen the original home computers, farcical though they were, and had glimpsed the future. Even at this early date, it was becoming apparent he'd been right. They were getting faster and more capable all the time. This thing called the internet he had spoken of so rapturously would soon be coming to homes everywhere.

He was still broke, though, since he worked for a startup, and so I was paying for lunch.

"OK, spill. We've already got entrees ordered, and you've barely spoken," I said to him as we waited. "Come on, if you can't trust me, who can you trust? What's got your head in a cloud?"

"Oh, it's just a marketing issue. We need to find a way to make our company stand out," he said with a shrug.

"Stand out how?"

This got a big sigh from Kevin and a sip of his Coke, a sure sign of cogitation from him. "Well, when we started, we thought we'd be ahead of everybody offering web-based emails. You know, a site you could go to, to house your emails rather than using the inbox built into your internet service. But now it seems as if everybody and his brother are going to have one unveiling soon. News stories and email all in one, just like ours."

"So, it runs on its own web page, and you, what, sign in to view your emails?" I asked sincerely.

"Yeah, but it looks like there's going to be at least five competitors rolling out this year with a similar model. We don't want to get lost in the shuffle. My boss has hinted that the one who comes up with a good idea to make us stand out is probably going to be a really rich guy after we go public," he said, sullenly swishing his ice cubes around in the glass.

I gave him my most charming pal smile and said, "Tell you what, give me dinner to think about it? Hey, two heads are better than one, after all. If I come up with an idea, it's yours gratis. You're the one who bought us all that Jolt for finals the one year, and that stuff wasn't easy to get back then, I figure I owe you at least an idea."

"You come up with one, dinner is on me," he replied.

We ate our dinner and caught up with how we were both doing. We had the same lives of most newly professional people: working hard, not making enough money, but with a sight of it on the horizon soon, et cetera. Neither of us were dating anyone seriously for the same reasons, which was no free time.

When the check came, I made to pick it up. Kevin grinned at me and said, "So, no great idea, huh?"

I acted surprised for a second, and then said, "Oh, yeah! I had one, nearly forgot! How about giving people groups? You know, for common interests or professions, and stuff. Like a room you host where people can come on your site to talk. It would help with doctors, for sure, but other people could discuss the things they like, like football, or old movies, or stuff?"

Kevin sat back, a stunned look on his face as he scratched his chin. He still said nothing as he leaned forward and swirled his ice cubes around a bit. Finally, a radiant smile crossed his face, and he reached for the check.

"Dinner is on me."

And so, we parted that night, he with his grand money-making idea, and me with the warm feeling of having done evil's grand work.

I can hear you scream at this page now, "That's it? You gave some computer wonk the idea for message boards????"

Please, hear me out.

The crippling of Doctor Richard Farnsworth might have cost a hundred, maybe a hundred and fifty people their lives due to being deprived of his surgical genius. It certainly cost him his. But past that, what did I do but create a great story to pass around in one of the various bars in Hell when I've been in my cups. Sure, it's funny and all, but still.

Do you really understand how much evil has been done by message boards? Within the year, Kevin's page was up and running at full force, and faster than that, political boards sprung up. People cursed each other and lied to each other every day. Physical threats were made by people named "Plumlover2000."

But it got better yet. Soon, there were web pages dedicated to lying! People began to distrust the old truth tellers in favor of lies they wanted to believe! Soon whole sites became dedicated to just people talking and lying to one another. Wars were fomented there, hate groups exploded as those lonely souls discovered they were not alone, and they began to recruit more to their sides. Murders happened, rapes, all kinds of splendorous things.

Some of my best work.

You see, my dears, this is what we demons REALLY want to do. We don't want to torture you. Well, we do, but we're smart enough to know that is only a fleeting pleasure. What we really want to do is let you create something you're proud of, we want it to be the best you can make or think of, and then, we want to convince you to screw it up for yourselves.

You split the atom, one of us haphazardly mentions its destructive force.

You create cars, we suggest tanks.

You create movable type, we suggest tabloids.

Now that's good clean fun, right there.

I got a commendation and a medal for internet groups. I can't wait for the next great and wonderful idea you have. There may be a demon among you right now, just itching to give you a suggestion on how you might improve it.

First Appeared in the "Merchants of Misery" anthology

The history of labor in this country has been a constant struggle between the men and women who do the work, and those that profit over it. In this country the safety of those workers has never been considered truly paramount. This is even more noticeable here in West Virginia, where mining disasters are just a way of life.

Blacklung

Waking up is never easy, it seems. The panic, the fear, fear, and recriminations. Uncertainty at its all-time high, you have to relearn everything you know in an instant. You learn to worry immediately about what you did to get here. Wherever here may be. It's always a risk waking up, you might not like the answers you get back from yourself.

Tommy Allison was not liking any of the answers he was receiving. He had been at a meeting with some union reps, arguing over benefits. He'd been taking pulls on his private flask that his assistant set up for him every morning. And now, he was here.

And here was very, very dark. Either that or he'd gone blind from bad moonshine. It was shine that was in that flask; he knew a guy.

Alright, don't panic, the best way to make a bad situation worse is to panic about it. First, assess your situation. Are you hurt? He went through a mental checklist and found that, except for being sore, he wasn't hurt. Where are you? Well, that was why he was sore, he had been laid out on a hard floor. Hard? His hand reached out, loose rock, dirt....

Those pricks!

They'd dumped him in one of the mines, he was sure of it!

Tommy sat up abruptly in the inky black. Those absolute bastards! That was a low move even for those union thugs! It was an idle mine too, no noise, no light at all. Well, they'd know just as well as he did which ones were idle at the moment. The union probably had just as much access as he did to the properties they were on.

He was angrier than anything right now. This was playing hardball. Well, if those dipshits thought it was going to work on Tommy Allison, they had another thing coming. Tommy Allison wrote the book on hardball. You don't go from red hat miner to being CEO of one of the largest mining firms in the country without being willing to bury a few bodies.

Slowly he got to his feet and began to gingerly feel around to get an idea of where he was, fuming the entire time. They probably thought they had a "good reason" for all of this. It wasn't his fault the negotiations on their damned pensions came so soon after the explosion, but Tommy could bet they didn't see it that way. The only reason he was negotiating was because of the explosion, and negotiating didn't mean giving them everything they wanted, damn it. Why didn't they even want to see it from his point of view? He was going to have to close a whole damned mine out of "respect for the family's loss." It was a good seam too, he was suffering here!

He had found the cart rails with his foot, which meant Tommy was close enough to the entrance, he might even be able to find a catwalk or something. It would be easy sailing after that if he could. Yeah, they forgot all right, forgot he used to work these mines himself thirty years ago, when he was a young dumbass, like the dumbasses they got to join their penny-ante union. Except, he was never that much of a dumbass, he had known how to play ball. He had pushed hard for a mine-wide vote, to make it a union-free mine when he was working down in the hole. Tommy told the other miners what he believed himself. It was stupid to part with hard cash to the union just to work, you made your money by the sweat of your own brow, stupid to be forced to give part of it up right to the union like that. It sure made him popular with the mine owners, that was for sure; he went through the ranks quick after that.

It would be a ton easier if he had light, so he had a rummage around his pockets. He had a little mini-mag on his keychain, and who knew what else. It was worth a look. A quick rummage yielded no wallet, no keys, two mints, and a book of matches. The book revealed all of four matches, and a scrap of paper tucked inside the pack, neither of which he'd had on him at the meeting. Unlike his wallet and keys which had been in his pocket then.

Tommy lit one with the idea to get his bearings. As it flared to light, his eyes went back to the piece of paper tucked into the book, which he unfolded with one hand holding the match aloft. Written on it in neat boilerplate handwriting were the words, "Burn In Hell, Allison!" Well, that was clear enough, nice of them to make their feelings crystal clear like that.

Glancing around quickly before the match went out, he tried to gauge where he might be in the mine. Guessing from the packed-down flooring, this part of the mine had probably not been worked in a very long time. It was packed from the passage of haulers, not loose from digging. That meant entrance level most likely, the lazy bastards hadn't even had the gumption to take him down very far. If it had been him doing the carrying, the victim would have woken up on a pile of coal dust underneath a side seam in the very bottom of the mine.

That's why he had to push 'em so hard. You give 'em an inch, they'd be laid out taking breaks for a mile. Tommy was a man who told the board he answered to that his mines would meet quotas, and damn it, he wasn't going back down in the mine again because they missed them. But if you listen to the union reps and MSHA, the poor babies needed breaks every ten minutes, even the ones who were only pulling double shifts.

He put his finger in his mouth to moisten it and pulled it out, holding it up in the air as he tried to guess which way the air was blowing. It would be blowing for the mouth, and out. Tommy felt some air, but not as much as he was expecting for what he thought would be pretty close to the entrance. Still, he had a direction now, so that made him feel better about things, and he even still had some matches in case he felt turned around. Things were looking up all right, and when he got out of here, he'd have every one of those pricks behind bars within the week. It gave him something to look forward to and a goal to work toward in the dark.

As Tommy was mulling over the terrible punishments he'd deliver, he tripped on something, he couldn't see what, and landed face first in the dirt! As he lay there gasping for the air the fall had knocked out of him, all he was thinking of was vengeance. The pain in his arm from trying to break his fall began to subside a little, air started coming back. Tommy didn't curse, and he didn't yell, he just thought, maybe he'd call in a few favors, phone up a couple of good ol' boys who don't like smart-assed union pricks either....

He had had the board shove the union on him in the first place. "Sign of good faith with the community," they called it. Cowards! One damned explosion and they lose their backbone. These things happen, it was a part of mining. You run the mine hard, you get dust, they want costs down, you cheap out on fans and filters, it blows up. Big deal! It's not like these ignorant hicks weren't busy breeding up the next generation of miners anyway. Hell, the explosion should have created a few immediate job openings.

It SHOULD have created some job openings. But the weasels on the board had ordered the mine blasted shut to boot. Out of respect for the dead, they said. Screw that, he'd personally sent flowers, that was plenty. When they blasted that mine shut, it was gonna cost HIM money and the "community" that the board was so worried about jobs. It was gonna happen any day now, he'd been so disgusted with the whole thing, he'd just signed the papers without looking at the date or the particulars.

He sat down now for a minute to take a small break from the hike. Too many years of good meals on the company account was his problem. Tommy hadn't been this deep into a mine in years except on a cart for an "inspection" here or there. Those trips were just PR, the old miner not forgetting his roots sort of thing, the equipment was all different now. Truthfully, half the time he had no goddamned idea what he was looking at on those tours. As long as the pencil pushers assured him that the machines ran coal faster, that was the important thing. Maybe in another ten years, they could automate completely and then the "community" could go pound sand if they didn't like how he ran his mine.

The problem with sitting still was the dark started to close in more. The weight of the mountain began to feel heavier and more oppressive. You had time to think about where you were, and the key to being able to be a miner was never thinking about where you were. A lot of them told the red hats, "You get used to it," but the simple fact was you never did. Tommy had to give his workers that, though, they manned up and faced their fears every day for a living. The key was to keep working, keep busy, don't stop to think about the inky void right beyond the lights, and never think about where you were.

After the explosion trapped those men, that was all they HAD left. Time to think about it.

Nope, he did not want to start thinking like that, time to get up and get moving again. Rest was for the dead, and Tommy was sweating too much to be dead. He slowly pulled himself up to his feet with a small struggle. He grunted a bit as he did, making a personal commitment to use that damned machine Darlene had parked in the living room "for his health" last year when he got out of here. Tommy used to jog through these mines, and now he was huffing and puffing at a walking pace, time to get in a bit better shape. He'd made a lot of money running these mines, no point just keeling over clutching his chest and letting other people enjoy his money for him. Lord knew there were plenty of useless leeches that would be glad to do it.

But that was a worry for later, right now he needed to get out of here. Depending on where he was when he hit the surface, Tommy might have to beg a phone call off one of the locals to beg a ride. But that wouldn't be a problem, not for Tommy Allison. Oh, sure they might tell all the reporters how much they hated him, but push comes to shove, they'd fold. Weaklings always did. They knew in their hearts that even with the explosion at the Stone Ridge mine, even with the inspectors hinting it was the company's fault, they'd never tell him no. You get it on record you helped Big Tommy Allison, you might actually make something of yourself. Get a job as a red hat in one of his mines, move the hell out of your Mamma's trailer, stop needing to deal Oxy to get by. The future looked bright. Well, brighter than it did if you told Tommy Allison no.

Tommy Allison had money, and money could buy you any damned thing you wanted in these hills. No, getting his one phone call from one of the local tumbledowns wasn't gonna be any issue at all. He just hoped he wasn't in one of the real out-of-the-way mines. If he got out at dark, he didn't want to traipse all over a mountain at night. He might have to hole up in one of the abandoned company buildings for the night. You sometimes got bears on some of the abandoned sites, and he wasn't going through all of this to end up as bear shit.

He had no way of knowing how far he walked in the floating world of absolute black. Nothing to gauge by, no landmarks to mark off the passing of each footstep. Tommy certainly wasn't going to light another match just to find out how far he could guess he'd gone. There was nothing for it but to keep trudging. Keep moving in the direction he'd picked. He knew in his heart that he'd picked right, nothing for it but to keep moving.

The overall feeling of the air changed around him. He reached out for the wall he'd been hugging against to see if anything felt different there. There was an overwhelming feeling of panic for a moment. He, he felt nothing there but empty air!

It took him a moment to recapture his calm enough to realize that was why the air felt different. He'd reached an opening, a junction. This was great news! It would be worth burning another match to not crawl around on the ground to discover what he needed. Tommy only needed to figure out which way the rails were going. He had to control his exultation now so his hand didn't shake or he didn't damage one of his precious matches. The way the side passages joined this one, the curve and the angle of the rails would confirm one way or another which was out!

He lit the match methodically, taking care not to look directly at it. The light was blinding even as it was, he had been in the dark so long. Tommy blinked repeatedly, trying to adjust his eyes as quickly as he could to get a good look around before the match burned out. But in the few moments that he had, Tommy saw exactly what he needed to see! It was a junction, and the rails coming in from the side passages, both, were angling gracefully to join with the one he was following. He'd been right! Straight ahead and OUT of here! The match burned his fingers as he stared at it in joy, but he barely even noticed any pain as he dropped it and put his injured finger in his mouth absentmindedly.

The sight of it put a little of the pep back into his step as he moved forward. Everything about this was miserable, but he was getting through and going over, the story of his life. Oh, my Mr. Union Rabble Rouser, you think this crap scares ol' Tommy Allison? Well, you can choke on it, buddy! When Tommy Allison got out of there, you'd be choking on it in jail! You keep telling everybody that will listen that Stone Ridge was his fault and he ought to go to jail, but he had enough inspectors on the payroll under the table, big Tommy would be skating out of this with a fine at the worst. But you boys thought you'd teach ol' Tommy a lesson, straight to jail, do not collect two hundred dollars, my boy!

The dirt around the rails had gotten muddy, forcing him to slop through now. That was a thousand-dollar pair of John Lobbs being destroyed in this muck. He was almost happy he didn't have a headlamp, so he couldn't see what they looked like now. He could feel the mud slopping over the tops, and through the stitching chilling his feet. Add something else to the offender's tab. But the positive note was, water meant he was getting even closer to the surface now.

It was odd, though, he'd expected more air this close. Temperature outside must be close to the mine temperature. Seemed like that was a bit chilly for the time of year. But, then again, he hadn't looked at a weather forecast, Tommy rarely did, so what did he know?

As he was walking slowly along, his foot and then leg slammed into a large rock on the mine floor, causing him to fall to the ground again. Pain shot up his leg to his brain, a pulse of red-hot shock emanating from his now bruised and probably bleeding shin! Tommy lay in what was now mud, clutching the wounded limb, short gasps escaping between clenched teeth.

He fought down his panic over it. When a mine gets shut down, well, rocks break loose here or there. For all he knew, it was something that fell off the back of one of the last crawlers to leave. When it's being closed, the last men out aren't exactly careful about things.

Nope, best not to think about the blood he felt dripping down his leg and be more careful from here on out. He'd probably been moving too quickly anyway in his hurry to get out. Tommy had to remind himself, he was walking around a mine, blind as any man with a cane, a dog, and a cup full of pencils down here. Heck, for all he knew, he wasn't bleeding at all, just some kind of phantom feeling from wailing his shin. That happened. No point in checking either, he couldn't DO anything about it down here. When it stopped and dried up and he was on the surface, it would remind him not to go easy on anybody over this!

As his toes prodded forward more carefully now, he noted more rocks strewn along the rails he was following. He made a mental note to come back and check this when this was over. If those chunderheads who worked this mine had left this much rock in the mouth of a mine rather than carry it the rest of the way out, he'd go through the books and find out who was last out and make them PERSONALLY come back and carry it out. Just because a mine is idle doesn't mean you might not re-open it. SOMEONE was going to have to move it at some point! Might as well be the lazy SOBs that left it in the first place.

Slowly plodding forward, Tommy thought he heard a squeak. Rats. You got them in mines, men bring their lunches in, and anywhere there's food, you find rats. Rather than being frightened by it, he took it as a good sign. In an idle mine like this, they wouldn't be going deep, they'd just be going to somewhere they remembered for shelter. Rats meant he was getting nearer to freedom!

The rocks on the ground were getting even more frequent. Even slowly moving one foot forward carefully, he was tripping more often. It seemed now, he was either tripping on a rock or getting sucked into the mud at all times. But soon it would be over, Tommy had to be getting close to the surface now. Soon he'd be able to see the moon or the sun, he had no way of knowing what time of day it was now.

He tripped again, hard, he could feel himself beginning to fall. Instinct took over and he threw out his hands in the dark to lessen the force of the landing. But, instead of falling all the way to the ground as he'd expected, he was suddenly jarred as he fell AGAINST something instead of down!

Leaning there, still partially upright, he started moving his hands against what he'd fallen against. Oh, god! No! This was rubble! The way out was blocked! It was blocked with rubble! Wait, don't panic! Panic is how you got lost and stayed lost down here! Careful, think it through. He probably just got turned around a little, but he needed more light than one match was going to provide.

He took off his jacket and began to feel around, looking for a loose seam or something. Finding what felt like a weak spot, he began to tug. Slowly there was the rending of cloth and the seam came free! Better yet, it felt like it had frayed some, the easier to light it! Slowly with utmost care, he frayed the edges some more, to make sure they'd light. The jacket was linen so it should go up pretty easily. He needed to work fast once it was lit. It was going to take a minute for the full sleeve to burn, but after it went, he was down to one match. He had to make this count!

By sheer willpower, he kept his hand from shaking as he lit the match. He tried not to look directly at it as it flared to light there in the abyssal dark, lest it blind him. With utmost care and deliberate action, Tommy slowly moved the flame over the frayed edges of his former sleeve. It was all he could do not to erupt in a bellow of triumph as the flames caught.

He picked the sleeve up and held it aloft to assess where he was. Oh, god! Directly in front of him was an enormous pile of loose rock! It went completely to the ceiling! A collapse! His eyes looked everywhere, his heart plummeted as he saw the rails he had been following led directly under the fallen section of the mine.

He caught something out of the corner of his eye, a sign! There! Bolted to the wall! Maybe if he could figure out which mine it was, he might remember enough of its layout to find a ventilation shaft or one of the other ways in or out. He could still get out of this! If it was just a stilled mine whose exit had collapsed, there would be other ways out. He had a rough idea how most of the company's mines were laid out, all he had to do was figure out which one this was.

He made his way with utmost care not to trip to where the sign was bolted in. Holding his makeshift torch as high as possible he read:

"Rules and Regulations
Stone Ridge #1 Mine."

Stone Ridge Mine.
The mine he had signed an order to blast completely shut.

Stone Ridge Mine had claimed the lives of nine men that day. Because of bad air, and unsafe conditions after the fire, they had only been able to reclaim seven bodies. For the other two men, Stone Ridge Mine became their tomb. Their families had left flowers at the mouth, and at the gate down by the road.

In the dwindling light of a burning scrap of cloth, an overweight man in his sixties is on his knees. His shoulders hunch as he sobs. He weeps because now he knows that Stone Ridge Mine is going to be the tomb of a third man. He knows that even if they knew, nobody will leave any flowers for him.

First Appeared in "Subcutaneous" #3

I've said before, a collection should have at least one unpublished piece in it. Just so it's sure to have something completely new. This piece has gone unpublished, unsubmitted really, because it was the most grueling personal thing I'd ever written. So now, I suppose you know something about me, childhood could have been better for one. Finally, I decided, "I'm old enough to know the futility of cowardice," and I went over it, and I'm including it here.

A Light on a Moonless Night

Sometimes, writing is the only revenge.

It was over. He was gone now so it had to be over. Sitting in the tub the boy sobbed, arms clutching at his frail-looking legs. They weren't frail, they were full of strength, but boys who are going to grow up very tall often look frail at ten years old. Occasionally Jim would let go of his legs and take the washcloth and scrub at himself vigorously until the humiliation brought back the tears in great racking sobs.

He was, if nothing else, confused as well. How could a friend do this to him? Jim hadn't had any older men in his life since the divorce, and the one that he had…. Just how could he do this to him? Terror also had its grip, that someone would find out. They might think he was a "fag" or god, that Larry would still "tell everyone you begged for it" like he'd threatened him.

With that thought came the resolve to get up out of the tub and dry himself off. If he stayed in the tub much longer, his mother might rouse herself out of her own daze and ask if anything was wrong. Better not to even get asked than try and think up a convincing lie at this point. Jim dried his stick-thin figure, put on some underwear, and went to his room. Thankfully the only friend he could trust, his little black cat Friday, was waiting for him.

Crawling into bed, Jim stared wide-eyed at the wall, petting the cat, but eventually, the rumbling purr of the animal, whose only life goal was to sleep next to him and be pet by him, lulled him. Eventually, slumber finally won out.

He woke up the next day to see Friday's dark-as-night face staring at him. Jim was happy as always to see that and smiled for a moment. But the black cloud of the night before washed over him, causing a sob to escape his lips, try though he might to keep the loss inside him. Friday started a little and Jim quickly reached over and scritched him under his chin. He was upset, no need to share it with the cat, most days the cat was all that Jim trusted.

Forcing himself up, he sat up in bed. Jim looked around the room, the light flooding through the ancient window. It all looked so much less sinister today. The white of the walls, even though it was a boy's room and therefore a mess, seemed clean to him. Getting up Jim searched about the floor, and found the least objectionably dirty pair of jeans there, and toddled out to see about breakfast.

He walked quietly past his mother's door. It was partially open and Jim could see inside. The room, dark, the light shining through the heavy drawn curtains swaddling the room in a deep maroon gloom. She was asleep, god knows when her medication would decide that she would join him. Jim didn't want to see her or anyone else right now, so he hoped he still had plenty of time.

First, he checked the percolator, it was half full. The thing was ancient but it still worked, and the nice thing was, it was easy to reheat and made strong coffee. He might be only ten but he'd already started drinking it in the morning. Jim also smoked, so did his mom, it was a cherished family tradition. He fished around in her purse and found a pack and snaked one out for himself.

Lighting a cigarette, he dug out the frying pan. Jim turned to the ancient refrigerator and brought out the eggs and some surplus butter. Scrambled eggs it was, quick, simple, and pretty good if he said so himself. Practice makes perfect. Mom didn't cook much anymore, so he had plenty of practice. This part of his day was going well, routine was good, routine was, well...routine. Jim could feel it all lurking at the back of his head like a monster, but for right now it was easy enough to go through all the motions of normal. Well, within reason of normal, things weren't "normal" any more a week ago, just, even less so today.

Jim grabbed his cup of coffee and his breakfast and toddled off into the living room. It at least LOOKED pretty luxurious. Dying factory town, low rents, plus some nice furniture from the breakup equaled a nice-to-look-at living room. The TV stood out, it was a complete piece of crap, but then again, they didn't have cable so how good did it have to be for network anyway?

Jim tried to keep his brain turned off as he ate his breakfast, drank his coffee, and watched cartoons. It was both the only thing really on, other than daytime talk shows, and all his wounded mind could handle at the moment. Nobody was going to get hurt like that on today's Scooby Doo. Jim knew he was putting off when he cried again, but it was his pain to put off. He certainly didn't want his mom to know, or anyone else for that matter. Nobody was going to EVER know how weak he was, how frail he was, how...... OK, stop that right now, no tears for now. There was a mystery to solve on TV.

The little box of a TV sat on a relatively nice oak end table which clashed amazingly with the horrid little TV itself, tragically. As young as he was, he fully appreciated how the mighty had fallen here. The derelict television that even the oriental makers of it wouldn't have in their own home sitting there perched upon that lovingly crafted antique summed it up nicely.

Jim found himself gazing at the fireplace again. A beautifully crafted mantelpiece that at some point a vandal had assaulted with the cheapest white paint imaginable. They had never lit a fire in it, but winter would get here sooner or later, so it would probably be left to him to get it going without burning them all to death. Lord knows he wouldn't trust his mom with the task. Jim wondered idly what was involved in getting wood.

He realized, starting, that he'd never actually checked the chimney itself. Here he was contemplating lighting a fire in it, and he'd never looked up it. At about this point the boy he really was, despite the cigarettes and coffee, kicked in a bit. Maybe there was something hidden up there, something really, really cool. You couldn't be sure until you checked. The Hardy Boys found all kinds of cool stuff in old houses. OK, maybe they WERE just books, but still, they had to get the idea from SOMEWHERE, right?

He let the idea percolate a little while around his brain. Really, the fantasy was way better than the reality. The reality was he was going to look up there and see nothing but sky and get nothing but soot in his face for his troubles. That's what life was about in his short experience, high hopes and ugly realities dashing them away. The hunt was better than the catch, the catch always sucked.

Eventually, though, curiosity got the better of his cynicism, so Jim got off the couch, setting his plate on another nice table. First, he took the metal stuff out, the grating he thought it was called, getting soot all over his hands. He'd probably be getting another bath soon today the way he was going if he didn't want Mom to freak out at him. Then Jim scooted his way in on his back to check.

As he had expected, what he mainly saw was stones closing up into some kind of pipe, and then sky beyond that. But, as his eyes adjusted a little, he thought he saw a spot where the sealant had cracked away a bit. There was something wedged in there! Reaching out as far as his thin arms could, he got his fingers around whatever it was. At first, it wouldn't budge at all, mocking his efforts. He leaned up even farther to get a grip on it, and wiggled it back and forth, it seemed to want to give a little. Patiently and slowly Jim worked it loose, his limbs burning from being stretched out that far in such an awkward position. Still, it didn't hurt as bad as some of the calisthenics in midget football and this promised to give him something, so it was worth keeping at it.

Finally, grudgingly, the object popped loose, and he fell back hard on the stone below him. Whatever it was jingled and rolled around on the stones themselves for a minute as he lay there trying to get back the breath he'd had knocked out of him. Eventually, Jim rolled on his side to start pawing around in the area where he'd heard whatever it was roll to. Jim still wasn't sure what it was that had been so important as to hide it in the chimney, but he had it now.

His hand fell onto it and he picked the small thing up. It felt to be a ring of some sort. Jim brought it out into the light and rubbed it on his shirt to see better what it was he'd found. He was going to have to change his shirt soon anyway, might as well get full use out of it. After diligently rubbing away at it for a while, Jim held the ring he'd found up to the light. The rubbing didn't clean off the soot of years that easily, but at least it let him get a look at it. It looked practically like costume jewelry, a thick band of what looked to be gold with a large red gem set in it. But it must be fake, he'd never even seen a gem that large before in his life! Probably some other kid had wedged it up there years ago.

His suspicions seemed to be confirmed the more he looked at the ring, it almost seemed to him that it might fit him. Jim was tall for his age, but still, a valuable ring shouldn't fit his slender fingers. Disappointment washed over him a bit, figures, nobody really finds treasure hidden in a chimney. Still, he might as well see if it fit him, that way it wouldn't be a total loss.

Jim slid the ring on, amazed at how well it fit. He looked at it for a moment on his finger. It was kind of gaudy, really. Pretty gay.... pretty gay, well, now he was too, right? I mean he must be after what happened, right? The hot rage and shame flushed his face, and tears began to run down his cheeks unbidden. I mean, that's what it meant to be gay, and here's this ring....and ...and...

Suddenly the ring flashed brightly! A blazing beam flashed out of the ring itself, which was pointed in the direction of the poker by the fireplace. The light blinded him it was so bright! After a second it was gone. It took another moment for his vision to come back to him, accompanied by spots.

He felt calm, not sad anymore, not mad anymore. Like it had all gone somewhere. He was totally calm for the first time since he had woken up. Then Jim looked back at the fireplace and saw the poker. "HOLY SHIT!"

The tip of the poker was glowing sullenly and turning black again, but the very tip of it was only a molten little blob. He stripped the ring off his finger in a rush of realization and set it down, which after a second seemed silly so he picked it back up. Then he looked at what had happened. The little blob of metal on the stones had cooled with a clinking noise, and the poker had turned back to black.

Jim thought about as fast as he could, not sure how much more time he had alone. His mom probably wouldn't notice this, she'd probably never given the poker a second glance anyway, and it wasn't too badly damaged. Thanks to the layer of dirt left by shoddy housekeeping, the blob of metal itself just popped off the stones. He would really need to think about this some, so until he found the time, he slipped the ring itself into his pocket and cleaned up the mess a bit so his mom wouldn't notice.

This would take some thinking about, and Jim decided he thought better out of the house, and more importantly with a candy bar. He found his mom's purse on the kitchen table and rooted around for coins. Soon enough, between her purse and rooting around the couch, he found enough for a pack of cigarettes and a Butterfingers, the perfect start to any young day. He buttoned up her purse, put the dishes in the sink, and went to get dressed to go out.

Tossing on a shirt, he decided his pants hadn't gotten that dirty, so he could leave them on. He flumped down on the bed for a little bit to pet Friday for a little while, letting the purrs wash over him, calming him yet again. Few things are worth as much to soothing an upset than a vibrating purr of a happy cat. But Jim still had plans, so after a bit he went down the stairs and out for the day. His mom wouldn't miss him much if she woke up while he was out, so he wasn't that worried about it.

Jim walked down the dingy sidewalk to the town's one store. It was an oddity, it had been a local lunch counter for one of the town's factories, and it still had the kitchen, but it had evolved to be a sort of general store as well. It had also had a small area with betting machines as well, bait if you wanted to fish the town's polluted stream, just about everything. It was a small microcosm of the town's last 50 years on display, really.

He found his candy bar first. Jim had done this routine dozens of times, and knew for it to be believable he had to go right for the candy first. Then he went to the counter, put down the candy bar, and then said, "My mom sent me down to get cigarettes too, just a second." Then he made a show of taking a folded piece of paper from his jeans and looking at it, and said, "She wants Marlboros." He gave the paper another glance and added, "Reds." Then Jim flashed a smile, to make it look like he was proud of himself for doing a difficult task. Adults ate that routine up, play dumb and innocent, and then pay up, what a good kid, running errands for his Mommy, right?

From there Jim wandered over to the local church, where they had a playground of sorts butted up next to the graveyard. As good a place as any to enjoy his candy and have a smoke. It was often quiet there. Jim was a big fan of quiet. There weren't many little kids in town, to begin with, and almost none in this part. The proximity to the graveyard probably creeped them out a bit, why build a playground here?

At least it was normally a good place to be alone.

That was when Richie wasn't heading through the graveyard right for him. Even he thought Richie was a bit of a dirtball, they were either friends or fighting depending on the week. The kid had issues. Today, unfortunately, was a "fighting week," so Jim could only groan inwardly as he saw him coming.

Richie came out of the graveyard and continued to head right at Jim, leaving no doubt as to his destination. Richie was a little bigger than him, with dark lank hair, probably because he didn't bathe very much. He wasn't that smart, or fast so as long as Jim kept away from him. He could probably pepper Richie with punches for a while until he got tired of it and went home or gave him an opportunity to run for it. Jim didn't really like fighting anymore. Jim fought all the time in school during the marriage's failing years, but now that it had ended so tragically he didn't seem to enjoy it anymore. Even though he won most of the time, he always felt like he'd lost somehow anyway.

Finally, his frenemy was in the playground. Richie sneered at him and went right for it, "Hey, faggot, you playin' with the little kiddie toys today?"

He'd heard insults like that from Richie a thousand times it seemed, but today, the word "faggot" put red over his eyes. He lunged right off of the swing he'd been sitting on and ran right at him. His shoulder slammed hard into the bigger boy like he'd been taught in pee wee football. The boys went down hard with him on top. There was an enormous exhalation of breath from Richie as he crashed into the hard ground.

From there he straddled Richie and just started pounding at his face, wailing away with everything he had. Richie was gasping out, "Stop! Quit it!" but Jim just kept punching away at him. It wasn't until he saw blood start to well out of Richie's mouth and nose that he came to his senses, and he stopped.

Jim was horrified by what he had just done. He could see the nosebleed, the lips already swelling up, and a telltale bruise that looked like it was going to turn into a black eye later. His breath was coming in ragged puffs as he gasped out, "Richie....I'm sorry!"

Jim leaped off the stricken boy and ran. He didn't stop running until he was behind one of the abandoned factories, back by one of the old loading docks. Little gusts of breath, like little boys sound when they ran as hard as they can, slowly subsided. When they finally gave way to something approaching normal breathing, he took out a cigarette and lit it, the first drag coming back out in an uneven stream of smoke.

He checked in his pockets, finding that his candy bar was crushed. Stupid Richie, why did he always have to bug him anyway? Jim set the wreckage down next to himself for later, before rummaging around in his pocket some more, his hand finding the ring. He wasn't thinking much about it as he slipped it onto his finger.

Stupid Richie, why did he have to call him that? He wasn't a faggot, now was he? That's what they called somebody who did that, right? But he hadn't liked it, he hated it. But that's what they called people like that, and Richie had just called him that.

Jim felt the tears rolling out of his eyes. His face grew flush and hot with the humiliation of it all. His anger was everywhere but had no direction; he hated Larry, he hated his Mom for bringing him here, he hated Richie for calling him that, but most of all he hated himself. He should have done something, he should have yelled out, he should have....

The ring blazed again, he let out a yelp, and instinctively his arm came up in an arc. Quickly he took the ring off his finger and looked in front of him. The dock railings were making a pinging noise as they cooled down now, with a molten gash running through all of them. The sullen angry red glow where they had once been joined slowly dulling to a sooty black, blobs of metal on the concrete a testament to their cruel treatment.

OK then, he was going to have to do something about that.

He walked home and went up to his room. He heard his mom in the living room watching TV, so she really didn't hear him come in, she always had the volume cranked. Jim was able to slip quietly into his room. First things first though, he pet Friday for a little bit as the cat sat on his bed waiting for him. Then he went over to his closet and hid the ring up on the top shelf there. Until he had any idea what it was, or how to possibly keep it from doing that, having it in his pocket would be like juggling explosives.

As an afterthought, he looked over to his bookshelves. That's when he saw the model. It was a '50s Chevy that he had been building. Larry had "helped him" with it. That had to go, and it had to go now. He emotionally felt cold and spent at the moment, but Jim instinctively knew that wouldn't last so that had to go right now while nothing meant anything. He took the model off his shelf and threw it in the trash can next to his bed. As an afterthought, he threw a bunch of tissues over it, so he wouldn't have to look at it again.

Jim needed to go out. He just needed to, he didn't need to deal with his mom, he didn't need to be here, he needed to go out. Jim slipped on a light coat and put his smokes in the front pocket. It was an old military jacket that had been his dad's. He quietly slipped into the kitchen and went to the fridge, grabbed a couple of raw hot dogs out of it, and slipped them into the inside pocket to eat once he slipped out.

As he was about to leave his mother's voice called out, "Where ya goin', hun?"

"Gonna go ride my bike some, Mom."

"Well, be back before dark, OK?" she said.

"Sure, sure," with that, he picked up his bike from the top of the steps and was gone.

And gone was the word for it, he was going to ride for a long while. Jim always did when he was upset. His HOME was a good ten miles away from where he LIVED. He wanted to go back there when he was upset. Things made a bit more sense that way. Despite that, he really wasn't able to see any of his old friends. If their parents saw him, they'd tell his mom. But if other people started flapping their jaws, that would mean child services getting a call, so she'd HAVE to yell at him for appearances. So instead Jim just rode, a lazy afternoon of country roads leading nowhere, and not a thought in his head.

On his way home, he stopped by Larry's parent's house. After a ride, he felt strong enough in his head to yell at him, to tell him this was never going to happen again. To tell Larry how much he hurt him. To get the confrontation he had in his heart over with. He knocked loudly and waited. He'd never really been here except for a moment or two before.

It was overhung with pine trees where the house sat back from the road. The entire area reeked of them. The air he breathed in was infused with the sappy turpentine smell of them.

Finally, after a few moments, the door cracked open just a hair. "Yes, what do you want?" asked the suspicious-sounding female voice on the other side of the crack.

"Is Larry here?" he asked, trying to sound pleasant.

"No, no he isn't, you'll have to go away," the voice said hurriedly. The lone eye he could see looked so very sad framed in the door there.

Then, the door shut. That was strange, she acted like Jim had done something to her, but really, he had barely ever even met her before.

So, he went to where he lived. Where else did he have?

Time passed, it's the nature of it. Larry disappeared from town soon after that. There were all kinds of rumors about it. He'd been sleeping with a married woman. He'd been killed. He'd robbed someone. It was still a small town even if it was an industrial one, after all, not a lot more to do but gossip. But the most consistent had been that his dad had made him join the army.

Stripped of his confrontation, Jim just tried to heal as best he could. He had a hard time making friends at school, but that could be just as easily a bi-product of them moving to a new school district, who could have really said. The new kid is always the weirdo, even if they're perfectly normal, and he certainly wasn't normal anymore. Jim also intensely distrusted adults, but who could blame him, really?

He'd also taken to carrying the ring in his pocket. Sometimes he could get it to do its trick without being angry and crying, and now he didn't get angry or upset enough to set it off automatically so it was safe. So, it felt kind of neat to be walking around with a magic trinket in your pocket.

Life was normal, for a given value of normal that is.

One fall day Jim was walking toward the store to get some cigarettes when he saw.......

Larry.

Larry was just hanging out, outside of the corner bar. Wearing a military jacket, just standing there. If anything, looking lost in his hometown.

Jim felt a rage looking at him. How dare he come back here? But almost instantly that went away and all the shame and sadness from what this monster had done to him welled up in its place. Jim realized tears were flooding down his red-hot cheeks and he didn't even care. He just stood there with his mouth open, his hands flexing and unflexing.

Suddenly, as if a beam of light had pierced the clouds and landed on him, Jim felt his salvation. He slipped his hand into his pocket and slipped the ring onto his finger.

"Hey, Larry!" he yelled, his voice cracking with the volume of it.

Larry looked up at him, and Jim did the only thing he needed to do now, he pointed the ring to the spot on Larry that still hurt him.

I had a brief moment while I was fascinated in writing buddy stories, the buddy story being one of the most venerable of tropes, you can't help but do it a few times, right?

Wrecking Amendment

"Get your game face on, we gotta go to work."

"Bullshit."

"C'mon, c'mon, hands off your jock and on with your socks."

"Bullshit, Sisp, we are on VACATION, you know, sun, surf, not doing our job," I pointed out, I thought quite reasonably.

"I lied."

"I thought you weren't allowed to," I said suspiciously.

"Alright, alright, I didn't know, hand on my heart swear, there was nothing in the press that even hinted. But you know the rules if it comes to our attention...."

"I know, I know," I sighed, resigned, "just let me get dressed, and let's go get breakfast."

Soon, soon he would have to continue the work. It got easier every time, thank god. It had been hard at first, against his upbringing, but Tannin had kept insisting. Saying it was a great work of power. He just kept reminding himself, he'd been promised quite a lot for this. You don't get rewards without sacrifice, you had to do one to get the other.

On a plus note, 95 helped a lot. Lots of potential participants and as a bonus, he'd always wanted to see the Eastern Sea Board. Coming up on the road, he saw the perfect place to stop for tonight. Great big ol' truck stop right near the Florida border. Lot of people, lot of people passing through. Lots of women. Lots of women working with some of those people just passing through in the privacy of a hotel or a sleeper.

Maybe one of them would work with him tonight.

"You're sure about this?"

"Awwwwww c'mon, Jimmy, be kind, I was looking forward to a week of clubbing and boogie boarding too, you know," said Sisp.

"So, what's the assignment?"

"Well, that problem I think I have partially figured out, he isn't here yet, so nothing would have hit the local news yet," said Sisp, putting on his official voice.

"We got an ETA?"

"Sometime tonight, I'd guess."

"We gonna get anything else?"

"Won't be able to tell until he's closer."

"All right," he replied, "we hunker in and wait for him. Nothing else for it."

There is a brief moment during the summer in the Southeast, just as dawn is breaking, where it doesn't feel so bad. The sky hasn't lit up yet like the inside of an oven. The air isn't soup yet with the dew being turned to humidity. Even the mosquitoes are sluggish and disinclined to bite.

You watch the sun peaking its way upward over the flat horizon, inching over the trees, and it all seems peaceful, if only for a moment. Within an hour the whole thing becomes a cacophony of heat and noise. But now, only a few birds and you.

The spell is broken by a loud splash in the southern Georgia swamp. A few of the logs floating in the water resolve themselves into something else. Definitely not logs, logs don't have that many teeth for starters.

The water around where the splash was erupts in a frenzy of thrashing activity. Then for just a little while longer, silence reigns again. In the deep south of Georgia and Florida, truck stops and gators are always open for business.

*****

Ever do something so bad that you beg and pray to god to forgive you, and let you forgive yourself?

Jimmy Mulligan had been a young Philly cop. He'd been on duty down on the docks when he thought he saw something near one of the warehouses. He and his partner went to investigate. All standard. Until they saw a bunch of guys loading crates right off one of the boats directly into small trucks. Jimmy was about to call it in when his partner told him to hold on and stay there. His partner vanished into the teeming facility, leaving Jimmy standing near the car, his hand on his gun. Cold sweat poured down the young man's back, but within five minutes his partner came out smiling.

"Get in the car, I'm driving," he told Jimmy bluntly.

As they drove off Jimmy asked, "What in the hell was that about?"

"Bonus just came early, bub, you scared the shit out of 'em, I'll tell you that," his partner said, foot down hard on the gas.

"Whaddya mean, Bill?"

"I'll explain in a minute, but first, we gotta roust a drunk and call in the stop, won't take us long to find one, but we gotta have some distance," Bill said.

After they had finally found what they were looking for on the edges of South Philly, they got out, did a "We oughtta haul you in" routine to a wandering drunk, and called in his name to dispatch to check for warrants. The Eagles had just let out, it didn't take long to find someone stumbling along. They got a minor reprimand for the fact they weren't scheduled to do crowd control and to get back out to their beat, but that was it.

When they were back in the car, Bill handed Jimmy an envelope, "Here ya go, kid, don't spend it all at once."

"What's this? What was this all about?" asked Jimmy, taken aback.

"It's about 500 bucks of 'I didn't see nuthin' and nobody,' kid, that's what it is."

"A bribe. You want me to take a bribe?"

"For who, for what, kid, we couldn't have gone in without a warrant. By the time we'd gotten one, there wouldn't be a reason to have one, any evidence would have been long gone out one of the other exits. There's just two of us and a lot of those. Nawww, this is 500 bucks of 'Fuck off copper' bonus money."

"I don't know, Bill......"

"I do, kid, there ain't crap we coulda done if they were bringing drugs in or jumping around customs if we go all Rambo on them, they had us outgunned by a lot. We call it in, just a lot of paperwork to find nothing and to make us look like dumbasses." Bill softened his face and continued, "Look, kid, I know you're still all gung-ho, but sometimes you gotta pick your battles, or let brass handle it. Know your limits before you find out what they are the hard way. Gettin' paid for a life lesson, there are worse things in life, right?"

"I guess so, Bill," Jimmy said. He was already envisioning the bills he could pay off with 500 extra dollars. You couldn't help but think about it in the city unless you were working as a suit in an ivory tower looming above the city.

"I know so, Jimmy, get the girlfriend somethin' nice and write it off to learnin'."

A few weeks later, the deaths started around town. Overdoses almost exclusively. It soon was readily apparent that a particularly hot dose of heroin had found its way into town. At first, that was easy enough to blow off, even for a wet-behind-the-ears idealist like Jimmy. Junkies getting killed by junk doesn't exactly bring a tear readily to anyone's eye. People breaking the law to take an illegal drug were being killed by it, crime prevention in a nut.

That was, until his cousin Robby OD'd.

His aunt went into complete mourning for her lost son. The whole family was devastated. It would turn out that Robby was a dabbler, not even a serious user, but overdoses don't ask for your life story before they kill you, they just do it.

That's when Jimmy got out his rosary, went to Saint Paul's to pray for forgiveness for what he could have prevented.

These days, he was working it off.

The large bridges of Jacksonville, Florida gleam in the night. The blue-lit bridge, the water, the skyline. It's the city's best time of day. Most of the day it hunkers down in the swamp it's built on and just seems to fester, but at night it gleams almost serenely and sensually.

Coming down into the city over the bridge drives a viper. Looking for a place to stay while working on the completion of its great work. The great work was nearing completion. This would take someone special. The kind of girl you don't find at a truck stop.

Ever wonder about serial killers, what drives them? What is wrong with those people?

Some of them are just people with screws loose, to be fair. Some on the other hand.... Hell is a hierarchy that demons run on: "Here is me at the top, whipping you down there." You have to earn your way to the really big projects in the work of manipulating humans unto evil. To get to the big time. Politics, televangelism, infomercials, the nuts-and-bolts terrorism that humans can inflict on masses of other humans, you need to be able to prove you can masterly manipulate on a small scale.

Say, one man.

Get a completely nondescript, plain Jane, milquetoast schlub to leave a trail of bodies from one end of the country to another, MAYBE you're finally ready to put together a mind-numbing, soul-deadening ad campaign for a fast food restaurant chain. From there who knows, you can be the voice inside the head of a major lobbying firm for a product that kills people by the scores. Maybe you can be the voice that convinces the young Senator who would have been President, who might have brought peace to the middle east, to send the dick pic on Twitter.

But you have to work your way up. Freelancing on that scale is seriously frowned upon. And when the higher-ups in demonology frown on you, you frown too.

Tannin had plans, and little nobody Mike Milwood was going to help him take the next step back up the food chain to big-time evil. No more of this convincing bullies to push little girls. One last horrific murder and he was already promised a chance to whisper in the ear of a promising megachurch preacher. He'd have that boy exhorting the faithful to mass hatred and misery in no time flat, and to send him millions of dollars for making them miserable with incoherent blind rage. Just needed a little while longer, and one more corpse. After that, who cared what happened to old Mikey? Half of them try to keep killing after the demon is gone, within a year they're sitting on trial, crazy as a bedbug.

This was all going to be two for the price of one, a ritual act that weakens the walls between the world of man and world of evil, and the kind of plan that, when the press figures it all out and spits it out on the news, makes people trust less, fear more, help each other less.

Sensational, and powerfully ritualistic.

The demon gives them the idea, the demon helps them keep from getting caught. Once the idea to kill is there, that's hard to get rid of. That's animal, it's lurking in everyone's shadows. Having the brains to not leave clues when wanting to do it, that takes a special cunning.

Demonic cunning.

Angels do not admit to hierarchy, everyone is supposed to be equally valuable in their service to the cause of good. Of course, that isn't true, but it looks good on a recruiting poster. Gabriel is not going to blow his horn, though, for every little ol' demon trying to work his way up back to the big time. He doesn't REFUSE per se, just as long as nobody asks him to.

That job falls to minor angels of note. Like Sisp.

It was Sisp that came to Jimmy in the midst of his grief and explained to him how he could wipe his debt and his guilt away. Find the demons and drive them out of their host. It wasn't as simple as just killing the host. Sisp had explained, "Once you drive out the demon, killing the human interferes with that person's free will. Frankly, it makes the bookkeeping a total mess. We used to try it that way, and then you get guys claiming the devil made me do it, and the damnedest thing is, yeah, they're right, the devil did. Kick the bastard out, and anything the twisted little weirdo does after that counts."

"So, any idea on ETA?"

"I think he's already here."

"So, what are we waiting for? Let's go get him," I said.

"Not that simple, Kemo Sabi. I don't have all the details, but I think this one has been working for a while now."

"And that means......"

"It means, he and his invisible partner have been buddy-pal for a while now, the demon on his shoulder has built himself a luxury condo. It won't be easy."

"So, we call in some help?"

"No time for it, if they've been together long enough, they could be close to the climax of the demon's plan. They pull off the final spell, the one that actually IS the final ritual, we lose our demon, and he has the power to get into way worse. He's killing a hooker at a time now, he could move up to race wars next week," explained Sisp.

"Well, what do we do?" I asked exasperatedly.

"Best bet is to lay low until I get the info I need and see if we can't find at least one holy object to use for the exorcism in this godforsaken oven."

"Oh, goody, sounds fun when you put it like that."

"But not until after three," said Sisp.

"Why?"

"It rains buckets almost every day between two and three, and I don't feel like getting you soaked, it's uncomfortable," said Sisp.

"Swell."

Mike was driving the car slow on the Southside today. He was scouting for something. A look, a design. A church front that would give him a certain something. Big money megachurches were not going to help him at all here. He needed an extra special girl for this next one.

This final one.

A good girl.

A pure girl.

A TRUE believer.

"Alright, I got us a lead on a holy object," said Sisp as they drove around Jacksonville.

"Why do I even need two, I've got the one I always have," replied Jimmy.

"Bit more of a feel for what we're up against here, you're gonna have to trap the carrier between two to get this monkey off his back, and you got one," answered Sisp.

"So, what are we looking for?" Jimmy asked.

"Haitian store, you would be shocked at how many of those voodoo odds and ends they have kicking around actually do end up with some power. They have one that ought to do nicely."

"What is it?"

"A rosary they have hanging up, offer to buy it for a couple of bucks. If they bark up the money tree, they probably don't know what it is, shouldn't cost you more than $25 at the tops."

"So, what is it?" asked Jimmy.

"Saint Relic if you can believe it, came over with a Spanish missionary way back, no idea how much is original, but enough is that it should have the juice we need," said Sisp.

"Care to tell me what I'm going to do with four breadfruits and two pounds of Malanga?"

"Now, we went over that, Jimmy, if you had just gone in for the rosary it would have looked weird. You got the internet, look it up. I give you holy advice, not recipes," said Sisp in a wheedling tone.

"Y'know, for a voice in my head you can be a serious pain in the ass, ya know that?"

"C'mon, Jimmy, that's not nice. You know what I am, that's just not nice."

"You're right, Sisp, I'm sorry. The heat is getting to me. I'd intended to be spending my days swimming, not shopping for Caribbean foodstuffs," sighed Jimmy.

"I know, buddy. We get this over with, we'll go find a place with nothing happening."

"Hi!" said the man in the car.

"Ummmmmmmmmmmm, hello," said the young woman hesitantly.

"Do you.... go to church here?"

"Ummm, yeah. Do I know you?"

"Oh sorry, my name's Mike. My wife and I just moved to town, and we're looking for a church. We're Episcopalians and, I've been looking at a few, and gosh, this one has such a wonderful old-world look to it," said Mike.

"Oh, it's a wonderful church, it's been here a very long time. Have you ever been inside?"

"Honestly can't say I have. We're still unpacking. I got transferred here for my job. Work in insurance. Your name is?" said Mike, smiling warmly.

"Tara, oh you have to come in, my uncle is the Rector," said the girl.

"Well, that's just great, Tara, let me park the car and you can give me the tour!"

"I got good news and bad news," said Sisp.

"What's the good news?" asked Jimmy.

"I know where he's going to do the killing," said Sisp.

"OK. What's the bad news?" Jimmy's voice now sounded suspicious.

"It's going to be St. Augustine," said Sisp.

"Well, that's fine," said Jimmy, grabbing his keys and jacket. "We'll beat him there, problem solved."

"That's the problem, he just left with his victim. He's in Southside, we're at 8th Street, he just left, and the whole distance there is a giant speed trap."

"Let's go and see if we can't make up enough time on the road to make a difference," replied Jimmy, heading for the door.

"Just be careful on the throttle, Jimmy, sitting on the side of the road waiting for a ticket is no way to make the heroic rescue."

A hidden part of Tolomato Cemetery, the venerable Catholic cemetery for Saint Augustine. Named for the Indian village that stood there. First, the monks took it over, and then they interred their corpses there. The British tore down the church but left the coquina limestone bell tower. Then it was given to Minorcan refugees by the British, then the whole thing was given back to Spain, and finally to the Americans who soon closed it. There were two unauthorized burials here in the 1800s but other than that, it's just for tourists to visit, not stay.

That are on record, that is.

There was another, buried on top of another corpse late at night, inside one of the stone, above-ground vaults. The flat marble lid just slid aside and the other body interred. The grave itself barely noticeable under the huge ancient oaks, hanging with Spanish moss.

There are other unmarked or unrecorded bodies in this graveyard. This one, though, has a woman atop the stone lid. She is both naked and unconscious. The man that put her there is also naked, for all that anyone can see in this part of the cemetery shaded from the moon and silky dark.

He makes sure her legs dangle from the end of the cold, worn marble. He is already obviously aroused. He goes to the head of the stone and lights two large black candles there. He is for all intents and purposes only viewing the show. Tannin is running this.

He picks up a long thin blade by the side of the woman. It would look like a British boot knife from the First World War if it wasn't for the jewel set in its pommel. He takes his place before the splayed woman again. He begins to move forward....

Jimmy threw every ounce of himself into the tackle! The naked man was borne to the ground with him. Unfortunately, Jimmy's momentum took him past the man, sliding a bit on the night-slick grass into a marker jutting from the manicured ground.

He began to stand up. Unfortunately, the man wasn't nearly as stunned as he'd hoped and was getting to his feet as well. Worse, the knife was still in his hand.

"Ummm, Sisp?"

"Nice tackle, Jimmy, good job," answered Sisp.

"We gotta slight problem."

"Yeah?"

"You know that vial of holy water I have, blessed by St. John Neuman?"

"The other holy object?"

"Yeah. The one I left in the car to make sure I tackled him......"

"Stall...."

"Planning on it anyway...."

The two men were both circling each other now. Occasionally, the naked man would thrust out with the knife, causing Jimmy to back away.

Mainly what the man seemed to be hoping for was to get Jimmy away from his impromptu altar. Well, and the hope that Jimmy would trip over a stone.

"Jimmy?"

"Yeah, Sisp?"

"Good news, you got to get him ten feet farther back from where you are. The grave where you can see the depression but there's no stone? Somebody was buried with a Saint's Vestments, probably goes back to the Spanish."

"Gotcha."

While Jimmy was distracted for a second looking for where he had to get the killer, the man lunged at him suddenly. There was a sudden bloom of red-hot pain! If he hadn't caught sight of the lunge out of the corner of his eye, the knife would have pierced right through his bicep where the man had aimed it. As it was, even with jumping back from it, the knife managed a gash on his forearm.

He needed to move things up a bit now, nothing for it. He'd start losing strength in that arm soon. He was already bare-fisting this, one arm wouldn't even be a fight. It didn't matter if he was clearly the stronger man! Looking at the man in the fitful candlelight, and the ambient moonlight, he put together his thoughts quickly. He needed to!

Grabbing his arm, he let out a yowl and stepped back rapidly like he meant to flee the encounter altogether. But then he stopped. The fiend smiled, seemingly smelling the blood, and the kill. Whatever he was worshiping wanted the girl, and Jimmy would make, if nothing else, a fine bonus to that. Jimmy started letting out a series of whimpers and forcing himself to take gasping breaths.

Jimmy's eyes were pleading with the man. The man smiled back at him with all the evil lusts of hell on his face.

The man lunged at him again with the knife aiming for Jimmy's side. Jimmy grabbed at the man's wrist, but rather than slapping the blade away as would have been expected or stepping away he yanked the man toward him and stepped forward with his left leg, sending the man sprawling, the knife bouncing from his grasp as he landed.

Right on the grave he needed!

Jimmy landed hard on the man, knocking the breath out of him. Then he flipped him over so he could look at his face and get his knees onto the man's biceps, pinning him painfully. The man looked stunned. He began to make a low yowling noise in the back of his throat, as the demon felt the holy object a few feet below him. The man tried desperately now to buck him off and unpin himself while Jimmy scrambled to get something from his front pocket.

The man now began to cry like a cat in its death throes, mouth wide open as Jimmy got what he needed out of his pocket. Jimmy took advantage of the situation. He stuffed the rosary in the man's mouth quickly. The man below him froze entirely, except for his eyes which bugged out hugely and grotesquely.

"That's got him, Jimmy!" cried Sisp inside his head.

The man's face lost focus, he ceased to move or struggle at all. Jimmy got up and walked over to where the knife had landed and picked it up. Then he walked the few steps back, knife in his hand. He collapsed down on the man hard, knocking whatever wind the monster had gotten back out.

Jimmy stared for a minute and raised the knife high!

"JIMMY, STOP!"

"Sisp, this son of a bitch is a complete monster, acing him would do the world a favor."

"Jimmy, we don't KNOW that. A few minutes ago, a demon was running him like a puppet. He might have been receptive, but we don't KNOW how much was him! Free will, buddy!"

"Screw that. I'm sending him to hell," Jimmy said, looking down at the man's now terrified eyes.

"That's the thing, Jimmy, killing him like this, it might get him sprung on a technicality...."

Jimmy's shoulders sagged at that, he knew about technicalities in any court. He looked back at the man and punched him with every ounce of strength he had in his good hand. His head jerked violently and when it came back, the eyes were closed. Jimmy reached down and felt his pulse.

"Alright, the bastard is gonna live."

"Good boy," sighed Sisp with relief.

"Keep your holy ghostly eyes open, I gotta get the girl dressed, and drop her off somewhere in Jacksonville before she starts bawling bloody murder. I don't want to have to do any explaining while I get this cleaned up."

Jimmy was sitting with his feet up in what was clearly a cabin. Deciding that, while it looked like he was completely in the clear on the situation in Florida, that was all good and well. There have been better ideas than hanging about while the authorities were investigating. He had as reasonable an explanation as anyone could ever hope for. He'd come to Florida to swim, he now had dozens of stitches in his forearm, tragic accident scraping against some exposed metal. Stitches that would not react well to salt water. Yes, I have had a tetanus shot, thanks, all the same, I just want to go home now.

He flicked on the news and flicked open a cold Devil's Backbone beer and sat back to take a load off.

"Today in a bizarre story that may lead to a serial killer. A Connecticut man was arrested in Daytona, Florida after an attempted assault on a New Jersey woman visiting the area with her husband, a member of the Devil's motorcycle club. Michael Milwood seen here in this undated photo had been stopped by Saint Augustine police weeks earlier after he had claimed that the reason they had found him naked was that he had been attacked by a never-apprehended assailant. After this latest arrest, police began to dig further, and now think that he may be involved in a string of murders......."

"Well, there ya go, buddy," said Sisp. "Free will strikes again."

"That's a load off my mind. Hopefully, that woman is all right and that's all he got up to," said Jimmy, smiling.

They both turned back to the TV. "In local news, the bodies of a couple in their early twenties were found today...."

"BULLSHIT!" Jimmy exclaimed, "Sisp, you PRICK! You set me up!"

"Jimmy, relax!"

"Oh, horseshit. 'Why don't you get some hiking in instead,' you said, and now here we are about to get drug into ANOTHER...."

"Jimmy, shut up a second!"

"What!" Jimmy exclaimed angrily.

"I checked, they drowned kayaking," Sisp said.

"They did?"

"Yep."

"No demonic anything...."

"Nope."

"Just one of them things?"

"Eyyyyyyyyyyup. Now," said Sisp, "enjoy your vacation, you've earned it.........dork."

First Appeared in Demons, Devils and the Denizens of Hell Vol 2

How about a ghost story in space? This happens, I start reading back issues of Analog and Azimov's, and next thing I know, I write some science fiction. So if you prefer that I "stick to horror," you know exactly who to blame for the deviation from the norm. This one's kind of fun in that I decided to slip all kinds of little Easter eggs into it.

Junker

Terry heard the seals in the process of being made. They had locked on, now it was just a matter of sealing the decon lock and popping the hatch. That was his cue that it was time to go to work. Finding the thing, piloting to it, that was the fun part. Getting it back to dock intact, that was where being Captain became a job again.

Junking paid the bills and kept the ship and crew moving happily along. Terry wouldn't give it up for the world, but once the hull of the other ship was breached and they were in, that's when the hard work would begin. It was tricky work, nobody could know all the operating systems out there, and Terry kept a lengthy library on file just for that reason. But even with his lengthy crib sheets, he didn't even pretend for a second that he always knew. You didn't know what you were grabbing onto and hauling off a lot of the time. It was an interesting bauble you spotted in the flotsam of the universe; what it was, you only guessed before you grabbed.

On the other hand, if you hit something new, the payday could be well and beyond mere salvage pay. The large corporations on every side wanted to one-up each other and come out with the next new thing in tech. Hitting an unknown operational system or an unknown drive and all of the potential advances it provided with little to no real research and development could be a triffidium mine of opportunity for somebody.

173

It was a great big universe out there, and nobody knew or had seen everything yet, not even close.

"Alright, Galmar, I'm going to gear up. As soon as we pop it, start getting me readings, alright?" Terry said, getting up from the command seat.

The translator he had implanted in him informed him that Galmar had just told him, "Alright, boss, I got this." He waved a thumbs-up at the Cellemmian, and Galmar responded with some sort of gesture with his one tentacle that Terry just assumed was an agreement.

He had to get suited up. Usually, they found these things to have some kind of usable atmosphere, but until they got samples from the entire ship and made modifications from their own tanks, everybody who went aboard the wreck was wearing a suit for the duration. It got even worse if they found something organic, they'd probably have to blow the whole air system out in that case. Terry stalked through the ship to the boarding area. His own ship was as bare bones as possible. Shaped and dyed plastex for an interior was fine, it cleaned easily and it was versatile. With at least three sub-systems to accommodate four different races on one ship, versatility was worth more to him than being pretty. The floor had minuscule ripples, to provide some traction, but other than that it was blank and boring. He got to the boarding bay in short order, his ship really didn't have much wasted space for the crew to move around. The various bits of machinery they needed to tow, or in the worst cases, cut down a ship for scrap, were a higher priority for the Shawnkerri than the creature comforts for the crew itself.

Aston was waiting for him. The big Relgian was already suited up, but he wore at least the breathing apparatus most of the time anyway. Terry had spent the extra coin a few years back to make sure the largest and the hairiest member of his crew at least had full native comfort for him in his own quarters, though. Some ship Captains made their crew pay for their own support systems as a term of hiring, but Aston was loyal as hell, all of the crew was, and Terry was to them. When they hit, the shares were always more than fair, and he made sure everyone's quarters were comfortable to them.

"What in the hell took you so long?" Aston demanded.

"Oh, I took a stroll to see the sights after I made sure we had our seals solid," Terry responded, grinning.

"I'm wounded! Like I have ever not done it right!"

"Except for that downed researcher in Iota Draconis," Terry said, pulling on his gear.

"Well yeah, except for that," Aston replied, grinning back.

Terry Jones, the only human on the Registry of Captains. It was Terry, not short for Terrance or anything, his parents were not that complicated people. At six feet two, his dark hair was the only short thing about him. He represented the next step in humanity's quest for the stars, so that made him complicated whether he wanted to be or not. The first human to actually finish the Combined Stars Corporate Academy. Others had gotten in, but they had all crashed and burned, in one case literally, before graduation. Terry had managed to pass in the middle of his class, which wasn't great, but he was the first human to do it.

He was also the first human born off Earth to even apply.

Not that all of that had gotten him very far for quite a while. It wasn't a prejudice in the classical sense, it was more that mankind hadn't proven themselves to the universe yet. When first contact had been made, the hopes and dreams and pride of an entire planet instantly had become, "Oh cute, they finally learned how to walk!" Or maybe that really was prejudice in any sense.

Maybe not that patronizing, but it felt that way at first.

Finally, light speed was achieved, man was riding high. The residents of Earth had finally figured a way to get into space without being torn apart by random bits of universe that were floating around out there, by way of the lengthy and painstaking construction of what amounted to a force-field tube. If random bits of universe keep getting in the way, the logic went, create a safe space. It must have been an amazing feeling, Terry had always thought, breaking out of the Sol system and getting ready to continue building toward the Gliese system. That's when the message came in, pre-translated for human convenience.

"Welcome, humanity, to the rest of the universe. Since you have gotten this far, we are prepared to help so that there may be no accidental blunders with factors you do not understand. Prepare to be boarded for the first exchange of diplomatic communications."

That first meeting had revealed much. It also revealed much more that mankind had not wanted to hear so soon after what should have been a moment of triumph. The part of the universe that counted as a loose federation had known about mankind for millennia, and those species thought humans were idiots. The representatives didn't come right out and say that, of course, but that was the gist of it. There had been a raging argument for an untold time about whether or not humans even counted as a sentient species. There had been numerous off-the-record nudges in human technology over the years to get them up to speed by concerned environmental groups, but it wasn't until the discovery of the printing press that various mining concerns had been willing to concede that humans WERE actually sentient. Stupid, but sentient.

They offered amazing new technology to the human race, but the way it was offered was a bitter pill to swallow. It basically had come down to, "Look since you're dead set on meddling, we'll teach you some basics so you don't break anything." Humans often teach their own children this way, and many of mankind's scientists recognized it for what it was. Especially the child psychologists, who were miffed for decades about it.

First came wormhole technologies that enabled mankind to expand its range immensely. It would have seemed more amazing if it hadn't come with the caveat of "maybe when you're older we'll let you play with a REAL spaceship." The wormhole ships that operated off of creating stabilized jumps through the fabric of space were in comparison to what the rest of the universe was using, the equivalent of a go-kart parked next to a Ferrari. Now the universe was attainable to humans, the kiddie-table universe, the mother of all mixed blessings.

Then they walked the human race through terraforming. Most of the solar systems near Earth had been left alone to give the human race room to expand if they ever got that far, much to the mining industry's chagrin. Now humanity had a way to get there, so they needed to make the planets circling those stars habitable. They also had a need. Despite all efforts, the Earth was still overcrowded, and polluted, and in need of some time to heal without an ever-increasing number of occupants.

It was on one of those colonies that Terry Jones was born to hydro-farmers.

His father had been raised in one of the huge cities in what had been America and had always dreamed of being able to move around in life without inconveniencing or being inconvenienced by people. So, when the colonies opened up, he convinced Terry's mother that this was their way to freedom. The lack of air pollution gave his father his first breaths of what he called freedom, the lack of light pollution from major cities gave Terry a view of the stars growing up. That gave him his own dreams, the ones that he followed.

He voraciously read the accounts of every human who had gone to the academy. He dug for clues in their stories, for how he could make his own story more successful. Eventually, he saw the worm in the wood. Those that had made it in had one of two qualities, either they were a crack pilot but weak on the science, the understanding of what was involved, or they were a total egghead lacking the intuitive instincts and guts to trust them that a pilot needed. He vowed to himself to have both of the qualities a pilot needed.

And he had been the first human to pass, if not with flying colors, at least with his colors still visible.

He had been hired immediately by one of the mining corps looking for good publicity. Possibly also to build a case that the humans had developed enough to be allowed to negotiate with companies like themselves about mineral rights in the burgeoning Federation of Humanity. It was a classic token hiring, and like all token hirings, once the press wasn't looking, advancement ended. No matter how hard he worked, and no matter how much more qualified he might be, he'd never risen above third mate on any ship he was on. He even stopped keeping up with his former classmates, it was depressing to hear about their ships and their crews while sleeping in a crew cabin.

Until Trago had come along, that is. Trago was a Serrian legend in business, and as such, he did whatever he wanted. Serrians all had a reputation for business. Trago left them standing still. Most of the major companies in the Combined Stars had the equivalent of shareholders, multiple owners of small parts of the company, usually through consolidations and purchases. Trago Incorporated had one major owner, Trago himself. While most of the major companies may pay junkers if they got something major, they never actually deigned to own those ships. They considered trash removal to be beneath them, but Trago didn't. Anything that made lots of money legally could never be considered beneath him in his eyes.

There were all kinds of rumors about Trago, which many suspected he made up himself, he certainly never discouraged them. He used to be a raider. The larger companies had been trying to buy him out for years but he laughed at them. He had even better flight systems he sat on just to keep his own fuel stocks high. All rumors, all things he neither confirmed nor denied.

Most interesting of all, he had always been an alpha specimen, and he'd always been male. Serrians changed sex depending on whether the other breeding stock in the area was dominant in a sex. It usually ended up with the younger but fertile ones protecting themselves genetically by linking onto stronger alphas, but not always. The rumor was, Trago had been born male and had always been the alpha in whatever cluster he'd been in and had stayed male.

One thing that was true, he was happy to save a bit of money and take risks without worrying about others prejudices. He was a master of recognizing when his competition wasn't being logical and taking advantage of it. So, one day, with one of his salvage ships having an aging Captain, and a first mate's opening, he saw a way to get a qualified applicant cheaper than anyone else. All he had to do was the thing nobody else seemed willing to do, ignore that Terry Jones was a human.

In time, the Captain of the ship retired, and Terry finally, after one of the longest waits by an Academy Captain Specialty Course Graduate, was hired on as ship Captain. After that, Terry had scrimped and saved every credit he'd earned. He didn't party with crewmates, he never gambled when in port, he put it all away. He had one more goal in life, to not only be the first human Captain, he wanted to be the first owner of a real ship. So, he bided his time, and he put away his money. He knew that Trago cut ships loose all the time, and he knew that he was slowly reducing his junker fleet. He probably wouldn't get out entirely, but it was proving to be more cutthroat than his growing reputation as a financial wizard needed. Better to have a couple of degrees of separation between himself and the bloodshed.

Trago had thought that Terry's clean living and spotless record as a Captain were signs that he was bucking to be promoted to one of Trago's big cruise liners, or some other business with a bit more spit and polish and pride. Nobody was more surprised than Trago when one day while at corporate for maintenance and a refit, his sole human asked to buy one of his soon-to-be-sold-off junkers.

Trago laughed and sold him the ship he was Captain of, the Shawnkerri. He even paid for the current maintenance it was in dock undergoing himself. He liked the young human and appreciated how hard he'd worked to get this far. It didn't hurt that it looked good on Trago: work for Trago, and you can go from lowest race in the universe to owning your own ship! There were other reasons, but for once in Trago's life he was welcoming a seeming rival to one of his businesses and wished him the best.

As soon as the hatch was popped, Terry went in first. He usually tried to be the first on. Never ask a crew member to take a risk you weren't willing to take yourself. As usual, Aston was right behind him. "Alright, buddy, get the air and gravity sensors set, and get the info to Galmar, so he can give Allas the mix we'll need to get out of these sweatsuits, OK?"

Aston grunted and began setting up. Terry started to look around. There was some kind of juice still running on the tub, the thing was dimly lit. The gravity didn't feel bad, he didn't feel like he could do any low grav bounces down the hall at least. So, whoever had grabbed this thing had been able to cut the propulsion systems out without gutting the secondary ones. That was going to make life a lot easier if they could get the air right and figure out the onboard systems.

He called back to Aston, "I'm going to try and find some kind of input on this thing so we can start getting system diagnostics. Hold down the fort setting up, alright?"

"You ever get tired of talking so damned much?"

"Love you too, Aston," Terry chuckled.

The hallways in the ship were thin in width and short in height, which made Terry thankful he volunteered to find some kind of port to wire up. Terry was over six feet tall, but Aston approached seven. He'd need him to work on the ship some, but why make him do it more than he had to if it was going to be this tight for maneuvering in?

He didn't recognize the materials, but then again, he hadn't recognized the ship design either so that was no surprise. This was not the normal run-of-the-mill-production puddle skipper though, Terry could see that. He saw taze marks burned into the shiny cream-colored walls, they were the only adornment or seam on them.

That explained what it was doing floating out here: raiders. Not everybody had gotten the message that this was now a happy, friendly, cooperative universe these days. There were still those who would work twice as hard for half as much, as long as they felt like it was stealing something. Getting over meant more to some than getting a lot. He'd gotten a tip on it from one of his spotters, locals in the system who ran telescopes and reference trajectories for him. Every junking operation had one in almost every system. If they hit on something large and manufactured but not moving for long enough, they contacted him with the tip. If it paid off, he'd slip them a percentage. Now he knew why it was just sitting here.

He just needed somewhere to plug in, or some kind of wave field that he could pick up that would let them examine the systems itself. If it had any kind of life left to it and could be used to help in towing, it was half the work for his ship and crew. He also didn't want to unload it for scrap materials, and then turn out it was the find of a lifetime. So, Terry crept down the hall, field detector in hand, looking for some kind of flight deck.

At this point, he was just following the taze marks. Logic was telling him that if the raiders had fought their way on, they would have gone for the bridge as fast as possible to prevent the captain from triggering an escape or even a last-ditch self-destruct. He winced when he passed what looked like open living quarters. He'd come back to check it, but for now, he needed to get Galmar a read on its operating system first and foremost.

After a t-junction, he kept following the marks, which led him to an open doorway. He could see instrument panels lit up in the gloom ahead, the bridge. The door should probably be shut, he considered, which made him doubt he was going to see any living occupants. He went in very tentatively and with a hand on his own tazer nonetheless. He wouldn't say his fears were confirmed by all of this. He wasn't afraid of it, but his suspicions were. It was the risk you ran if you operated in the backwaters.

Terry came out onto the flight deck. Instruments were lit low as if it was running on auxiliaries. On the floor, the crew lay dead. He looked down at the two figures lying there, they looked like husks. Bipedal, some form of bone structure there; after that, the details blurred. The skin was now gray and almost beginning to crumble, which made him wonder how long this thing had been sitting here to have that level of decomposition.

It would have to wait. First and foremost, he had to get linked into the ship's system grid. This was going to end up being easier than he had anticipated. There was a taze burn in one panel with circuitry now exposed. He didn't understand how it was laid out, or even how it was constructed. He didn't need to, all he needed to know was that he had a possibly exposed connection.

He brought out his scanner, which registered where the best place to hook into the system was. High reading meant it was very exposed, low enough meant you were scanning a non-metallic rock that wouldn't conduct if you shoved a thousand volts into it. As soon as he so much as waved it in the general direction of the console, the lights on the scanner started lighting up.

"Galmar," he said into the mic on his helmet.

"Reading," the Cellemmian replied through his headphones clearly.

"I've got some exposed electronics, I'll be hooking you in in a moment. Aston, you set up the air sensors yet?"

"Any second, Mister Impatience," Aston said back.

Terry moved the scanner around until it was almost burying the lights on the reading. Looking closely, he saw circuitry he didn't recognize, but it didn't really matter. They only needed to connect on, and let the computers and Galmar figure it out from there. So, he took the leads off the scanner and stuck them in place with some glistening circuit tape to a couple of likely spots according to his readings. As long as they were close enough without too much interference, they'd be able to start getting readings from it.

Job well done.

"Alright, Galmar, you're hooked up, so start with your magic. Aston, I'm going back to you, we've got DBs unfortunately, so probably raiders. I'll let Allas try and species ID them and decide on quarantine, she has a degree in that sort of thing."

"Degree in multiple species physiology, she works as a ship's mechanic, what a universe," Aston chuckled.

"We all do double duty, Aston, we've got a small ship."

It took him a few moments but he was soon back with Aston. "Alright, let's jet and let the wonders of technology do its work, while we go get some grub," Terry said, patting his friend on the back.

"Works good enough for me."

When they got back on the ship, Aston went right for his chambers. Terry went to the engine rooms looking for Allas. Allas, that was the other thing that Terry cared about, as in Allas his girlfriend. Also, as in, Allas the daughter of the man he'd bought this ship from. It was weird, but not like it might look. He had known Allas in school, except that she'd been a he then. He'd been in the Captain program, while he/she had been in the Engineering wing. He only found out she was Trago's daughter a month after she'd been hired on to the Shawnkerri. When he was still a Captain, and Allas, now a she, was another crew person. It wasn't like her qualifications hadn't been tip-top, Trago wanted her to earn her own way, and learn the ropes from the bottom up.

When he bought the ship, he'd given the crew a chance to walk, and stay with Trago's company, saying Trago had OK'd it if they came or if they went. If they stayed with the crew, Trago would still give them their severance package for leaving his company, and from there on, they'd be drawing paychecks from Terry. Terry had expected all of them, especially Allas, to walk. He'd almost cried with gratitude when they elected to stay as a crew.

Allas and Terry as a couple were just, well, one of those things that happen. You spent all your time with someone, and you got to know them. If anything, the fact that he vaguely remembered Allas as a he in school was probably the thing that made it take as long as it had, really. It wasn't like Allas wasn't lovely, with deep luminous blue skin, and a thick luxurious set of almost hair-like crest spikes leading down her back. Other than that, visually, at first glance there weren't that many differences between the races, bipedal, etc. etc. Terry had even suspected, during the offer to keep the crew, that Trago had hinted he might not be absolutely devastated to have Terry for a son-in-law. They even had compatible atmosphere needs, which was major. Even with all of that, it had taken a night out together getting inebriated in port.

The next morning when he woke up groggily in his bed on the ship, it wasn't just him for the first time in forever. He hadn't minded, and he minded even less when even after the coupling, the friendship they had was as strong as ever, if not stronger. He hadn't even minded when she had admitted she'd had a crush on him since coming on board as a crew member. He hadn't minded that despite the similarities, and the promises that with medical care she would stay a she, they most likely would never be able to mate according to a geneticist they had consulted once. As far as he viewed it, as long as Allas was satisfied, he was deeply in love with his best friend, so there was nothing TO mind. He was first and foremost a ship Captain; it had been what he had always wanted out of life until he and Allas had become more than friends. Now he knew that what he wanted was to be a ship captain, with Allas by his side.

She was in the engine rooms, probably getting initial readings from the alien ship they were latched onto when he came in. He slid up behind her as she was hunched over the computer and kissed her on the neck softly.

"Mmmhmmm, that feels nice. I bet you do that to Aston all the time," she teased, smiling, as she leaned back to rest her head against him.

"Not anymore. I got sick of getting hair in my teeth," he teased back, grinning.

"I'm sure he pines for the good old days," she said, turning the chair to look at him.

"Are you starting to get anything from Galmar yet?" Terry asked, his face turning serious.

"It's just starting to trickle in, it'll be hours before I can make any diagnosis of what we're looking at," she replied. "So, what does the inside of it look like?"

"Well, ignoring that it's outside of any of Combined Stars' models, it's not that far off from what we're used to. Seems to be mainly touchpad and voice command operated. Unfortunately, this," he said, resting a hand on her shoulder, "is one of those runs I think we're going to need your other skills on."

"Bodies?"

"Two that I found, possibly more. Before we can even hope to stabilize the air in there, we need to know if we might be breathing spores or some other poison. That, my dear, is for the person with the degree that includes anatomy and biology. By which I mean, you."

"Damned raiders!" Allas spat. "I absolutely hate these type of scrap jobs, they're always so sad."

"I know, hun. But if we get some good new tech out of it, we could sell it, and settle down somewhere without a care or a bill in the world," he said with a grin.

She smiled back and said, "Liar, I couldn't get you off this old tub if I tried to cut you out with a laser cutter and you know it. Alright, is there anywhere on that ship I could do a hard and fast series of autopsies on them?"

"There's one room that hasn't been checked yet that I saw, it's close to the hatch. As long as it doesn't have anything vital in it, we can probably force shield it after you're done. Flush the air system for foreign bodies in the air if we have to, and work in something approaching comfort while we decide what to do with the ship," he said.

"Any rush?"

"Nah, we've all had a busy day, getting here, getting it latched, and setting up the diagnostics. I think to a degree, it's quittin' time, babe," he smiled.

"Oh goody, shall we dine on the veranda?" she joked.

"I was thinking dinner in bed."

Terry went onto the ship alone at first, after they'd all eaten breakfast the next day. He wanted to get the bodies situated in the living quarter room he'd seen the day before and to see if there was anything in there that might work for autopsy tables. This was all hard and fast work, but nobody welcomes a ship into port with unidentified aliens and a promise of "Well, I guess they might be safe, don't know really."

When he went into the room, he made another gruesome discovery, two more bodies. Smaller ones. He didn't get sad at these kinds of things anymore. In his line of work, you brought in the victims of raiders far too often to be sad every time, but smaller usually meant children. No matter how hardened you might be, seeing children was worse. Trago had told him the best thing to do was to try and help the authorities catch the murderers, "Son, I always have the cops go over a ship after I bring it into port. It don't cost you anything, and if they can find a clue, maybe you might help the dead get some peace. It gives you a reputation for honesty, and if you ever get out of junking... though I guess with your racial handicap you probably won't, still, an honest reputation can grease a lot more wheels than money."

He looked around. This had obviously been the crew quarters, kitted with six bunks, all of uniform sizes. There didn't seem to be anything personal about it, which seemed odd, but maybe there had been rules, and personal gear was stowed somewhere else on board. They were hooked into the ship's systems enough to affect the gravity on board, so he'd had Galmar reduce it some to aid with moving the two bodies on the control deck into here, so he could do it without dragging Aston or Allas in. He'd been holding off on altering the air supply on board until they had sealed off this room so whoever was on board would be in a full suit. No point in forcing a lot of air in, just to find out the bodies contained some disease that would cause them to have to jettison all of it, let alone the risk of backdraft contamination into their own systems.

Once it was set up, he made his way back out to the latch and to decon. He could have stayed on board, but it had no point. Allas didn't like him hanging about when she had to do something like this, she said it made her feel like she was "creepy" somehow. This kind of work was why she'd gone into ship mechanics for her father, and the academy, after her first graduation from med school. It was why she had decided to work for her father, despite knowing it would lead to accusations of nepotism. Little did she know that her medical training would add to her value so much.

Now that he had the other ship hooked up anyway, he could start writing out different course plots on board the Shawnkerri while Allas worked. It all depended on what they found, of course. If the ship had some capabilities of autonomous movement, it might be able to travel with his ship, loosely tethered through a warp bubble. If not, they would have to drag it along like a tug, through a wormhole. Even that was contingent on whether it was worth tugging. If the operating systems seemed to contain nothing special, it would make just as much sense to find a local boneyard and ditch it there for scrap price. He didn't mind coming up with contingency plans really, it was the captaining part of his job after all. It could get a bit tedious, but trying to get top dollar for minimal cost was really the name of the game.

Everything was peaceful on the ship. Galmar was running diagnostics on the other ship's system, which occasionally led to little muttered curses from him. Aston was checking the connections to the decon bay and the tentative connections to their prize for when they stabilized the air. All three of them had tasks, all three bent to them.

That's when the screaming started. He had the tele-links on speaker while he was working to keep track of everybody and to be there when he was needed. The screams suddenly started loud and clear. They were from Allas! He leaped to his feet and ran from the lock. Aston was in the lock at the time and geared up. He could see through the hatch, the Relgian already had his helmet on and was popping the hatch to get into the alien ship! Terry grabbed at his own suit and was thrusting himself into it as soon as he got to the lock. He still had to be careful and methodical getting geared up. It was tough to go slow now, but his suit wasn't impervious to damage.

Terry slammed the helmet over his head, and before bothering to seal it, he barked into the com, "Aston! What in the hell is going on over there?"

"She's OK, boss, I'm bringing her out now. I think she just fainted. We'll find out together once I get her back on the Shawnkerri, OK?" Aston grumbled in his ear.

Terry paused, and before taking his helmet off, he said, "Alright, buddy, I'll be right on the other side of the lock when you get here."

When Aston reopened the hatch and stepped in, Terry could see Allas with him. She was awake now and being helped along by their friend into the decon link. She saw him through the clear plastex staring at them and gave him a weak thumbs-up. After they had run the decon procedure, the hatch to the Shawnkerri finally opened and in stepped Aston and Allas after what seemed an eternity. Allas fell into Terry's arms, sobbing into his shoulder for a moment.

Eventually seeing she'd be fine, Aston said to lighten the mood, "Oh, I see how it is, you hug her. Me, I don't get nuthin'. She runs to you, she just laid there and didn't say a thing when I got to her. I see it all now!" He smiled at Terry and gave him a huge wink.

Allas got herself together a bit and turned to him, giving him a wan smile before saying, "Thanks for the rescue, you big lummox!"

"Anytime, if I let anything happen to you, the Captain would mope terribly, and nobody wants that," he smiled back.

"Allas, what in the hell happened in there?" Terry demanded.

"Tell you what, hun, can we do this on the bridge? It will give me a chance to compose myself, and I won't have to repeat it for Galmar. I know we could use the tele-link, but I want to be able to look at everyone."

They all followed her up to the bridge, where Galmar was already humping toward them, using his tentacles for a quick form of locomotion. The two large eyes in his bulbous head looked directly up at Allas as her entrance brought him up short. "Are you OK, my dear friend?"

"I'm fine. Well, I'll live at least. Since we're all here, I might as well say it now," Allas began. "I saw it."

"Saw what, my dear?" asked Galmar as he humped back over to his padded terminal chair.

"It. The massacre. All of it," Allas replied.

"But how?" asked Aston, frowning.

"I don't know, I really don't. I was finishing up the autopsy and was getting ready to seal up the room so we can blow the ship's air out. By the way, you were right, Terry, totally alien, nothing in the list of known species, so I'd go with the blowout. I can't safely say it'll be fine in there. I turned, and I saw it all. The boarding party coming aboard, the firefight, after the hatch was opened. I'm positive, the two bodies in the room were children, Terry! They were hiding when they were killed!" Allas sobbed. Terry moved quickly to her and held her until she subsided again.

"Alright, Galmar, there's something to watch for, they must have set some kind of recorder when they knew they were being boarded. Try and figure out what in the hell triggered it, OK," Terry said softly but firmly.

"We're getting there, boss, I almost have some sense of the system. If it's in there, we'll find it," Galmar replied.

"Good, we get a read on that, we have rock-solid evidence on the raiders. Nothing like a tri-d replay of you doing the crime to sway a jury," Terry said. "Alright, gang, Allas, you've done your bit for now," he continued, addressing them all, "first off, blow out anything and I do mean anything in there after we seal that room. We don't know they left anything contagious in there, we don't know the species, but then again, we don't know they didn't. Aston, you and I are gearing up and sealing it solid. Galmar, can you give me at least a rough idea on what connects to that room, wiring and air ducts and so on so we can seal that too?"

"I can get it off our own grid reports, we've been able to get a visual on the structure from our side," Galmar said, turning back to his controls.

"Alright, let's get it done."

Terry was sitting in the new ship. He had jokingly started calling it the 'Mary Celeste,' a joke based on an old Earth ghost story. In theory, he was calibrating with Galmar. They had gotten into the ship's systems enough to find a series of smaller thrusters that could be used to steer the ship and could possibly be used to enable it to keep up with the Shawnkerri enough to be able to use a warp bubble without it needing to be dragged along. If it could match a smallish velocity to the Shawnkerri, the Shawnkerri's ability to warp field generate should be enough to enfold both ships.

It was tedious work, though, and both Galmar and he were just about ready to call it a day. He'd brought along a portable audio player and was listening to music from his native Centauri G. The little readout box was bouncing the sound signals around the cabin so well that it almost sounded like he was back home. Terry swore that the only reason he brought the device along was to bone up on some lectures he had stored on it, to keep up with the latest news in shipping, and to use it as a communications device, but he secretly had scores of music and comedy files on it.

"Alright, I've got the last readings," Galmar's voice came through the portable, quite ruining the chorus to this particular tune.

Terry waved the music off with his hand and responded, "Alright, Galmar, I'm off to decon, and then I want to see if Allas wants to watch something on the tri-d tonight." With that, he waved off the little chip device that was sitting on top of the bridge console and got up to go to the hatch.

The sound of the hatch opening and closing was in the distance. There was only the twilight of the ship's controls slowly dropping to sleep mode, as the ship realized there was no longer a physical presence in the room. Then, without a sound, the lights on Terry's portable device lit up, followed by music flowing into the empty room.

It had reached the big day now. They had decided that the Mary Celeste's systems were unique enough that it was going to one of Trago's yards. Trago would see they got top dollar for it, and residuals on any patents that could be gotten from it. Terry didn't trust Trago with absolute conviction, but he certainly trusted him more than most of the other yards.

The decision had been made, by him, that he and Aston were going to do what flying needed to be done on the Mary Celeste to match the pace and position that Allas and Galmar set in the Shawnkerri. He and Galmar had worked many hours on it, so in theory, both ships' initial thrusts were synced enough that all that really needed to be done was to be there in case of emergency once the flight paths had been set. But still, if this junker was going to break up on anyone, it would be him. He'd already made a point that Aston had first dibs on this ship's escape pod if anything went wrong. It was what being a captain came down to at the end of the day. It was your ship, it was your responsibility.

Terry was sitting at the controls, looking out at the front view. He didn't see anything, or hear anything. Rather, he FELT something, something almost electric, right behind him. He looked over and saw that clearly, Aston had felt it too. They both slowly turned in their seats. Standing behind them were three shimmering figures.

They were short and thin, their eyes were large and soulful, seated in finely featured, drawn faces. Fine-featured, except, oddly they had large (what Terry could only guess were) noses that looked almost like tubes hooking over their mouths, which belied their otherwise delicate bone structure. Their skin, if it could be called that, he wasn't even sure they were really there, was an orange hue. They were also completely hairless. There were three of them in descending height.

The tallest of the three seemed to speak, but while its mouth moved, the sound almost seemed to arrive directly in their ears with no intervening distance. "Hello, crew of the Shawnkerri," it intoned solemnly in flawless Galactic Common.

Terry just looked at them slack-jawed for a moment. In his years of towing junked ships, he'd never had a dead crew show up before! Aston was making some kind of hand gesture that Terry guessed might be to ward off evil on his planet. Finally, he managed to say, "And, umm, you are?"

The figure appeared to smile and said, "Our names would be quite untranslatable, but I suppose Salax is close enough for conversational purposes. I know to call you Terry, so it should be only proper for you to have a name to call me by. This is my mate, Drallest, and our child, Bonnat."

Terry couldn't stop himself before he blurted out, "But there were four bodies."

The creature's face looked stricken at the comment, as did its mate and their child. Finally, it said, "I should explain. Our species only exists in a physical organic state for part of our life cycles. What you might call, 'In the flesh.' At a certain point, the flesh drops away, leaving the electrons that it housed to continue on their own while retaining the essence OF the individual."

"So, when the raiders...."

"Shot us with their weapons, they only managed to destroy our cocoons. Our youngest child... was too young to make the transition and... died the ending death prematurely," the tall creature said, his head dropping and his eyes clouding with pain.

"I'm sorry, I really am. We were hoping to use the ship, and what we believed was a ship log to try and bring the raiders to justice," Terry said.

"Ah, I believe I must also apologize. What your young lady saw was not actually a projection of any normal kind. We were using our energy to replay what had happened. We had hopes that maybe you would be the local constabulary yourselves since we could not speak your language, we had hopes of showing you the events that had happened," Salax said.

"But how can you speak Common? You're not like anything I'VE seen before," interjected Aston.

"Your Captain, Terry, left a small communication device on board the ship," said Drallest, "we have all studied it and ran it through the ship's computers here on our ship to impart the knowledge to us. Being in this form, once it was deciphered, it could be directly fed to us with full retention."

"Handy trick," replied Terry, "but look, what are you doing in this quadrant anyway? There are a few inhabited planets, but this type of backwater is rife with raiders."

"We did not realize that when we came. Why we came? Our own culture has grown stagnant. Our long lives have made us content with our own planets and the safety they provide, and we have ceased to explore. The idea that we could possibly live for a thousand of your years has paralyzed us with fear of risking so much time and life. We have ceased to learn new things. We frankly think we know it all already. Since Drallest and I are, were, still of the mating phase, we decided that before we became another blissed-out, smug set of electrons producing nothing but philosophy, we wished to explore. So, we came here, to the absolute fringes of our race's known explorations."

"Ours too," Terry interjected. "So, cards on the table, I suppose this means you'll be wanting your ship back, huh?"

"Actually, we have little need of it now, in our current state. If lines of communication exist, we can easily ride them to new destinations. We could have stayed with your ship without you ever knowing we were there unless you did a full diagnostic down to energy fields. We only wish that you could deliver us to some well-civilized planet in your empire so that we may learn and observe," Salax said.

"So, you want us to give you a lift?" Aston asked incredulously.

The three beings conferred a moment by, for lack of a better way of saying it, melding their projections together for a moment, and then pulling them back to normal. "Yes, exactly."

Terry sat there for a moment, his brow wrinkled as he considered it. He might be breaking god knows how many laws by unleashing an alien species that hadn't gone through quarantine. Of course, for all intents and purposes, they were dead, at least legally. It wasn't like any other race had the subatomic particle option available to them, so technically he wasn't doing anything wrong. He also felt like he owed them SOMETHING for what had happened to them.

"I keep your ship, right, and any tech we can use off it too?" he asked.

"Of course."

They had just dropped off the little family on a small planet a few systems away. One of those places just connected enough that they could explore to their heart's content, or whatever you would say they had now's content, but still distant enough nobody was likely to notice them. They had worked out a way to communicate with the Shawnkerri in case they wanted to try a different world, or in case Terry managed to track down the raiders in question, and they needed some kind of testimony. Terry worried about that a bit since their testimony would be proof that Terry's crew had smuggled in aliens until Salax pointed out, they could always say his family had not let Terry's crew know of their presence.

Now it was just him and Allas, alone in their room watching a movie on the tri-d. She was snuggled up tight to him tonight. He figured, with the scare they had given her, she was probably glad to see the aliens gone off the ship, and he couldn't blame her. If it had been him they had decided to give that horror show to, he'd have been tempted to break contact with the Mary Celeste and let the whole damned thing float off into the void.

"Terry?" she said quietly as she ran her fingers through his chest hair.

"Yeah, hun?" he said, not taking his eyes off the movie.

"Remember when we talked to that geneticist?" she asked.

"Yeah, he charged us two hundred creds to let us know he didn't think we could compatibly create offspring from mating. Then offered to make us a test-tube child, for a HUGE price. Rotten shyster!" he grunted out.

"I think you should tell him to give your money back," she said.

"Why? Just because it isn't good news doesn't mean you get your money back," he replied, looking down into her eyes.

"It's just, seeing that he was wrong..." she smiled.

First Appeared in Schlock! Winter Quarterly 2016-17

The Hills Are Alive

Josh Adams had had it. The whole rat race, and frankly the whole human race. It wasn't that he actively disliked people, he could be quite social in the right setting. No, that wasn't his problem. Just society in general that he'd had enough of. He'd tried everything that was supposed to make you happy: money, dating, hobbies, the whole thing, especially money. But day after day he found that he spent more time hiking alone, and less time even watching TV, let alone getting more connected through the internet. Every day it seemed he was less a part of his surroundings and spent more time wanting to get away from them. He'd experienced society, and now he just wanted to leave it behind him.

At 29, after five very good years at the firm, he hatched his plan, and for the next three years he'd worked on it. OFF THE GRID! Alone in the woods. No people, no bother, no preservatives in his food, no pollution, no commute, no bad sitcoms, no more crappy dates, no more crappy bands, no nothing of nothing. Peace, quiet, solitude, and all of his hard work going to live a healthier, happier life.

For the next three years, Josh busied himself accruing money like he always had. But on the weekends, his time was his own. He spent his time on his dream. First buying a plot of land deep in the woods of Appalachia, a spot nobody was interested in, miles from anything but a dirt road. Then he bought tools, cleared as much of it as he could without upsetting too much. Then he built a cabin. This was something the internet was useful for, why re-invent the wheel? Look up the techniques he needed and go do it. Heck, it was easier for him than for his forebears,

193

with a chainsaw for starters. Then starting a garden and learning to can the results. He took classes on hunting and fishing and practiced on his weekends. He built a still and re-directed part of a stream for the water that would serve both the house and the still itself. When he wasn't at the cabin doing the hard work to make it function, he was on the internet in his apartment doing the hard research to make it work.

This was going to be functional; he was absolutely determined to make this actually work. Josh put in solar panels, he put in a largish library for a cabin. Since a huge MP3 collection wasn't going to be of much use, he bought a mandolin and found someone who taught lessons. He got a gun and lots of fishing equipment, bought farm implements, built a shed for them. He was building his future, and he went after it with gusto.

The most amazing part of it, though, was that it made his everyday life more tolerable. He'd hatched his escape plan and he found himself becoming happier even at his job, which mainly seemed to consist of getting people with lots of money to put it where his bosses wanted it to go. But Josh became more personable and pleasant and, if anything, much better at it. As the cabin progressed to the point where you could enjoy it, he'd had a few of his closer friends up on a "fishing trip" and they had joked with him over beers that he reminded them of some kind of "prepper." But they'd had fun themselves overall and went back to their houses, and jobs, and wives, and kids with tales of the fish they'd caught and the joy they'd had. For a while the cabin became a tradition. They'd go up a couple of times a year with him, and for a bit of free labor helping him work on it, they could safely become mighty hunters and fishermen in the wilds of America.

The last half year had really been just the wrapping up. Taking his savings and socking it into low yield but ungodly safe investments. Josh was leaving society and all, but just in case, having money to come back to would certainly help re-integrate into it and all. His employers had actually been sad to hear he was going. Since he'd put together his plan, he'd actually become one of their best brokers. People seemed to trust Josh much more now. It was probably that soft-sell approach. He didn't NEED people to believe him anymore, and it made him that much more believable. There had been some unpleasantness with his parents and an ex-girlfriend and a threat of commitment, but Josh had had his lawyer explain it to theirs that going off the grid, especially as well as he'd planned it, was not actually "insane" in any way. His lawyer had jokingly said to him that he almost wished he was going to right before the whole thing was dropped.

One day, though, the planning and preparation were finished, the cabin and its garden and small copse of fruit trees he'd planted were ready and fully self-sufficient, he finally believed. So, Josh sold off his remaining expensive belongings, bought a few more supplies, and deposited the rest of it into a high-yield account at his bank, with some slipped into checking for emergencies. Finally, he parked his Phaeton in the small parking lot he'd built next to the nearest road, gathered up his remaining supplies, and started the long hike up the track he'd worn over time, to his final escape from society.

It turned out, society was something you had to wean yourself off of. He was very thankful he kept some money and the car. For the first few years, Josh learned he'd forgotten to build a forge, for starters. He got it done, and now scrapped the river his stream fed into for metal once a month. What people discarded that found its way into the river could be remade into needed bits and pieces. He needed gas for the chainsaw and a backup generator for a while as well, but soon he was using his ax more and his chainsaw less, and he found that for most of his needs the solar panels were more than enough, especially after he figured out beekeeping and started making candles with the wax. For some time, he also found a desire for women, and whiskey that didn't make you feel like your eyeballs were on fire. But his desire for women lessened with age or maybe just absence, and eventually, he was using the fruit from his trees for more gentle libations. Not to mention he started to grow a plant that would get him in serious trouble if anyone really cared about him anymore. It not only made fine rope and cloth but would make an evening go away in a most relaxing manner.

His friends still came up for fishing trips for a couple of years, but even that began to slough away. The easier the cabin was to live in, the less they seemed interested. His parents had visited him once, he'd had to meet them at the road, and they had refused to make the trek all the way to the cabin. He'd spent the afternoon at a local diner being berated about how much a college education costs, and why he was using it to live like some kind of doomsday nut. The afternoon ended with his mother in tears and his father telling him that if he ever came to his senses, he remembered where they lived.

Occasionally he'd get a letter in his box in town, along with the statements of how his investments were doing for him. Sometimes Josh even remembered to write his parents back, for whatever solace they thought they needed. His investments were doing quite well. If he ever did "come to his senses," he could probably go right into retirement in a town like maybe Hinton.

But that wasn't going to happen anytime soon. The chemicals of modern food left his system, and his digestion improved. Days of hard work hunting, fishing, farming, and making repairs on his homestead honed his muscles into wire cables. Nights spent reading the library he'd amassed for himself broadened his mind far beyond the concept of money changing hands. He'd even taken to writing some. His hair and beard grew out and thickened. Josh was almost unrecognizable as the clipped and trimmed office creature he had been. For loneliness, he'd gotten a dog out of a pound for companionship after the first year. The dog did some hunting on its own and slept by his feet every night. Josh slept the exhausted sleep of the honest man every night. Mentally and physically, he felt more healthy and secure than he'd ever felt in his entire life. He looked forward to every day and what he was going to do wandering the woods, society be damned.

"Kid, it's time."

"Aww c'mon, I don't want to."

"Tough, you gotta learn how to hunt some."

"But why?"

"Why? WHY? Cause it's your responsibility as a higher creature, kid. We don't hunt them sometimes, they overbreed. They start destroying everything. We HAVE to hunt 'em out some out here. Sure, this is kind of their land, but it's ours too, and part of taking care of it means hunting them and controlling the excess population, that's just part of nature."

"I....suppose."

"Then you're supposin' right for a change. Now pay attention and be quiet for a change. There's been one around here a bit lately, I've been watching it. Now, if you get your head right, you can make yourself blend right into the background. I swear, they never even see you until it's too late. The one that's been wandering around here is a killer, so it definitely needs to be put down anyway. Now when we hear it rustling around, pay attention to me, and do exactly what I do. If you do it right, I swear they practically walk right on up to you begging to be put down."

"Really??"

"No kidding! I'm a lot older than you, bucko, I've done this a couple of times, learned it off them what came before me, same as you are now."

There was a rustling in the bushes and then they saw it. It walked unconcerned toward them, seeming not to see them at all. As it neared them, they saw the fur covering its face and its teeth flashing in the sun. But not at them, it really didn't feel the predators, not the least aware of them at all. As it got close to them, it tripped on something, a rock or something in its path it hadn't noticed, and then the most amazing thing happened. It LEANED, it actually LEANED right on the older one of the two, like it was sacrificing itself to the greater good.

There was a loud and sudden creaking noise, as the hunter flung its limbs around its prey! The prey struggled and cried out. It attempted to thrash about to get free, but to no avail at all. At this point, its cries, and the tree's own movements startled a group of birds from the tree's upper limbs which took flight complaining at the disturbance. There was another loud crashing noise. Leaf mold and dirt was flung aside as the tree's roots ripped up and out through the soil. The roots also wrapped themselves around the victim. It created a hole from the violence under the tree itself. The tree seemed to rear back slightly and then flung its bleating and thrashing victim into the hole. Almost instantly the roots and some of the dirt settled back in place. There were muffled screams for a few moments, but shortly, even those were silenced.

In short order, the forest sounded like the peaceful woods again, bar the soft scraping of the smaller roots reaching out and smoothing out the leaves and the dirt over the base of the tree again, so even the most careful observer would have deemed the area undisturbed.

The Hills Are Alive

"Is it always so horrible?" the younger of the two trees asked.

"Horrible? Kiddo, that thing barely felt anything. One less of the vermin roaming around the woods hacking down your relatives, my little acorn. You wanna grow up big and strong like me, don't you?"

"Well, yes, of course."

"Well, there's lots of good nutrients on them really shaggy ones, and that's nothing to shake your leaves at."

First Appeared in "The Stray Branch" Winter 20-16-17